The Price of Sin

The Price of Sin

Samuel L. Hair

www.urbanbooks.net

Urban Books, LLC
78 East Industry Court
Deer Park, NY 11729

ISBN 13: 978-1-60162-498-7
ISBN 10: 1-60162-498-0

First Printing May 2012
Printed in the United States of America

10 9 8 7 6 5 4 3 2 1

Distributed by Kensington Publishing Corp.
Submit Wholesale Orders to:
Kensington Publishing Corp.
C/O Penguin Group (USA) Inc.
Attention: Order Processing
405 Murray Hill Parkway
East Rutherford, NJ 07073-2316
Phone: 1-800-526-0275
Fax: 1-800-227-9604

The Price of Sin

Samuel L. Hair

Two things that will make a person act right: A good ass-whippin' or a good prayer. Our actions on earth determine our destiny.

—Samuel L. Hair

Chapter One

It wasn't that the pastor's sermon didn't interest Deja—she just found it difficult to focus on his words with fine-ass Garnell Sutton sitting right across the aisle from her. Although she nodded her head a few times, she barely heard a word that Pastor Gardner said, but instead caught herself cutting her eyes to the left more times than she was willing to acknowledge.

The first glance had sincerely been out of just being aware of her surroundings, which was when she happened to notice him. The second had been to size him up, including the third finger of his left hand, which bore no band. On her third glance, they caught eyes; and from there, Deja's thoughts switched from halfway spiritual to purely sexual. "Mmph, mmph, mmph," she moaned almost inaudibly as she crossed one leg over the other. She flexed the muscles of her hot spot, thinking about the "blessing" she thought she might receive in getting to know him better.

"Lord, forgive me," she barely whispered, feeling guilty for the sexual feelings that arose within her as she sat in the sanctuary. Deja believed that her natural affection for a man and desire for sex was indeed God-given, but too many times Pastor Gardner had chastised his congregation over the pulpit for operating in the "spirit of lust," as he put it.

But why did you put all this heat in me if you weren't going to give me a husband to go with it? She cut her eyes to Garnell again and bit down on her bottom lip. "Lawd, ha' mercy! Help me to stay focused," she mumbled in prayer. "But I wouldn't mind, Lord, if you hooked a sister up with someone who loved you and who I could love," she ended. She never thought to ask God for someone who would love her back.

Across the aisle, Garnell felt his manhood throb as his eyes traveled from Deja's stiletto-dressed feet, to her ankles, to the hem of her above-the-knee skirt, and then visualized the rest. Without even realizing it, he licked his lips seductively; imagining himself suckling on her rounded size D's, but then jumped a bit when he noticed that she'd been looking dead at him. Initially he felt a wave of embarrassment, but it dissolved almost as quickly as it came, when he noted the unmistakable lust in Deja's eyes. It was the ever-so-slight lift of her brow that gave it away. Inwardly he chuckled to himself while he turned his head back toward the pulpit and nodded, but not because he agreed with what the preacher spoke.

Yeah, she diggin' me, he told himself, hiding his grin. During the sermon, he shot his eyes back over at Deja a few more times, dreaming of foreplay, until Pastor Gardner reached a high point in his sermon and bellowed with such authority that it demanded both their attention—at least for the moment.

"Beware of wolves in sheep clothing!" Pastor Gardner yelled, having noticed the nonverbal flirting that was taking place right in the sanctuary. Having founded, twelve years prior, Abundant Grace Fellowship, a former grocery store building transformed into a place of worship, David Gardner was a watchful shepherd over his flock. With a congregation of less than a hundred faithful members, not much slid by him on a Sunday morning. His fixated stare convicted Deja, since she'd been a long-term member. She cleared her throat and dipped her head, pretending to be intrigued by a Bible verse. "They look good to you and possess pretty eyes, athletic bodies, good hair, straight white teeth, and they'll say all the right things at the right time. They'll give you deceptive winks and smiles, but watch out; you're bein' set up for devastation and destruction!"

He cut his eyes over to Garnell, who he knew had a wife, regardless of the fact that he wore no ring. "You see, it doesn't bother some folks in here to fool around with someone else's husband or wife! You don't know and probably couldn't care less if that individual is married, a nonbeliever, a whoremonger, a fool, unemployed, a deadbeat dad, or a recoverin' crackhead, 'cause you're too interested in the physical.

"Let me tell you something, physical characteristics and materialistic possessions do not define a person's character. There are dedicated members in here this very moment lustin' right from the pews. Women checkin' out men, and men mesmerized by women in tight, inappropriate attire, looking like they dressed for the club instead of God's house! You see, these days, folks done made church a place to hook up and find a flavor of the week." Pastor Gardner gave Garnell a second lengthy stare. "Men comin' up in here seekin' a vulnerable Christian woman for a one-night, fornicatin' stand, and it's sad to say that more than likely he'll find it. Can I get an amen!"

It was the elderly mothers of the church who waved wrinkled hands in the air and shouted "Amen, Pastor!"

"It's tight, but it's right!" another said from behind Deja.

"Some women come to church to seek a spiritually filled Mr. Right, but I'm here to tell you that everything that glitters ain't gold, and most of the time it ain't even glitter! Be careful what you pray for, because you just might get it! And what looks good to you may not be good for you! And the grass ain't always greener on the other side, you know. We've gotta be inwardly strong and outwardly focused. People come to church these days for all the wrong reasons! When some folks leave church, they're cursin' and lyin', and drinkin' liquor, and hookin' up with people of the world, and lookin' for some type of sin to indulge in! Church just ain't what it used to be!"

Just a few rows away from the pulpit, Garnell shot to his feet and clapped his hands, feigning his support and agreement with the path Pastor Gardner was on, in an attempt to throw him off. "That's right," he yelled from his seat, causing Pastor Gardner to turn his scowled face directly toward Garnell.

Garnell had learned church behavior well and could hang with any Bible-toting, fancy-footwork-dancing, suit-wearing brother there. "You tellin' the truth, Pastor," he added for effect, but different thoughts circled his mind. *Who the hell does he think he is? He ain't got a heaven or hell to put nobody in. Practice what you preach, Mr. Preacher man, because I know damn well you're doin' somethin' you ain't s'pose to be doin'. Just like the rest of those devilish preachers, you're in it for the damn money. Yeah, why don't you preach about church bein' a get-rich business?*

Both you and I know that all you gotta do these days is know how to talk good, be able to recite a few scriptures, and rent a raggedy-ass building to preach from and in a coupla years you'll be buyin' up universities and shit, sellin' front-row seats, and watchin' through hidden cameras to see how much money people be puttin' in. But you wanna judge me for gettin' what these hoes givin' for free? I don't think so. Even

King David dipped up in some pussy that was out on display. Ain't nothin' wrong with that shit."

When Pastor Gardner swiped a wave of sweat from his brow, Garnell shifted his eyes to Deja for a split second. Just as he'd hoped, she was watching. He knew churchwomen loved fresh meat in their hopes to catch a 'saved and sanctified' man. He learned that from watching his own mother's futile search for love in the rows of church pews. Anytime a new man crossed the threshold of his childhood church, he watched her immediately going into her act of not-so-innocent flirt, more than typical meal preparations (inviting him over), and late-night tiptoeing while sneaking him into her bedroom when she thought Garnell was asleep. Because of what he'd seen, and learned, Garnell never had to go too long without a piece of pussy. He knew all he had to do was show up on a Sunday morning, at any given church, and pussy would be thrown his way no sooner than the service started. And he didn't mind giving the ladies the blessing they desired. *Naive ass,* he thought. *I'ma wear that pussy out.*

"Folks in here texting, and cell phones ringin'. . . ." Pastor Gardner's voice trailed away. "Church just ain't what it used to be! It's filled with front-row professed Christians and back-row sinners! You'd better check yourself, people, before you wreck yourself! The devil is present and busy as I speak, seeking out the weak ones!"

Pastor Gardner was on fire, pacing the length of the stage, speaking loudly and emotionally. The organist began to follow the pastor's squalling with a series of chords, causing other parishioners to leap to their feet. "I guarantee you that a person who looks at an individual in a lustful manner, instead of seekin' out the heart of that individual, is brewin' up a recipe in his godless mind for disaster! The Bible tells us to be equally yoked in our relationships! A true, pure-hearted Christian and a worldly person is not a match the Lord condones! We should be wise enough to distinguish wolves in sheep's clothin'! Keep in mind that Satan has more disguises than you can ever imagine, and he's filled with charisma and charm. That's part of his plot! He'll laugh with you and agree with you! There's no extreme Satan won't exceed to captivate you, but the Good Lord has the ability to do incredible things for us imperfect people if we allow him to!"

The drummer took a seat behind his set, struck licks on the snare and cymbals, and maneuvered his foot against the bass drum pedal, which was all it took to send several of Pastor Gardner's members into a running, jumping frenzy.

"Hallelujah!" Deja threw her head back and yelled, joining a few ladies in the aisleway. She leaped in the air a few times, her breasts bouncing beneath her blouse.

Damn! Garnell thought, catching a glimpse of her plump ass as Deja ran several times in a small circle like a dog chasing its tail. *I bet that's sweet right there!* He didn't want to, but he remembered where he was and forced himself to look away. He turned his head to the left away from a jiggling, gyrating Deja and right into the face of what had to be the homeliest woman he'd ever seen.

"He talkin' 'bout you, you know," Eureen Francis snapped. With the music blaring from the organ, drums, and various tambourines, Eureen didn't worry about the volume of her voice.

"Excuse me?"

"You heard me! You sitting right up in this church tryin'a find who you gonna attack next, but I see that devil in you!" she sneered.

Eureen's hair was as tangled and stiff as steel wool, pushed back from her forehead with what looked like a sweat sock passed off as a headband. Her skin was pecan brown and terribly scarred, as if she'd lost a thirty-year battle with acne. Her eyebrows were thick and unruly; her lashes looked to be tied in knots; her chapped lips, smeared with a bright fuchsia lipstick that in no way complemented her skin tone, were tightened into the smallest O she could form. What made her even less attractive was her nasty, grouchy disposition, aggravated by hard times—although her husband made a substantial amount of money—hardheaded children, and the lack of a hard dick, Garnell reasoned to himself.

"Don't make no sense how you sitting up in here looking at women like you in a strip club," she continued to scold.

Garnell sighed, shook his head, and then picked his Bible up from the pew. He wove his way through several people who still filled the aisles, with their hands lifted, excited about the words they heard from the pulpit. A part of him did want to stay, to at least get Deja's number, but he knew there'd be another time.

With a disapproving grimace on her face, Eureen let her eyes follow Garnell down the aisleway and out the sanctuary doors. She found herself distracted the entire service in watching Garnell watch Deja. Truth be told, although she was married, she was quite jealous that she never got male attention, not even from her husband. With a paper fan, she pushed air across her ample but sloppy bossom.

Since when did a big, soft pair of titties stop being enough to get a man's attention? she wondered. If Garnell had looked her way, even a little bit, she would have kept her comments to herself, but since he had not . . . Well, it just didn't make no sense for him to be acting like that in the house of the Lord. She was going to have to talk to the pastor about this.

Shortly after Garnell had made his exit, the service ended. Pastor Gardner always took the time to greet his congregation afterward. He stood near the exit, shaking hands and politely greeting parishioners as they left.

Eureen made it her business to be one of the last to leave the sanctuary. She had an earful to give her pastor and didn't want to be rushed along by anyone else wanting his attention.

"How are you today, Sister Francis, and where's your husband?"

"I don't know where he's at, but he needs to be out tryin' to find some damn Viagra!" Eureen shamelessly and candidly replied.

Pastor Gardner gave her a stern look. "You'll need to respect the house of the Lord, Eureen."

"Forgive me, Lord," she mumbled, glancing up at the ceiling. "'Scuse me, Pastor, I'm sorry, I'm just so frustrated," she uttered, linking arms with him and pulling him out the front door. "Come on out here so I can say what I need to say without the church being struck by lightning."

David Gardner chuckled as he allowed himself to be led to the sidewalk just outside the doors of his church, but he freed himself from Eureen's grasp no sooner than they got outside.

"He just ain't the man he used to be. Ain't no spark about him no more. Bad thing about it is that he act like it don't bother him! Now I don't mean to tell you my personal business, but I'm sick and tired of Monroe not being able to get a hard-on! I need you to talk to him, Pastor."

"Sister, you should have enough womanly power to work that out yourself. I don't meddle in people's bedrooms," David commented.

"Well, I need some help! Sister Franklin told me that Brother Franklin took one of those Viagra pills and said he kept a hard-on for three straight days! That's what I'm talkin' 'bout, Pastor! Thrill me—you know what I mean? Hell, I want it so good that it'll make me jump up and grab the chandelier! I wanna be hit doggie style, froggie style, from the side; I want him to ride the hell out of it! You know what I mean?"

"Eureen, I want you to—"

Eureen didn't allow him to finish his sentence. "I know church ain't the place to be talkin' 'bout nothin' like this, but I'm fed up and some serious changes need to be made quick! When I told Monroe to go find some of that Viagra, and I'll buy him a year's supply of it, he talkin' 'bout he can't take it because of the blood pressure pills and the other medication he's takin'! I don't need no damn excuses, Pastor. I need resolutions! He say's the Viagra may cause internal complications or a stroke, but what about my needs? I ain't but thirty-six years old, and the fire is still burnin' down below! I need somebody to put it out, Pastor. That's what I really need! I been tryin' to hold on and remain faithful, but this mess is gettin' old."

"Sorry to hear that, Sister Francis. I can see this situation is stressful and irritating to you, but there are other ways of producing pleasure for your partner, and vice versa, without using dangerous drugs."

"I'm tryin' not to sin," Eureen tagged on. "Now if I wasn't saved and tryin'a honor my marriage vows, that fine brother who was sittin' beside me today woulda had hisself an eyeful. 'Cause I know howta hike my skirt up too, and do the huckabuck."

David couldn't help but laugh as he watched Eureen "cut a step," adding extra movement to her hips.

"He sho was filling his eyes up with every other nasty-cracked hoochie in there, shakin' her titties all in his face!"

"Sister, Sister, Sister," David called, having heard enough. "You just need to go home and have some honest conversations with your husband. I'm sure you two can work through this. In the meantime, put on the whole armor of God, stay strong, and quit allowin' the devil to have so much influence over your mind. Keep on praying, Sister; it'll work out." He chuckled. "Something remarkable and pleasurable is destined to happen."

Eureen frowned. "I been prayin' 'bout this for months and ain't a damn thing happened yet! And if something don't happen quick, I'ma be filing for a divorce. I'm gonna find me a young man who can put that thang on me all day and night long! Rock my boat every which way, and then put me into a sweet, long sleep. I think they call it 'thug passion.' He ain't gotta work; he ain't gotta bring nuttin' to the table. All I want him to do is to do me. I want him to lay pipe all night, and I mean all night," she babbled, envisioning Garnell manipulating his manhood inside her walls. "Hell, I might even buy him a Cadillac and a hip-hop wardrobe if he hit it right, and I ain't lyin' either, Pastor. That's jus' how bad I need it!"

"I'm sure you do, Sister Francis, but as I said, lose those devilish thoughts and try to work things out with your husband."

Eureen rolled her eyes; then she was silent for a few seconds as she began to fantasize about having sex with her pastor.

"Pastor, I bet you ain't got no problem pleasin' Sista Gardner, do you?"

"The first lady and I keep our private life private. You should do the same. Now if you'll excuse me."

Felicia Gardner walked up to her husband and took his arm.

"I was just coming to look for you," David said as Felicia latched on to his arm. He pecked his wife's lips and winked. "Sister Francis, we'll see you Wednesday night."

"All right, now," Eureen responded before turning to go to her car. She took note of Deja and two other young ladies chatting in the parking lot. "Tight-skirt-wearing heifers," she mumbled. She strained to hear a bit of their conversation as she walked by.

"Did you see how he was all into the message?" Jasmine commented. "That's what you want right there, a man who's rooted in the Word."

"Girl, he was staring your big ol' Beyoncé booty down," Tracey added.

"Good! That's why I wore it, to get some attention," Deja said with a giggle. "I'm glad it worked."

"Oh my Lawd, there goes that ugly-ass troll, Eureen. What kind of momma names their child 'Eureen'? That's too close to urine, and her face be looking like she smell piss all the time!" Jasmine cracked, causing laughter to erupt from her two friends.

Eureen looked over at the women without stopping her movement, although she heard their words and cackling.

"And why don't she do something with those Herman Munster eyebrows?" Deja asked. "She look like she got two big, fat caterpillars sitting on her forehead."

"I'ma pray for y'all two." Tracey giggled, unlocking her car doors. "We ain't been out of church a good five minutes and y'all talking about your sister like that. Come on, because they stop serving brunch at two o'clock."

The three ladies got into Tracey's Camry and wheeled past Eureen as she seated herself behind the wheel of a Kia Sorento, which always had to be prompted at least three times before it would actually start. Not feeling like experiencing the embarrassment that day, she sat for a few minutes, pretending to search through her purse for her keys, or acting as if she were talking on her cell phone, whenever someone walked by, until she was practically in the parking lot alone. Before she started the vehicle, she sighed, thinking about the comments her so-called sisters had made. She pulled down the mirror on her visor and assessed her face. She licked, then smoothed a finger over her brows, silently admitting that they did need a bit of grooming. Just that little bit seemed to help. For a moment, she wished she were as pretty as the trio that had just left. All three of them had beautiful, healthy hair, in varied lengths, flawless skin, and figures like video vixens. Eureen looked down at her rounded belly, which sat on her lap, covered by a flowered smock of a dress. Stacked on her stomach were two out-of-shape titties, which really needed the support of a good bra, at the very least. Then she remembered that none of those women had as many children as she did. Jasmine, the only mother in the group, did have two girls, but Eureen had twice as many, so she had a perfectly good reason why her body was now misshapen.

"At least I got a husband," she mumbled, pushing the mirror back up. "So forget them bitches. 'Scuse me, Lord." She paused for a few seconds. "Next time that man come strolling through here . . . he gonna be looking at *me!*" she vowed.

Chapter Two

"So what's the deal with Shamar? You still raising a boy along with your two girls?" Tracey asked before forking a mouthful of lasagna between her lips.

"Why do you have to say it like that?" Jasmine rolled her eyes and sighed as she sipped from her wineglass. "Slide over," she huffed. She and Tracey were seated in Deja's living room for their weekly girlfriend pow-wow.

"I'm just asking." Tracey shrugged and covered her mouth with a napkin as she spoke. She balanced her plate on her lap as she slid to her left to make room for her friend on a chocolate-colored sectional accented with turquoise pillows. "There is such a thing as miracles, right?"

"Girl, you know if something had changed with that situation, I'd make sure it was on the five o'clock news."

"I just can't believe you keep taking care of a grown-ass man like that," Deja quipped. "I'd rather stay single than have to carry around a two-hundred-fifteen-pound baby."

"Yeah, but you also gotta settle for a vibrator for a boyfriend," Jasmine shot back. "Either that or keep repenting every Sunday while you pray for a man."

"Having no man is better than a sorry man—any day of the week," Tracey teased. "I don't mind stocking up on batteries. That's a lot cheaper than paying someone's way through life."

"Shut up! *For the Love of Ray Jay* is on." Jasmine pressed the volume button on the television remote, effectively switching the focus off her marriage, although the thoughts lingered in her mind privately, well after she'd left her friends for the evening.

Shamar and Jasmine Murphy had been a couple since sixth grade and were now in their early thirties, with ten years of marriage under their belts. They had six- and seven-year-old girls to complete their family unit. Jasmine's income afforded them the privilege of living in the middle-class bracket, and they resided in a recently built two-story, five-bedroom, four-bath home in Sunnymead Ranch, California. They rented because Shamar's credit was so bad that they weren't able to buy. She drove a late-model Navigator, and Shamar sported a pre-owned but meticulously maintained Jaguar. He kept both vehicles clean enough for any dealership showroom floor.

Judged by the photo of the four of them encased in an acrylic frame dangling from her keys, they looked like a model family, and Jasmine worked hard to maintain that perception. Only Deja and Tracey knew the real deal. Jasmine prided herself on her education, eighty-grand-a-year salary and A1 perfect credit, but her husband, on the other hand, barely made it out of high school, sporadically took on brief assignments at a temporary agency, and had a credit rating so low that even the payday loan establishments would think twice about giving him money. Despite his brilliant mind, Shamar was a lazy, wavy-haired pretty boy who still had a firm grip on his momma's apron strings. He was Cyreese's only child and she had spoiled him beyond repair, producing nothing more than a grown baby instead of a productive, responsible man. Because of his mother's lifelong pampering, Shamar believed that he didn't have to do a damn thing but keep up his physique, keep his hair neat, and keep his wife sexually satisfied. His perception of a good day was lounging around the house playing video games or watching movies, while Jasmine brought home the bacon, paid all the bills, and kept him and the kids well dressed.

No matter how many times Jasmine asked, petitioned, and even begged her husband to do what a man is supposed to do—which, to her, meant get a job and provide for his family—Shamar refused.

"What for? You got that on lock, baby" was his response. "You make enough money for the both of us," he'd argue. That was before he fattened her belly with two babies. Jasmine was sure that her announcement of both pregnancies would cause Shamar to rethink his priorities.

"Or at least set some," she'd mumbled to herself. Her thoughts and her words had been futile, and had fallen on deaf ears.

No matter how often she broached the subject—sometimes with caution, other times with loving support, but most of the time fueled by sheer anger—Shamar's response was consistent.

"What the hell I'ma get a minimum-wage job for when you ballin'?"

"Because that is what a man does!"

"Naw, that ain't all the way true. I know plentya men that's letting they woman do the damn thing."

"Like who, Shamar?"

"Like Oprah and her dude. He ain't bustin' his ass to add his two cents to her millions."

"Probably because they're not married. Besides that, you don't know what that man does. He done wrote books, ran businesses, and all kinds of stuff."

"Yeah, whatever. That ain't shit to all that money Oprah making." Shamar paused in thought for a few seconds; then he shot out again in his defense. "What about ol' boy that Angela Bassett is married to. You don't hear shit about him, 'cause she handlin' shit. Rollin' down the damn river being Tina Turner and shit."

"She's married to Courtney B. Vance, who's an actor himself and has played on all kinda shows," Jasmine argued, pressing her lips and folding her arms across her chest.

"So you tryin'a say he make more than her? He famous like her? Don't nobody know that nigga."

"I'm not saying he makes more or less than her; what I am saying is that he got a damn job, unlike your broke ass!" she screamed.

"I don't have to listen to this shit!" Shamar would say at the end of every similar conversation, if it could be called that. "I'm outta here! I'm goin' to my momma's house."

"Get your ass out then!"

Jasmine could no longer count the times they'd had that same argument, with the same ending. Shamar would go running to Cyreese's arms, where he would spend up to a full week, blaming his wife for his shortcomings and greatly magnifying hers. And Cyreese, believing that her son could do no wrong, always took his side, not caring that there were two sides to every story.

"Her high-saditty, rat-race-runnin' corporate ass," she would mumble, balancing a cigarette between her lips. "Don't make sense how she rushed to get married, but ain't rushin' to be a wife. I swear, if you ain't come round here and get a good meal, you be done withered away by now."

Cyreese cooked like it was Thanksgiving whenever her son ran away from his own home to the temporary solace of hers. She'd fill his belly with rich meals of ham, slow-roasted chicken, cabbage, spinach, corn pudding, stuffing, fried potatoes and onions, and homemade rolls. Shamar would never admit it to his mother, but Jasmine was just as skilled in the kitchen as Cyreese.

"That's all she do is work, Ma. She don't be thinkin' about us. I gotta be the momma and the daddy. Clean up, cook, and take care of the girls; help them with they homework, make sure they get to school on time, all-uh that. How I supposed to do all that and hold down a job? If she stayed her ass at home like a wife s'pose to do, I could get a job. If I went and got one, ain't no way I could go every day. I'd have to call in every day just to make sure the house don't fall apart."

After listening to Shamar go on and on, Cyreese would be even more convinced that the struggles of her son and daughter-in-law's marriage were all Jasmine's fault, and she would often call and let Jasmine know just that. It made her blood boil, but Jasmine never showed an ounce of disrespect toward Cyreese, completely concealing her strong aversion for her mother-in-law.

Chapter Three

Tracey got home from work just in time to hustle for her ringing phone. She glanced at the caller ID before answering, smiled a bit, and then picked up the handset.

"Hello," she huffed, dropping her purse and keys on the kitchen table. She wedged the cordless handset between her face and shoulder, freeing up her hands to wind her long, silky hair into a bun on top of her head.

"Hey, baby," Jermaine answered.

"Hey, Jermaine. I'm so glad you called."

"You know I had to call to see how my baby was doing."

"I like that." Tracey's smile could practically be heard through the phone.

"How was your day?" he asked.

He was used to Tracey complaining about her long hours as an assembly-line worker, but he asked daily and listened intently, on guard for any qualities or characteristics she shared with his ex-wife, Karen.

Karen had been beautiful to look at, but her other qualities were unbearable. She was extremely loud, drank excessively, and had an unmanageable drug habit, which caused her to do unspeakable things in search of her next high. She was the type of woman whom the family hated to see coming, knowing she would get drunk, talk loudly, and curse out three to six, if not all, of her relatives. It was nothing for her to become violent and call her own mother "a bitch." She wouldn't even think about an apology. Her obstinate, bullheaded attitude toward signing the divorce papers cost him a little over $2,500, which he figured was a small price to pay to regain his peace of mind and control over his household.

It took Jermaine nearly two years after that to get back out into the dating scene. Even then, he was gun-shy about jumping in with both feet. Nonetheless, loneliness began to set in, and he'd become tired of occasional one-night stands and empty relationships, if they could be called that.

He had run into Tracey one Saturday as he picked up a few items from the grocery store.

"Hey, girl!" Jermaine commented, spotting Tracey at the deli counter.

"Jermaine! How you been?" she asked. They had known each other for several years, although they'd never embarked on a romantic adventure. "You still driving trucks?"

"Yeah, I am." He nodded. "How about you? What you doing these days?"

"I'm still down at the plant," she answered, "and doing braids on the side."

He now assessed her features as she talked, wondering how he'd overlooked her before. But then again, with him constantly being on the road, and being married, he hadn't really been open to other women. Since things had changed for him, her smooth skin, well-toned body, and beautiful smile appealed to him. She went on for a few minutes, catching him up to what she'd done in the past few years, which didn't amount to very much at all. However, that didn't matter to Jermaine at the moment.

"*Matter of fact, Momma an'em cooking out this evening; you should come by and say hi,*" *she offered with a smile.* "*They gon' have a lot of food, and you know we gonna kick off some spades and dominoes.*"

"*Uh . . . I'm home for the next couple of days and could use something to do. I think I will.*" *Jermaine accepted.* "*They still stay in the same house?*"

"*Yeah, you know my momma and daddy ain't going nowhere.*" *She rolled her eyes and waved her hand at the notion.*

"*Okay. I . . . um . . . I'll be glad to come by. Thanks for the invite.*"

"*You welcome.*" *Tracey pushed her basket only a few feet away before Jermaine stopped her.*

"*Tracey, I . . . uh . . . I 'ma just come right out and ask you, are you seeing anybody?*"

Tracey pressed her lips together to hide a smile. "*Not at the moment.*"

Jermaine nodded silently; then he commented, "*Good. I'll see you tonight.*"

It was a dinner date Jermaine was glad he had accepted. Over a plate of grilled ribs, chicken, and hot dogs, homemade potato salad, roasted corn on the cob, baked beans, and packaged rolls, he and Tracey hit it off. He was pleased to know that she was drug free and had steady employment. She attended church regularly, although he didn't care much for the church part. Feeling like God had let him down more than He'd answered his prayers, Jermaine had very little faith or reverence for Him.

I made it through the hard times without God, so what I need Him in the good times for? She can love the Lord all she want, long as she don't try to push that religious mess on me, he thought. *At least she is somebody that got some damn sense,* he decided.

***

He and Tracey had been seeing each other, going on two months now, and he was enjoying the ride, minus the fact that Tracey was slow with sharing her pussy with him like he wanted. The most she had done was let him eat her, and it had taken him an hour of coaxing by bumping and grinding just to be able to do that.

Once I work this magic on her clit, ain't no way she ain't gon' want some dick to top it off, Jermaine figured.

When Tracey gave permission by opening her legs wide, and displaying a complete bare pussy, he buried his face between her legs and went to town sliding the length of his tongue along her flesh, gently and slowly licking and sucking her clit, causing her to moan and shiver.

Oh, I'm 'bout to make this church girl cuss, Jermaine told himself, using his tongue and lips to their fullest potential.

And just like he anticipated, Tracey's orgasm began to kick in and she started cussing like a sailor.

"Um, damn, that shit feels good. Damn," she slurred. "Oh shit, ohh, aw, ahhhhhh, shiiit!"

Within minutes, she came, and Jermaine sucked and flicked his tongue on her pussy even more.

Unable to take the overwhelming pleasure, Tracey tried to scoot away, but he had her legs locked and she couldn't get away.

"Shit, baby! Oh, oh, stop, stop!" Tracey gasped, but she encouraged him to keep eating. "Awwww, you gon' make me come again! Oh shit, Jermaine! Ohhhhhhh, Jermaine. What the fuuuuuuuck!" she cried, thrusting her hips wildly against Jermaine's face and pushing his head deeper in her pussy until she came a

second time. With a series of tremors, she collapsed, fully satisfied.

"Jermaine, I love you, I love you, I love you," she uttered, out of her mind in ecstasy. Drained, she pulled the covers around her, legs now closed, trying to catch her breath and smiled. "Where in the hell did you learn how to eat pussy like that?" she panted.

"Self-taught, baby, self taught," Jermaine bragged.

"Whatever," she answered, chuckling; then she closed her eyes and moaned. "That was so incredible."

With the confirmation that he'd more than pleased her, Jermaine hoped she would reciprocate by riding his dick until he burst. He curled up against her, sucked on her nipples, and pulsed his throbbing erection on her thigh as a signal. He waited to see what was next. When she didn't respond quickly enough, he tried encouraging her.

"Come on and take a ride on this dick, baby," he whispered.

She gave half a smirk, keeping her eyes closed. "Baby, you know I'm saving that for marriage."

Instantly Jermaine was disappointed, but he didn't give up so soon. "Come on, girl. You know you want somma this. Get on and get a little bit of heaven on earth." He wrapped his hands around her ass and gently pulled her closer to him, bumping the head of his dick against her secret place.

"Un-uh, Jermaine," Tracey whined. "You know how important waiting is to me."

"Well, what the hell I'm s'posed to do with all this dick right here?" Jermaine pulled the covers back, exposing his manhood, hoping she wouldn't be able to resist the sight of his juicy stick of hard meat. He pulsed it a few times to lure her.

"Mmm." She grinned and licked her lips. "Don't think I don't want to, baby, but I promised myself after my last boyfriend that I wasn't gonna let nobody else up in me until he gave me his last name."

Not having intercourse was Tracey's version of celibacy, and it was a standard she swore she would keep until she was wed. She had decided on this after having given herself in several ways to several men in hopes that one would find her worthy of marriage. As many times as she'd heard the adage "why buy the cow when you can get the milk for free," she thought it was bunk, until she realized that she was still on the market and passed over. Now believing that there was definite truth to the statetment, she vowed to hold out. And in her mind, having her pussy licked was not the same as giving away the milk for free.

Jermaine sighed. "Well, can you just give me a little bit of head, baby?" he asked, beginning to pump his dick slowly with his right hand. "Just a little bit," he practically begged, hoping Tracey would think " just a little bit" didn't sound as bad as just straight-up sexing. "A little bit ain't gonna hurt nothing," he added. "That ain't even really like doing it."

"Baby, no." Tracey's response was soft but adamant.

"All right," Jermaine said, giving up with a heavy sigh. "Shit," he mumbled under his breath.

He pulled himself from her bed, walked naked to the bathroom, closed the door behind himself, and masturbated until he achieved some level of relief and satisfaction, although he was sorely disappointed. When he returned to Tracey's side, she was fast asleep. He lay down with his back to her and pulled the covers up to his chin.

*"Damn church girl. I don't know if that's a fuckin''
plus or minus."*

Nonetheless, Jermaine liked Tracey.

He called to check on her daily while he was on the
road.

When he was home, they spent practically every
night together. He ate her pussy every time they were
together, but he was forced to make himself content
with his hand and a bottle of lotion. Every now and
then, Tracey would give him a hand job while he
sucked her titties.

He tried to crack her sugar walls a few times, but
Tracey simply refused. The last thing he needed was
for a woman to cry rape on him, so he decided to wait.

Chapter Four

"So when will I get to meet your beautiful family, Brother Sutton?" Pastor Gardner posed to his new parishioner.

Garnell rubbed his chin and looked down at the carpet, pondering his pastor's question. "To be honest with you, I don't know when I'm going to be able to move them out here," he answered, regarding bringing his family from the East Coast to California. "I can't do that until I can find another job. Right now, I'm staying with my uncle. I'm grateful that he put me up; but to be honest with you, it ain't no place to bring my kids, you know?"

"How old are your children?" David asked as he and Garnell walked down the hallway toward a small classroom, where a men's group meeting was being held.

"My daughter is two, and my son is, uh, just about six month now." He paused for a few seconds, pretending to think about his family. "I hated leaving them in South Carolina like that, but I had to come out here and try to make a better life for us," he lied. Truth be told, he'd walked out on his wife just days before she delivered their baby, when she'd found out Garnell had gotten two other women pregnant and had confronted him with it.

"I can't believe you are accusing me of this stupid shit!" he bellowed. "If you don't trust me, then I don't need to be here!" He hadn't seen his wife since that day, fleeing the scene of his crimes.

"So what have you been able to accomplish since you've been here?"

Garnell shook his head almost painfully. "I wake up every morning, waiting for that call to come through." He paused again. "All I can say is, it ain't came through yet. But I can't give up, though. I gotta do it for my family."

David patted Garnell on the back. "Don't give up, man. It'll work out."

"Yeah, I keep telling myself that," Garnell murmured.

"Do your best to get them here quickly," David advised. "It's a dangerous thing for a man to come to church alone. Especially, without his wedding band." The latter part was said in reprimand, signified by his lifted brow.

Garnell bit his bottom lip and quickly stuffed his left hand into his pants pocket.

The two men passed by a room where the female church members were meeting. While David made eyes at his wife, Felicia, Garnell sent a bit of a nonverbal message to Deja. She tried to act as if she didn't notice, but she saw the tiny tilt of his head, which she equated to a hello. She didn't hold their eye contact. Instead, she immediately looked away and reached for her purse on the floor. Being careful not to move her lips, she whispered to Tracey, "Girl, look at the door."

Tracey turned her head amazingly fast. Deja was surprised her girlfriend's neck didn't snap. "Not all fast like that!" she squealed, poking her friend in the thigh with the end of her ink pen.

"What? You told me to look. That joker is fine!"

"I know." Deja winked. "He single, too. He was just looking over here at me. I hope I run into him when service gets out. I got some digits I need to give him."

"I know that's right," Tracey commented. She focused her attention back on Felicia, who was leading the women's group session that night.

"Now, some of you are still single, so just put this in your goody bag for later," she said with a wink. "You married ladies, you can't get married and forget how to turn it on—amen!"

"That's right!" a woman answered from the back.

"The Bible says marriage is honorable and the bed is undefiled. So, ladies, you have to know how to keep it hot in your bedrooms." Felicia leaned against a podium and winked at the audience of women. "I mean, let's keep it real. Sex was made for marriage, right?" She didn't wait for a response. "So if it was made for marriage, why you gonna wait 'til you get married and then *not* have the best sex of your life? What kind of sense does that make?"

Some of the women in the room giggled and guffawed.

"Now, when you were single, God had mercy on you when you were droppin' it like it hot and doing all kind of tricks and backflips and standing on your head, doing splits and all kinds of carrying on for a man who wasn't even yours. Then you get with your husbands and you want to freeze up and act like you only know one position," she said with a sista-girl twist of her neck. "Come on, ladies," she said, encouraging affirmative expressions.

"That's right, First Lady," Eureen agreed, slapping a high five with the woman next to her.

"Learn how to turn it on for that man!" Felicia continued. "If he wanna see you in some stilettos and a thong, you better put 'em on and strut it like you know what you doing!" With a hand planted firmly on her hip, Felicia strutted across the front of the room like a model in a pair of black stiletto pumps with four-inch silver heels. "Stop going to bed wrapped up in a flannel blanket with buttons down the front, talking 'bout, 'It's cold,'" she mocked. "You better learn how to heat it up!"

Eureen sat in the back, scribbling furiously on a notepad, trying to capture everything Felicia shared. Her eyes were wide with eagerness; she was desperate to do whatever she could to change her sex life.

"Let me tell you, Sisters, sex and marriage go together! Ain't no one without the other. Stop being tired and having headaches and talking about the kids done wore you out and the boss done got on your last nerve." Felicia slumped her shoulders and feigned exhaustion, walking across the room a second time. "'I'm ti'ed tonight. My head hurtin'. I'm sleepy. Let's do it tomorrow.' Then that man wait patiently 'til the next night, expecting you to deliver on your promise, and here you come with your broke-down self with the same old excuses," she reprimanded. "What you think that man supposed to do? How many nights you think he gonna sit around waitin' for you to get yourself together? Honey, you better drink you some kinda energy beverage and get it poppin'!"

More laughter, guffawing, and amens erupted from her listeners.

"Now, I told you when you came in here, I was going to keep it real with you, didn't I?" Felicia asked. "So I don't want none of y'all runnin' to my husband talking 'bout 'Passssssta! First Lady offenn-ed me,'" she said with a country twang. "'Cause for some of y'all sisters, I need to make it real plain. Is that all right?"

"Go 'head, First Lady!" the women encouraged. "Tell the truth!"

"Some of y'all sistas just need a makeover!"

Howls of laughter exploded from the group.

"If you can't get his attention, you need to look in the mirror and figure out why," Felicia offered. "He married you, didn't he? So he saw something he liked. Maybe it was your eyes, your behind, your hair. It mighta been your toes with that fresh French pedicure on them," she suggested. "But he saw *something* that he liked. Don't let your *something,* whatever it is, get all broke down and ran over. Keep that *something* fresh! Keep him looking at that *something!*" she ordered. "Now we gonna do a little exercise." Felicia opened the storage cabinet of the podium and pulled out a mirror. "Most of us carry some kind of compact or mirror in our purse," she started, showing a hand mirror to the group. "I want you to dig that mirror out right now and take a honest look at yourself and I want you to make a note of three things you can go home and change tonight," Felicia ordered.

Obediently, Eureen dug through her shoulder bag and found a small makeup compact. She flipped the lid open and assessed her features. Again she took note of her bushy brows, scarred skin, and chapped lips. She looked at her hairline, which resembled clusters of tiny peas. Although she couldn't see her entire body, she considered her wardrobe, which that night was an oversized T-shirt, a pair of faded leggings, and a dirty pair of pink rubbery plastic shoes known as Crocs. She inconspicuously examined the crust on the back of her heels while Felicia continued to talk from the front of the room. Eureen looked at her nubby fingernails, some of them lined with dirt, and all of them uneven and unkempt. She saw her belly poking forward and her dimples on her thighs showing through the thin fabric of her leggings. She began to make a list on her pad of her observations.

"Now, I'm not gonna ask anybody to share your lists, but if you got more than three things on your list, chile, you need a makeover! Don't be ashamed, though; that's why we all here. Sometimes you just need someone to help you through, amen!"

"That's right," women commented.

Eureen quickly finished her list, tore it from her pad, and stuffed it in her purse. She took to heart all the things that she had written down.

"Ladies, learn how to fix up what you have, and then work what you got!"

Felicia strutted another time in front of the ladies with purposeful and determined steps and an extra thrust in her hips.

"Work it, work it, First Lady!" cried one woman.

"All right, now!" squealed another.

"Look at your neighbor on your left and on your right. Tell them, 'Girl, you need a makeover so you can work what you got!'" Felicia instructed.

With laughter, the ladies followed her playful direction.

Eureen didn't exactly appreciate being told this by the women who flanked her sides, but she conceded, anyway. Once things settled a bit, Eureen began to study Felicia. She admired her short, choppy hairstyle of spiky strands standing wildly yet impeccably groomed on her head. Her mocha skin was smooth and creamy, and her makeup was flawless. Arched brows punctuated her words as she addressed the ladies, and long lashes fluttered on her lids. A neutral-toned gloss covered her lips, giving her a sexy and natural look. Her large wedding rings captured light from every angle and was nearly blinding at times; but other than that, Felicia's jewelry was quite simple. A pair of diamond studs graced her earlobes, and an elegant cross necklace hung between her collarbones from a white-gold chain.

Felicia was dressed admiringly in an appealing two-piece fuchsia suit with intricate black-and-silver embroidery, which flattered her size-ten figure. The skirt stopped just at her knee, which rose to almost midthigh when she sat, but she kept a large matching handkerchief nearby, which she would use to lay across her lap if she needed to take a seat. She wore patterned panty hose on her legs, which had definite sex appeal without making her look whorish. And her stiletto pumps brought the entire outfit together in perfection.

I could look like that, Eureen thought. She began to envision herself as a sexy diva, turning heads wherever she went. She reached up to her hair, pretending to scratch her scalp, but she actually was feeling for new growth in her mixture of relaxed and natural hair. *I can look like that,* she told herself again. Felicia talked on, but Eureen was more focused on how she planned to change her image within the next week. Before she knew it, Felicia was saying a closing prayer and dismissing the group. Eureen took her time gathering her things. Instead of going to claim her children from the children's church area, she lingered a few minutes to chat with her first lady.

"First Lady, can I talk to you for a minute?"

"Sure, Sister Francis." Felicia nodded with a smile.

"First, that was real good what you said tonight. Everything was real good. I like how you kept it real."

"Well, thank you. Sometimes we need to be transparent with each other."

"I just wanna ask you, um . . ." Eureen looked away in embarrassment. "Where do you buy thongs from, and don't they hurt your booty? I mean, don't that little string 'bout cut you in half?"

Felicia couldn't help but giggle a bit. "No, they don't cut you in half, and they are actually quite comfortable when you have on your right size."

"For real?"

Felicia nodded. "You can buy them anywhere you buy panties. I don't know where you shop, but you should be able to find them at Victoria's Secret or even Walmart. They can make a world of difference in your marriage if you start wearing them," she said, winking.

"I need all the help I can get in that department," Eureen confessed. "You said a lot of stuff that I'ma do, 'cause it do be kinda cold in my bedroom and I'm sicka that," she started to explain.

"Well, honey, you got the power to turn it around," Felicia answered, giving Eureen a quick head-to-toe once-over.

"I wish I had your figure, though, 'cause that made sense what you said about how we look and stuff. You right, though. My husband did marry me for something, but them babies did something to me." She chuckled.

"You can undo it with a little work, and maybe it's something you and your husband can do together."

"That sounds good," Eureen commented pensively, thinking what she could do at home to reignite a fire that had gone out long ago. "I have another question, if you don't mind."

"Sure."

"Is it a sin to use stuff? You know, like sex toys and stuff."

"I don't believe it's a sin, but it's definitely a decision that you and your husband should discuss and decide upon together." Felicia touched Eureen's arm lightly. "Quiet as kept, it can add a few sparks, you know what I'm saying." She grinned.

Damn, you and the pastor freaks like that? Eureen thought; although outwardly, she only let out a bit of a giggle. *Pastor be tearing that pussy up, huh?* "Thank you, First Lady," Eureen finished, giving Felicia a small hug. "Let me go down here and get these kids; then I'ma go home and work it!" With a hand on her hip, she twisted away.

"Work it, girl, work it!" Felicia encouraged.

On her way down the hall, Eureen passed by Garnell talking with Deja at the water fountain. Her first inclination was to roll her eyes at him, but then she thought better of it. After her makeover, maybe she could catch his eye. "Not that I would cheat on my husband," she said out loud, but inaudible to anyone other than herself. Instead, she gave Garnell a weak smile, slightly hoping that he would only vaguely remember how nasty she'd been a month ago in church. However, he completely ignored her.

"So I'll give you a call tomorrow," Garnell said, ending the conversation between himself and Deja.

"That sounds great." Deja nodded with a smile.

"Let me walk you to your car," he offered. "It's gotten dark outside and we can't take safety for granted."

His chivalry impressed Deja. *That's what I'm talking about,* she thought. *A man who knows how to be a man.*

Chapter Five

Monroe Francis was an egotistical man, excessively interested in his appearance, his status, and his assets. According to him, the only thing wrong in his life was he was married to a woman to whom he was no longer attracted, primarily because he didn't believe she matched him intellectually; and secondly, she seemed to refuse to take care of herself.

He found that he could barely talk to Eureen without her becoming confused or asking him to break the conversation down into layman's terms. Eventually he found it easier just to keep his thoughts to himself.

On the physical side, he was tired of trying to run his hands through what she called "natural hairstyles." She seemed not to know that it took brushing her teeth to get rid of morning breath. Her wardrobe of oversized T-shirts and sweats were reprehensible, and he thought he'd go blind if he had to look at another supersized pair of what he called "drawls" and a dingy matronly bra.

He and Eureen married when they were both eighteen. He didn't have a dime or a roof to offer her, but she loved him, anyway, and believed in his ambitions. They lived with her mother while Eureen worked two jobs, even while she popped out babies, to let him study and work toward his business degree. Monroe graduated with honors from UCLA, and then he spent another three years taking risks and gambles in the real estate market. When he finally closed a deal that netted him $500,000, this sale was the true launching pad for his career as a broker. Since then, he'd made hundreds and hundreds of thousands. Maybe even a couple million. He just didn't believe in sharing it with his wife.

She didn't do the work; she doesn't deserve the reward, he thought. The success of his career had turned Monroe into a despicable and extremely selfish man.

Now instead of embracing her with the unending and immeasureable love he'd promised on his wedding day, he resented Eureen. Other than providing her with a home, and a used car to get her back and forth to her job as a cashier at a gas station, his assests were off limits to his wife. The only thing that kept him from leaving was the thought of having to split his wealth with her.

In addition to Monroe's accomplishments and wealth, he was an extraordinary lover, but he had long ago stopped making love to Eureen. He found his pleasure in other women . . . and sometimes with men, including his favorite lover, Paul.

Monroe met Paul when Eureen had dragged him one day to a church-sponsored cookout. He spotted Paul from afar, but Eureen did the formal introductions. Since they were both in the same line of business, Paul and Monroe's conversation was effortlessly comfortable.

As Monroe and Paul casually chatted, Paul caught his vibe of interest. He also saw the way he looked at his wife with disgust in his eyes, although Monroe kept it from being displayed on other areas of his face.

Paul decided to probe just a bit. "So how long have you and Eureen been married?"

"Too damn long." Monroe grimaced as he answered. "I don't know what the hell I was thinking when I married her plain ass." He was careful to manage his volume, remembering that he was surrounded by "church folks," but he didn't respect Paul enough to delete his profane words in their conversation. "She has no ambition or drive. All she talks about is Jesus and the Bible, and she's just let herself go." His eyes followed her around the park ground as she balanced two paper plates in her hand and piled them with food for her youngest two children. The other two followed closely behind, able to fix their own plates. "Look at all that damn fried chicken she's getting, knowing that salad would be her best choice."

His comments made Paul both uncomfortable, because of his loose friendship with Eureen, and also strangely excited at the same time due to his sexual preference.

"I don't even enjoy sex with her anymore. She's too big, and she's too big." He chuckled at his own play on words on her overall size and her widened vaginal walls. "And she's too much of a prude, you know what I mean?"

Paul nodded with a smug smile, fantasizing in his head about the wild experiences he could share with Monroe. "Yeah, I do, but you know—just like in business, you always have options."

Monroe smiled slyly. "You got a business card?"

Paul didn't hesitate to slip his hand into his pocket and produce his printed information.

"I'll call you," Monroe promised, tucking the card in his pocket and patting it with a lustful grin on his face.

For the rest of the afternoon, Monroe was caught up in fantasy after fantasy of sexual acts with Paul. "Shit. He make a brother think twice about sleeping in on Sunday mornings," he uttered under his breath, not wanting his wife or, for that matter, anyone else close enough to hear his spoken thoughts.

Since Monroe generally rejected Eureen and her
beliefs, she had been elated when he agreed to come
with her to church the following Sunday. She was completely unaware of his motives. She clapped her hands
and sang praises louder than she had on any other Sunday, several times hollering "Thank ya!" and patting
her face dry with a handful of tissues she had minutes
before filled with snot. Silently she bowed her head and
prayed, *Thank you for changing him, Lord. Take him
deeper and deeper in you.*

For the sake of appearances, Monroe hid his dis-
pleasure when Eureen reached over into his lap and
squeezed his hand.

*Thank you for my husband, Lord! Thank you! And
forgive me for lustin' after other men and stuff. I know
I ain't supposed to do that 'cause that is just like committin' adultery. Please forgive me and give me a new
love for my husband. Help me to seek you more so I
can be a better wife to him.*

Eureen repented from her lewd thoughts of infidel-
ity. Believing Monroe was on his way to finding the
Lord, she overlooked his unpleasant demeanor and
their practically nonexistent sex life. She committed
herself to becoming more involved in the church, instead of spending her time studying her Bible privately
and in prayer, which allowed Monroe the freedom and
flexibility to see Paul whenever he liked.

Eureen did notice that he was keeping later hours
at work; and whenever she called him, he was always
extremely busy and had very little time to talk. The fact
that he rarely made time for a simple hello greatly disappointed her, but she took it in stride, believing that a
change was coming.

"I'll call you back. I'm working on a deal and there's
lots of money on the table here" was his general re-

sponse. "It's a man's world, and a man's gotta do what a man's gotta do."

"And you better keep in mind that it's nothing without a woman," she humorously replied but gained no response from her husband other than the familiar click of the call being disconnected. She eased the handset down with a heavy sigh and fought back tears for the next twenty minutes or so, until she got an idea.

Clearing her throat, she called Monroe back. As soon as he answered the phone, she spoke as seductively as she could. "Baby, I need to see you. Real bad. Can I come by there for a few minutes? I'll make it worth your time," she cooed.

Monroe grunted, at first. However, since Paul was in a meeting that was running late, and Monroe was unable to get his daily lunchtime sexual release, he figured he'd take advantage of the offer. *If I close my eyes, I might be able to forget that it's Eureen,* he told himself.

"What you got for your big daddy?" he replied, surprising her, but making her smile.

"Can I ride you, baby?" she asked. "Or do you wanna hit it from the back?"

"Only if you suck this dick right," he demanded in a teasing tone. "If you suck this dick right, you can get anything you want."

"I can do that, baby. Right there in your office, up under your desk, while you taking phone calls."

"Oh shit. Now you talking." He moaned and ran his hand over his dick, giving it a squeeze.

"You gonna eat this pussy?" she asked, trying to sound like a temptress. *Forgive me, Lord, for using this foul language, but he is my husband,* she thought, feeling a twinge of guilt.

Monroe had no intention of actually having oral sex or intercourse with his wife. He was only concerned with his own selfish pleasures; because of that, he was willing to play her game. "Yeah, baby. Have that shit smelling like pineapples and coconuts. I like tropical fruit—you know what I mean?"

Pineapple and coconuts? How I'ma do that? I'ma have to stop by the freak store and see what they got in there. She wasn't about to blow her opportunity to get something she so desperately needed. "Yeah, baby. I can do that."

"Have that pussy fresh for me, baby. I'm hungry and in the mood to eat off your fruit tree." He chuckled.

"I'll be there in thirty minutes," she promised.

Eureen hung up, feeling excited and a bit moist. Quickly she wet her hair, smoothed it down with a fruity-smelling gel, and slipped into a sundress. She pushed a pair of dark shades over her eyes, jumped in her car, and rushed to an adult novelty store to look for some flavored lubricants, hoping no one would see her.

Eureen had never been in an adult store before and was both appalled and turned on by some of the items she saw. She tried to hide her embarrassment when one of the salesgirls, scantily dressed, approached her.

"Hey there! Can I help you find something?"

"Um . . . I . . . uh . . . I—I was looking for something that comes in a pineapple and coconut smell," she stammered.

"Do you need it to be edible or more like a perfume?"

"I don't know. What you mean?"

"I mean, do you plan to have it licked off?" She winked. The words tumbled easily from the woman's mouth, but Eureen was too embarrassed to look her in the eye.

"Yeah, something like that."

"Okay, we have a whole line of flavors right over here."

Within a few more minutes, Eureen paid for her purchases. She was headed to Monroe's office, grateful he had finally taken time out of his busy schedule to let her come by. Her plan was to have sex with him and then tell him just how much the Lord loved him and encourage him to come with her to Bible Study that week.

Once she got to his office building, she slipped into the ladies' room and smeared two fingerfuls of the lubricant across her lower lips, then on her nipples and then on the lips on her face. Right away, she felt a warming sensation in her panties, which made her rush to Monroe's office door. She knocked twice and turned the knob, finding him seated behind his desk on the phone. He barely even looked her way but continued his conversation without as much as acknowledging her presence. She took a few steps over to a leather sofa that was against the right wall, but then she had a better idea.

With Monroe still on the phone, she approached him, dropped to her knees, and undid his pants. He invited her to continue by widening his legs while he carried on his conversation. Once Eureen enveloped his head in her mouth, he quickly wrapped up the call.

"Ahh," he moaned, leaning back in his chair. "Mmm, suck that dick, baby."

Eureen glanced up for a second, observing the closed eyes, opened mouth, and furrowed brows on her husbands face. The sight both motivated and excited her. She moaned along with him and circled her tongue around his head as quickly as she could.

Little did she know, but behind his closed eyes, Monroe was envisioning his secretary giving him the blow job, not his wife.

"Oh shit! Suck it, baby." He was moaning louder. "Let that dick hit the back of your throat," he coaxed.

Obediently, Eureen filled her mouth with as much of his manhood as she could take; in return, Monroe's reactions became louder. She dipped and bobbed her head to capacity a few more times, and then she tried to pull away to straddle her husband. He wouldn't let her, though.

Before she could get his dick out of her mouth, he felt her slowing and weighted her head with his hands. He then thrust his hips forward. His movements were gentle and fluid initially, but every stroke brought a little more force and a little more speed and a little more selfishness, until he had a firm grip on Eureen's head. He was nearly choking her with his dick.

Eureen was no longer controlling her own movements, and her eyes began to water in her struggle not to gag. Her hands gripped Monroe's thighs in an effort to gain some level of control; but at this point, he couldn't be stopped.

"Shit, baby! Shit," Monroe hollered, gripping Eureen's head even more tightly as his dick exploded a stream of cum into her mouth. He was frozen for nearly three seconds; then he began to ease into a collapse, with his breathing heavy. He didn't notice, and wouldn't have even cared, about the tears cascading down Eureen's face.

Ashamed, she quickly stood to her feet, turned her head away from her husband, and smeared her tears with the heels of her hand. She was no longer turned on.

To add insult to injury, Monroe mumbled as he zipped his pants, "Take your ass on outta here."

Completely demoralized, still not facing Monroe, Eureen used the neckline of her dress to wipe her nose before picking up her purse and heading toward the door. She rested her hand on the knob and thought about why she'd come there in the first place. Of course, she'd wanted to add a little spark to their sex life, which she felt she'd failed at, but she also wanted to tell Monroe how much Jesus loved him.

I can at least do that much, she thought.

She inhaled deeply; then she turned around. Monroe was just picking up the phone to make a call. "Monroe, wait a minute."

"What?" he responded drily, still holding the receiver in his hand.

"I can't leave here without telling you that the Lord loves you."

Immediately Monroe rolled his eyes, but that didn't stop Eureen.

"Instead of focusing so much on your business, you need to put God first, because the Bible says, 'What does it profit a man to gain the whole world and lose his soul,' and I don't want your soul to be lost. I want you to start coming to church more, not just an occasional Sunday." Eureen paused in anticipation of a response.

"And I want you to get your ass out my office, like I said two minutes ago," he spat out.

Chapter Six

More than a week had gone by, which was the longest Shamar had ever stayed away from home. While Jasmine's daughters had pretty much gotten used to Shamar pulling frequent disappearing acts, they became unsettled when more than seven days had gone by.

"Daddy will be home soon," Jasmine told the girls every time they asked about Shamar's whereabouts. "He's just helping Grandma with some stuff."

Truth be told, Jasmine wasn't quite sure herself that Shamar would be back. More accurately said, she was sure that he would return, but she wasn't sure that she'd allow him to stay.

Two nights later, Jasmine approached Shamar no sooner than he crossed the threshold.

"Hey," he mumbled, dropping an overnight bag full of dirty clothes on the floor.

It was just after ten o'clock, so the girls had gone to bed, allowing Jasmine freedom of speech without being overheard.

"Shamar, this isn't going to work anymore," she said. "I've given it a lot of thought, and I feel like I've given you enough time to get yourself together. I'm tired of taking care of you, and I won't do it anymore."

Taking a seat on the couch, he let his wife's words go in one ear and out the other. Jasmine wasn't saying anything he hadn't heard before, so he picked up the television remote and turned to ESPN. "Don't nobody wanna hear that bullshit," he said under his breath, but still loud enough for Jasmine to hear.

"Well, you ought to want to hear it," she said, planting her hands on her hips. "Somebody need to tell you something besides your momma!"

Shamar didn't so much as look her way.

"How you call yourself raising daughters when all they see you do is sit on your ass and flip through channels, instead of getting a job! What kind of example are you setting for them for when they start dating?" Jasmine challenged.

"Whatever." Shamar stood and shuffled to the kitchen to get a beer. "What the hell did you cook tonight? I'm hungry."

"Are you even listening to me?" Jasmine's voice changed octaves. "I said I'm sick of you! All you wanna do is fuck, wash cars, and play those damn video games. I cannot and will not tolerate it any longer! I need a real man, and a real man would step up to the plate and provide for his family, instead of dodging his responsibility every chance he gets! You ain't no man. You ain't nothing but a mama's boy, and you disgust me."

Shamar slammed the refrigerator door; then he pounded on it with his fist. "Listen, Jasmine, do we have to go through this shit again? I just walked in the damn door, and here you go! Don't you ever get tired of bitchin'? Don't your tongue ever get fuckin' tired? I ain't in the mood for this shit! Take a chill pill and holla at me later. I'm goin' to bed; I'm tired."

"How you just gonna walk off from me while I'm talking! It's bad enough that you leave the house anytime you damn well please and stay gone 'til you feel like comin' back. Then when it's time to man up, you run! What the hell?"

"You know damn well I ain't got no job skills and degrees like you, and I ain't neva been smart like you. I ain't one of those brainiac-type dudes who can just up and get a job like that!" Shamar snapped his fingers, emphasizing his point. "And when I do happen to stumble across a job, I give you my whole damn paycheck, so what you trippin' off of? You're the one who wanted to live in this expensive-ass house, tryin' to look good to your friends and family and keep up with the Joneses, not me! You're the one who wanted that Cadillac truck and buy me a fuckin' Jaguar! Hell, I could've settled for any old car to get me from point A to point B, and we don't need a house this damn big! Shit, we coulda lived at Momma's house, but no, you wanted to live a lifestyle of the rich and famous. Then you got the nerve to complain about high-ass bills and shit, which you created! It ain't my fault, Jasmine. Blame your got-damn self!"

"You don't want nothing more out of life than to sit up under your momma?" Jasmine wanted to throw a few choice words to describe Cyreese, but she thought better of it. Shamar had never put his hands on her, but if he ever would, talking bad about his momma would be the one thing that would make him do it. Giving him a disgusted stare, Jasmine shook her head and continued speaking. "You're pathetic, Shamar. Sometimes I can't believe I allowed myself to fall in love with, and have kids by, a pitiful excuse of a man like you. You're a poor example of a man, and you're a poor example of a husband and father!"

"I'm tired of your got-damn mouth, Jasmine! You're always downin' me because you got a good job and pay all the damn bills! I ain't gonna keep lettin' you talk to me any kind of way! Fuck this, I'm packin' all my shit and movin' back to my momma's house!" Shamar stormed upstairs, mumbling obscenities, infuriated by things not having gone as he planned. He had wanted to come home, have make-up sex, and go to sleep.

Jasmine followed him and continued her tirade. "See, there you go! You ain't been home five damn minutes and you ready to run off again. Well, pack then, nigga! There's the fucking door!" She pointed down the staircase. "I'm sure your momma's waiting for you with a damn pacifier, some footie pajamas, and a warm bottle of milk—or is she gonna pull out one of her saggy titties for you to suck on, 'cause you ain't nothing but a grown-ass baby!"

Shamar stomped his way to their bedroom, entered the walk-in closet, and yanked clothes from their hangers.

"You're nothing but a spoiled-ass mama's boy, Shamar! You'll never be able to stand on your own feet! Your sorry ass is gonna be all twisted when she's dead and gone! You call yourself a man just because you got a big dick! Well, let me tell you something; there are bigger and better ones out there! Yeah, you hurry up and get your shit! Move to the left, nigga, and make sure you don't forget anything, because I don't want you coming back! And give me my car keys, my house keys, and my credit cards! Call your momma and tell her to pick you up, and tell her to hurry the hell up!"

"Fuck you, Jasmine. Kiss my pretty yellow ass!" Shamar barked, slamming a set of keys to the floor, just barely missing Jasmine's bare toes.

Jasmine spun on her heels and threw herself face-down across their bed, trying to hide her sniveling. She buried her head in her crossed arms and prayed through her tears.

Lord, what am I doing wrong? I don't get this. Your Word says a man who don't work don't eat, so why

can't Shamar just get a job like a man supposed to do?
I've tried encouraging him, incenting him with super-
freaky sex, finding him job hookups, and everything I
know how to do, but he refuses to work! And then he
loves his momma more than he loves me. A man s'pose
to leave his momma and daddy and cleave to his wife.
He not cleavin' to me; he cleavin' to her. I'm sicka that,
Lord, and I just can't take no more.

Shamar emerged from the closet and shuffled around
the room, opening and slamming drawers. "Gon' tell me
I ain't no damn man. Who da fuck you think you talking to?" Shamar was speaking more to himself than to
his wife. "I break my neck, making sure this oversized
house stay clean and shit, and make sure your car look
like something for you to flaunt your ass in the streets.
I make sure these girls get to school on time, and I go to
the parent-teacher conferences and shit, but that ain't
worth shit."

Jasmine never moved or said a word.

"Bye," he uttered, and left the room.

Jasmine listened keenly to him go down the stairs
and out the front door. Even then, she didn't move,
feeling too overwhelmed and emotionally tired. She
pulled herself together and rolled over on her back, her
mind swimming in a sea of thoughts as she stared at
different spots on the ceiling.

Besides being lazy and unconcerned about household issues—that is as far as Jasmine was concerned
—Shamar had been a faithful and family-oriented man.
Not once had he even thought about cheating on Jasmine, although his looks gained him plenty of attention. He turned heads wherever he went—from both
single and married women—but he turned down every
single sexual offer that came that way, completely satisfied with his sex life at home.

And without question, Jasmine loved him very much, but she was just simply fed up with carrying the entire load of providing for their family.

Jasmine pushed a long sigh from her lips as she thought about the girls. What were her kids going to think when they knew she'd put their father out? It was actually hard for Jasmine to take something from them they loved so much; but hopefully, they would understand after she explained exactly why their father was no longer living with them.

Jasmine often had entertained the thought of divorcing Shamar because of his "I don't give a damn" attitude, but she always dismissed it, replacing the thought with hope and prayer. She wanted nothing more than a perfect marriage and family, which to her included a good, understanding, working husband who contributed at least half, or maybe even 75 percent. But, hell, at this point, she would settle for just 10 percent to start.

Her phone rang, startling her. Although she didn't feel much like talking, she took Deja's call, anyway. She quickly caught her up to what had taken place over the past hour. Most times, Jasmine kept her friends out of her marriage business, but Shamar not having a job was a secret to no one. Sometimes she found her situation unbearable and just needed to vent.

"So I sent his ass to his momma's house, girl. He go runnin' over there all the damn time, anyway. I'm through with him."

"Yeah, whatever, Jasmine. If I had a penny for every time you and Shamar broke up, I'd be a millionaire!" Deja replied humorously, but truthfully. "He'll be back in a couple days like he always does; I'll give him three at the most."

"Why can't you guys support me on this, like girl-friends are supposed to do? Why do you have to be so damn sarcastic and negative?"

"Can you blame us? Think about it, Jasmine. You're too damn smart and educated, and have too many positive things going on in your life to be with a loser who can't find two brown pennies to rub together. Plus, if he could find them, he too damn lazy to bend over and pick them up. He's just hating on you because of your accomplishments. You did the right thing, but like I said, I give it three days max before he's back."

"I've been seriously weighing my options; because as it stands, things aren't ever gonna change with him. I just don't want to make any sudden decisions that will hurt the kids in the long run." Jasmine sighed.

"So what you gon' do? Hold on to a worthless loser to make the kids happy, but make yourself miserable and stressed the hell out, paying all the damn bills? Or do you drop him like it's hot and be optimistic about your and the kids' future?" Deja challenged.

The question caused Jasmine to silence herself in deep thought.

Deja pressed forward. "If you ask me, you're hurting the kids even more by having an unfit man raise them, but let me shut up and stay out of it, because you'll end up being mad at me for telling the truth! You'll take him back, like you always do; then you'll be mad at me and not talk to me," Deja added.

Jasmine released a long sigh. "I'm just fed up, girl. I tried being optimistic, but nothing has changed. For the moment, I need some 'me' time to sort things out. Lord knows I tried, and I've been more than patient with Shamar," she stated. "But he just too damn comfortable doing nothing and too satisfied with those once-every-three-months, dead-end, minimum-wage jobs."

"I don't know how or why you put up with his foolishness this long," Deja replied. "Honestly, my recommendation is a place called 'Fast Divorce,' if you're serious. He better be glad I ain't his damn wife. I woulda been changed my last name back to my maiden name."

"Well, this time, I'm not letting him come back."

"What are you going to tell the kids?"

"I'll tell them he's on a road trip or something."

"Summer might believe something like that, but you know Winter is way more intuitive and will know something's up."

"I'll deal with the kids, Deja. I've gotta take one thing at a time. I'm just sick of this happening."

"Things happen for a reason, Jasmine. Keep that in mind. Shamar is a sorry example of a family man, anyway! He's lazy, and he's a mama's boy at that. That woman has more control over his life than he does."

Jasmine sighed.

"To tell you the truth, girl, you set yourself up for a letdown, because you knew all about him before you married him. You've gotta partially blame yourself."

"Chill out, Deja. You're sounding more and more like my mother. You are supposed to be consoling me, not criticizing."

"I'm just givin' it to you straight 'cause I love you," Deja claimed.

"Anyway"—Jasmine's tone matched the rolling of her eyes, which Deja couldn't see—"I've gotta call my job and tell them I'm taking a few days off so I can get myself together. I'll call you later."

"Okay, but don't be stressing out behind that mess. You did the right thing. Life is too good and way too short to be trippin' off a worthless nigga."

"Thanks for listening. I'll talk to you later."

No sooner had she hung up the phone, than she heard Shamar coming back inside. Quickly she ran her hand across her eyes, smearing away her tears. Then she flipped back to her stomach and tucked her head back into the crook of her arm, pretending not to have moved a muscle. She heard him slowly make his way up the stairs, then into their bedroom. Shamar eased his weight onto their bed and removed his shoes; then he lay back, right next to his wife.

Silence hung in the air for nearly ten minutes. Jasmine actually had begun to doze off a bit, but finally Shamar spoke.

"Babe," he called softly.

Jasmine didn't answer, wanting him to think she'd fallen asleep.

"Jaz," he called, slightly shaking her.

"What, Shamar?" Her response was muffled, since she didn't lift her head.

"Look, babe, I love you," Shamar whispered, but got no response. He ran his finger across a small strip of skin that was exposed where Jasmine's shirt didn't meet the waistline of her pants. She enjoyed the tingle it caused, but she didn't move. "I love you, Jasmine. I know I fuck up all the time, but, baby, I'm sorry."

He turned his body to her and nuzzled her neck as his hand slid beneath her shirt and caressed her back. He rubbed for a few seconds; then he nudged her head with his own to get her to look at him, which she did. He met her lips with his for a slow, indulgent lingering kiss.

"I'm sorry, babe. I'ma try to do better." He kissed her again. "You got every right to be mad at me, and you right. As a man, I do need to do better for you and the girls." The more he talked, the better his hands felt. Jasmine began to be aroused. "I'ma look for something this week, a'ight?" He paused momentarily for a response, but Jasmine didn't move. "I'm talking about a real job. Not just something at the temporary office—you know what I'm sayin'?"

This time, Jasmine nodded silently.

"I love you and the girls, baby," he continued. "And this is where I wanna be. Not with my momma." Those words brought a slight grin to his wife's face. When Shamar saw it, he planted more kisses on her and pulled her to him, which she obliged, returning his affectionate actions. "Mmm," he moaned. "Bring me my sugar cookies."

He and Jasmine made love for several hours and fell asleep in a wet, messy heap, completely consumed and in love with each other.

Chapter Seven

With his regular church attendance and steady job, Garnell hoped that he was proving to his uncle Wilbur Sutton that he truly was ready to do the right thing in life and was simply fed up with facing the consequences that crime, drugs, and basic street life produced. When he showed up on his doorstep two months ago, he had professed to his uncle that he had come to the reality that there was nothing in the streets but jail or death, and he had grown tired of living like that.

"Good evening," he said, coming in after a Sunday evening service and finding Wilbur sitting in the kitchen, finishing up a plate of what had been smothered chicken, rice, and black-eyed peas. Wilbur grunted with an old man's scowl and continued eating. Garnell set his Bible on the kitchen counter and then took a seat across from his uncle. He sighed happily, thinking about Deja. "I'm a changed man, Uncle Willie," he said with a slight grin.

Wilbur pushed his empty plate to the side and lit a cigarette; then he lit into his nephew. "And you expect me to believe that shit," he spat out. "You got a mutha-fuckin' rap sheet long as my arm, and that make you a got-damn high-risk muthafucka." Wilbur took a long drag on his cigarette as he glared at his nephew. "But 'fore my baby brother shut his eyes in death, I promised him that I would look after you, and that's the only got-damn reason I'm letting your criminal ass stay here."

"Yes, sir," Garnell replied respectfully. If he didn't need a roof over his head, clothes on his back, and food in his belly, he would have told the old man to shut the fuck up; but since the last thing he needed was to be living on the streets, he stayed humble. "I appreciate it too, Uncle Willie," he mumbled, studying the grain pattern of the kitchen table, where the two men sat.

"Where my muthafuckin' rent money?" Wilbur extended an aged hand, which was greasy and worn from working a lifetime under the hood of vehicles. With his other hand, he pulled a half-smoked cigarette from his lips and smashed it into a butt-filled ashtray, which sat in the middle of the table.

Garnell hated that Wilbur smoked. It messed up his clothes, and thus messed up his game with the churchwomen. That's one thing he knew a God-fearing woman would run from in a heartbeat—a stale, smoky-smelling man.

"I got it," Garnell answered, immediately reaching for his back pocket for his wallet and pulling out $200. "Here you go."

Wilbur snatched the hundred-dollar bills from Garnell's hand, folded them together, and put them in his shirt pocket. "I ain't gon' be looking for your ass every week to get my money neither. When I crack my eyes open on Saturday mornings, you better make sure that shit sitting right here on this got-damn table right up under this muthafucka right here," he commanded, slapping the ashtray against the tabletop. "You hear me?"

"Yes, sir." Garnell nodded. "I'm 'bout to go out for a little bit." He rose to his feet, not wanting to hear any more of Wilbur's choice lecturing.

I don't know who the fuck he think he talking to; I'm a grown-ass man, Garnell thought, but he knew better than to let the words escape his lips.

"And don't be bringing no shit to my house or your ass gonna be on the street," he threw in. "I ain't gon' give a damn 'bout what I promised your daddy. He need to come back from the grave an' whup your black ass, just for the hell of it."

Garnell didn't comment, but only reached for his keys and headed for the door.

"Your ass bed' not so much as run a got-damn stoplight in that car either," Wilbur warned.

"Yes, sir." Garnell closed the door behind him and sat in the car for a few minutes, just thinking. Living with his uncle, he felt like a thirteen-year-old child all over again, but it was better than being at a homeless shelter, and cheaper and cleaner than a motel. Wilbur also allowed him the use of one of his many vehicles he'd acquired from customers abandoning their vehicles after sending them to his shop for repair. Another benefit was that Wilbur was a well-dressed man when he went out, and he and Garnell happened to wear the same size. Garnell just needed to put the garments in the cleaners before he wore them, in order to get the cigarette stench out; and then again after he wore them, to prevent being cussed out. In addition, he thought he could always lie and tell women that he'd moved in with Wilbur to help him out financially.

Garnell pulled out his cell phone and dialed Deja's number, newly acquired after a few more after-service chats. "Hey," he stated, "it's Garnell."

"Hi," Deja squealed, grinning to herself. She was pleased that he'd called.

"You busy?"

Deja contemplated what her response should be in a split second, not wanting to seem too available or desperate. "I was actually about to cook dinner," she lied. Most nights, Deja skipped dinner or ate out, not wanting to put forth the effort to prepare a meal for one.

"Whoa, whoa, whoa!" Garnell chuckled. "Before you start rattling pots and pans, I wanted to see if you wanted to grab something to eat with me."

After a few seconds of hesitation, Deja agreed. "I guess I could stand a break from the kitchen."

"So I'll pick you up in about thirty minutes?" he asked.

"How about I meet you," she suggested, not yet comfortable with Garnell knowing where she lived.

"Sounds great," he agreed. "See you at Ruby Tuesday in a half hour," he added.

I hope her ass got some money, Garnell thought, reminded that he only had a few dollars to get him to his next payday. He was hoping that Wilbur would have let him slide on the rent that week, but he had no such luck.

Right on time, Deja met Garnell at the restaurant. She greeted him with a warm hug. Deja was dressed in a flowing halter dress of red, black, and yellow. A pair of red stilettos graced her feet. Her hair was pinned in a loose, sexy updo, and large hoop earrings and beautifully glossed lips completed the look.

Garnell lightly pecked her cheek and inhaled her aroma. "You look amazing," he commented, taking special note that she wore no bra. He avoided the urge to lick his lips seductively while he escorted her to their booth. Once seated, he stared at her adoringly, until Deja blushed. "I'm sorry; you're just so beautiful."

"Thank you, Garnell." Deja smiled with confidence, feeling beautiful and sexy.

Garnell narrowed his eyes a bit and folded his bottom lip into his mouth, showing her some degree of his sexual attraction; then he cleared his throat, as if coming to himself. "Let me stay focused," he commented, taking hold of the menu, although that was far from his intentions. "You want an appetizer?"

"Sure!" She nodded, enjoying his attention.

Garnell ordered a plate of golden-brown fried shrimp, tossed in a fiery yet sweet chili sauce, and two soft drinks, although he would have preferred something from the bar. As an entrée, Deja chose a dish featuring sautéed baby portobello mushrooms and artichokes in a Parmesan cream sauce over a fresh grilled chicken breast. It was served with steamed broccoli and white-cheddar mashed potatoes. Garnell settled on a well-seasoned nine-ounce sirloin, cooked well done, then topped with blue cheese crumbles, onion straws, and Boston barbecue sauce, sided with a baked potato covered with bacon bits, butter, sour cream, and cheese.

"So how long have you been in California?" Deja asked, sipping from her drink.

"I was raised here," Garnell answered truthfully.

"So you've been here all your life, then, huh?"

Garnell nodded his lie, stirring through his iced beverage with his straw. He left out his transitions to several state prisons, which ultimately landed him on the East Coast, where he met and married Stephanie, and then left her there with two kids.

"Ever been married?" Deja asked, reaching to take hold of a shrimp.

"Hold on, sweetheart. Let me bless the table first," he offered, impressing Deja. Garnell said a simple prayer; then he dipped a shrimp into its sauce and offered it to Deja's receiving lips. "To answer your question, nah," he lied, again, which set the course for their entire conversation.

Garnell told one lie after another, making himself look like the perfect man for any woman. By the time dinner was over, he had worked ten years on the same job as a pharmaceutical sales representative, then manager, then regional manager, which allowed him to travel the country. In his mind, he was telling the truth: He had sold drugs first on his block, then his neighborhood, then throughout his city. He had traveled from state to state, but with shackles on his feet, and a gun in his face.

It's up to her to figure out what I mean, he told himself.

"You got kids?" she asked.

"Can't have kids without a wife," he answered. "I've always been too busy traveling and stuff to settle down with a family; I've just been focused on my career." Garnell added to his story that he'd allowed his uncle to come live with him after his uncle's house burned down to the ground, and the older man didn't have homeowner's insurance.

While he spoke, their server brought the check. "Thanks, man," he said, picking up the folio as soon as it hit the table. He glanced at the printed paper; then he reached for his wallet.

"He's been having a time getting back on his feet." Garnell shook his head. "It's my daddy's brother, and ever since I lost my dad when I was eight, I really gravitated to my uncle. I can't leave him out there like that, you know?"

"Wow, Garnell. You are something else," Deja commented, having believed every word.

Taking advantage of her being caught like a fish on a hook, he smacked his fingers against his forehead. "Oh my God," he said almost inaudibly.

"What's wrong?" she answered, finishing up her dessert of moist buttermilk-and-walnut cake, layered with cool cream cheese and accented with a dusting of toasted coconut.

Garnell sat in pensive silence, his eyes darting randomly around the room.

"I'll be right back. I need to go to my car right quick." Garnell went to the parking lot to act out his drama; then he returned two minutes later. "I'm so embarrassed," he said, sliding into the booth, shaking his head with a sigh.

"What happened?" Deja asked a second time.

"I've lost my debit card," he announced, taking a second look in his wallet. "And I don't carry cash; it's too dangerous."

"Oh, don't worry about it, Garnell. I got it," Deja offered.

With Garnell showing her he had so much to offer, she didn't want him to walk away, with the thought that she had nothing to bring to the table, so she was delighted to pay the bill. Quickly she dug through her purse, pulled out her wallet, withdrew a few bills, and set them on the table. "That should be enough for the tip too."

"No, please let me get that. That's the least I can do," Garnell insisted.

He picked up the cash, gave Deja whatever would be considered change from the check, and then added a twenty from his own pocket, giving Deja the impression that he was a big tipper.

"You're a lifesaver. I promise to make this up to you." He maintained a humiliated look. "I was really hoping we could catch a movie tonight, but I can't even afford to take you out on a real date without my debit card."

"Oh, I got it!" Deja waved her hand in dismissal. "You can pay next time," she added with a giggle.

Feigning reluctance and agitation that he was unable to pay for the evening, Garnell agreed. He easily could have won an Academy Award for his performance. "I feel like a worthless jackass," he mumbled.

"Don't feel that way, Garnell," Deja replied, grabbing hold of his hand. "We're only human and these types of things sometimes happen. Please stop letting it bother you. I've got everything covered this time. Like I said, next time it's on you, or will there be a next time?"

"Are you kidding?"

"Well?"

"Of course, there'll be a next time, and many, many more, I hope."

"I saw how a couple of the women at the church have looked at you, so I just need to know if I'm entering myself unknowingly in some sorta unspoken competition."

"Is that how you feel about me?" He held a serious look.

"Not really, but I know that women can be flirtatious and promiscuous when they see something they want."

"Listen, Deja, I've always been the dedicated type, you know. I devote all my love, my time, my heart, my mind, my soul, and my money to the person I'm with; and I expect the same in return."

Deja nodded with a smile. "I can do that."

Despite Deja having spent close to a hundred dollars, she still had a good time and was looking forward to many more. She couldn't wait to get home to call Tracey and Jasmine to tell them about her new acquaintance, but a better idea suddenly popped inside her mind. To her, she had possibly, finally met Mr. Right.

As for Garnell, until he accomplished his ultimate goal of moving in with a woman who would put up with his shit, he would not be 100 percent satisfied. Wilbur had given him just a small window of time to get his shit together and move on, and his time was quickly running out. If Deja wasn't the one, somebody out there was.

Chapter Eight

It took two hours, but Eureen finally emerged from the beauty supply store with two bags full of makeover items. She took a seat in her car and grinned at her purchases: two full lace wigs—one curly and one straight—some adhesive, hair grease, a bottle of moisturizer, a few bottles of nail polish, a foot file, a jar of hot wax, and some new cosmetics.

"You sure you know how to do this?" she asked her fourteen-year-old daughter, Mezzi, who had a natural, yet ghetto-fabulous, knack for styling hair.

"Yeah, Ma. I do it for girls at school all the time. Plus anything would be better than how your hair looks now," she added.

"Don't make me slap you, girl," Eureen warned. "I'm still your momma."

"I'm just saying, I been asking you to let me do your hair."

"Well, today's your lucky day."

Mezzi sucked her teeth. "But why you pick the day I s'posed to be going to the movies with my friends, Ma?"

"You need to be grateful that I let you go out with them skanks at all. It shouldn't take that long, right?"

"About an hour."

Mezzi started on her mother's head as soon as they got home, hoping she'd still have time to go out with her girlfriends. She parted and braided Eureen's untamed coif into neat rows, greasing her scalp in the process. When she was done, she covered Eureen's hair with the wig cap, cleaned around her hairline with alcohol, then placed the wig on her head and glued it in place. Mezzi trimmed the lace, brushed it out, and then handed her mother a mirror.

"Oh my goodness!" Eureen exclaimed, examining the silky strands of hair that appeared to be growing from her scalp.

"You can part it and style it and stuff," Mezzi mentioned, running her fingers through the faux hair. "Nobody will be able to tell that it's a wig."

Thoroughly impressed, Eureen smiled with a new and extremely high sense of confidence. She stood to her feet, snapping her fingers and wiggling her behind.

"Go, Ma! Go, Ma," Mezzi chanted, encouraging Eureen's behavior. "Now sit down and let me get those eyebrows."

Eureen obeyed her daughter and, after a bit of yelping in pain, was again pleased with the results.

By the time Bible Study rolled around, Eureen felt like new money. She had squeezed her body into a reshaping undergarment, which smoothed out her bulges and rolls, lifted her breast sand behind, and gave her an incredible hourglass figure. Then she put on a red pencil skirt with a black sleeveless blouse with cascading ruffles down its front. She was a bit uncomfortable, but she put on a pair of her daughter's Baby Phat platform pumps. She used her hallway to practice walking in them. Although she felt a bit awkward, she was ready to take the chance.

As gracefully as she could, Eureen attempted what she thought was sauntering past her husband, who was dozing on the couch, and picked up her keys and purse. Monroe peeled his eyes open momentarily, taking notice of the backside of a woman he didn't recognize.

"Who are you?" he asked lazily as a lustful grin spread slowly across his face.

"Don't worry about it," Eureen snapped as she whisked her head around, revealing her face.

"What the hell!" Monroe exclaimed, stunned at his wife's transformation.

"You ain't been interested in me all this time, so don't look this way now."

"What is that mess on your head," he slurred with a chuckle, partially breaking down Eureen's confidence, but then she quickly remembered he hadn't so much as looked at her in almost three years.

"Carry your ass back to sleep," she growled, and wobbled to the front door. "I'm going to church."

"Did you cook me some dinner first?"

Eureen slammed the door behind her, got her balance, and headed to her car. Instead of playing her usual Shirley Caesar tape, she tuned her car radio to an R & B and hip-hop station, where Mary J. Blige was singing "The One." She wasn't familiar enough with the lyrics to sing along, but she listened and bobbed her head, glancing at herself in the rearview mirror every chance she got.

As she pulled into the church parking lot, she turned her stereo down, tuned it back to the gospel station, and parked her car. She saw Deacon Derrick Kelly waiting in the lot to escort women safely inside, as he normally did, and smiled in anticipation of his reaction when he'd catch sight of her. Normally, Derrick pretended not even to see Eureen because she just wasn't attractive enough for him to make the effort; but when she stepped a single foot out of her car, he was forced to do a double take.

"Oh shit!" he mumbled to himself, giving her body a once-over and liking what he saw. "Look-a-here, look-a-here!" Instead of turning his back and going the opposite way, Derrick strode over to Eureen's car and waited for her. "Good evening, Sista! God bless you. Let me make sure you get inside all right."

"Good evening, Deacon." She grinned, flattered by his sudden interest. "Thank you." Eureen picked up her Bible and purse from the front seat.

"You look very nice tonight," Derrick commented respectfully, although his thoughts were far less than respectful. "You been working out?"

"Something like that." She kept her stride slow and even, as not to embarrass herself in the heels, and tugged on her skirt a few times as she walked.

"Well, that's good. We all need to take care of this temple made of flesh." Derrick chuckled. He glanced behind Eureen to catch another eyeful of her ass; then he cleared his throat. "Yes, sir. Gotta take care if it." Like a gentleman, he opened the door of the church for her and she walked inside. "Enjoy the service."

Derrick tracked back outside, adding Eureen to his list of women he planned to fuck, looking around him to make sure no one would see him give his dick a squeeze. Because Eureen had shared her business with one too many people, Derrick knew that she was itching to have a solid piece of dick. He wouldn't have to do too much to seduce her into letting him give it to her.

Instead of sitting near the back, like she normally did, somewhat ashamed of her appearance, Eureen sat boldly in the second pew, wanting to make sure that both the pastor and the first lady caught sight of her and her new look. She would never admit it, but she was a bit self-conscious about the other female parishioners glancing over at her and seemingly whispering. She made herself dismiss their utterings, knowing she looked good. She had to try extra hard to hide her grin.

"Let us stand to our feet to honor the Lord," Pastor Gardner instructed, ready to open the service in prayer. Eureen popped up like her name was Jiffy. She slung her straight locks behind her with a quick twist of her neck and let it fall again as she bowed her head. She barely heard Pastor Gardner's words; her thoughts were consumed with her own perceived beauty. From out of nowhere, a song popped in her mind.

"I'm a, I'm a, a diva, hey!" She sang it over and over in her head, not knowing any more of the song made popular by Beyoncé. When she caught herself, she mumbled a half-second prayer for forgiveness.

Jasmine slipped into the sanctuary fifteen minutes after church started and quickly took a seat beside Tracey.

"What did I miss?"

"Nothing really. He's just getting started good."

"Good. Girl, Shamar came back home," Jasmine shared.

"I heard. That's good," Tracey commented.

"Girl, please," Jasmine said, rolling her eyes. "That mess ain't good."

"What do you mean?"

"I'll tell you after the service," Jasmine promised. "Oh my God! Is that Eureen Francis up there with that headful of weave?"

"Yep." Tracey nodded. "She shoulda come to my house. I woulda hooked her up, sho'nuff, but it's a start."

For the next hour, the congregation tuned in to their pastor's teaching. As usual, his topics seemed to step on the toes of their private lives. He'd been on a series focusing on family structure, where he talked about the roles and responsibility of the man, which had Jasmine darting her eyes nervously, avoiding eye contact. He talked about loose, fornicating women, and that had Tracey squirming in her seat. Still, she didn't feel too bad because she didn't consider herself, technically, to be having sex with Jermaine, even though she was now considering moving in with him. Pastor Gardner revisited men with ulterior motives, which made Garnell nervously pat his foot and stare at the printed words in his Bible without really focusing on them. His point about women scheming and planning to cheat on their spouses made Eureen look the opposite way of the pulpit, which is when she caught eyes with Derrick. There was almost a sigh of relief from the congregation when David Gardner finally dismissed the service.

Tracey and Jasmine gathered their things, making idle chatter until they got outside. "So what's the deal with Shamar?" Tracey asked.

"He's back home, but he still ain't got no job."

"Girl, I done told you—"

"But he has been looking . . . for real this time," Jasmine threw in, cutting Tracey off. "He just can't hardly find nothing. You know he ain't hardly worked ten days in his whole life. Don't nobody hire people like that, but McDonald's. We were both hoping for a little better than that."

"You want me to talk to Jermaine? He said they always looking for drivers on his job, and they pay you while you in training."

"What you gotta do?" Jasmine asked, fully interested.

"Other than have a driver's license"—Tracey shrugged—"I don't know. I'll ask him when he calls tonight."

"Girl, look at Eureen!" Jasmine shrieked, taking note of Eureen's instant hourglass figure. She whipped Tracey's shoulders, pointing her in the direction of Eureen, who stood cackling with Felicia Gardner. "Oh my

God! What happened to her? When did she get a body like that?"

"Oh snap!" Tracey's eyes nearly popped out of her head "She look good! I wonder what she talking to the first lady about."

"Who knows, girl, you know she half crazy with her mean self. Anyway, please ask Jermaine about the job thing. I wouldn't mind Shamar being gone a few days a week. Does it pay good?" Jasmine asked.

"Girl, yeah. Jermaine makes good money. Every week he break me off a few hundred dollars just because," Tracey bragged.

"What! You must be givin' up that good-good if he dropping dollars on you like that."

"Nope. I told him I wanted to wait until I got married."

"And he didn't run away?"

"No. We still seeing each other. He calls me every night; and when he's home, he spends all his time with me. Girl, you know if they love you, they'll wait. That's a man right there."

Jasmine's look was suspicious. "You sure he ain't shoppin' at another grocery story."

"Yeah, I'm sure. Girl, he sho know how to lick the pussycat too!" Jasmine giggled, falling into Tracey's shoulder.

"So you gettin' without givin'? Nasty heifer!"

"Don't hate."

"Ain't nobody hatin'. I'm married, remember?"

The two ladies strained to hear what Felicia shared with Eureen as they walked by the pair.

"Yeah, that really helped me to look at myself differently and make some positive changes," Eureen said, flinging her hair.

"I see." Felicia bobbed her head.

"My husband still ain't paying me no mind, though. I need the Lord to give me patience and strength. Next I'ma gonna go 'head and try them thongs."

"You do that, Sis." Felicia winked and accepted her husband's arm as he walked up and pecked her cheek.

"Y'all have a good night." Eureen watched Felicia walk away, studying her behind for panty lines. "Hmm." On her way to her car, Eureen gave some thought to stopping by Walmart and picking up new underwear.

Chapter Nine

"Y'all, come on in!" Tracey welcomed Jasmine and Shamar into Jermaine's home, where she was hosting a dinner party centered around an NFL game. "Deja and Garnell are already here."

"Hey, girl," Jasmine greeted. "This is nice!" She slipped out of her shoes, adding them to the footwear lined up just inside the door, indicating that none were to be worn inside Jermaine's home.

"'S'up, Tracey?" Shamar followed suit, inconspicuously absorbing his surroundings, which weren't decorated like a typical bachelor's pad. He didn't say anything, but he was impressed with the marble flooring and a tan sectional, with matching recliners and matching drapes. The place was spotless and gleaming as if Mr. Clean himself had made a house call. *This shit is laid,* he thought. *Driving trucks pay like this? Sign me the hell up!* He had already planned to talk more to Jermaine about the job opportunity while they were there, but even more so now that he'd seen a bit of the house.

"We're down in the basement, where the big TV is. Come on this way."

"Girl, we want a tour first!" Jasmine demanded with a laugh. "I didn't know your man was doing it like this."

"Can't tell you everything," Tracey teased. "Come on." She led the couple upstairs on thick carpeting to two fully decorated guest bedrooms, with a full bathroom adjoining them, a well-equipped home office, and a room with mirrored walls that housed a tread-mill, elliptical machine, several dumbbells, and Bow-flex home gym machine.

Tracey led them through the master bedroom, fea-turing a king-sized four-post bed, a box window, com-plete with plush seating and elaborate draping, two walk-in closets, and a beautiful double-sided fireplace, which provided heat and ambience in the bedroom; then they headed right over to a double-sized Jacuzzi tub in the bathroom.

Shamar nodded his head in silence and let his wife do all the verbal oohing and aahing for the both of them.

This nigga ballin', he thought.

They took a back staircase to the first floor and ended up in the kitchen, where granite countertops with sil-ver flecks gleamed alongside stainless-steel appliances. A large island was covered with food, although Tracey and Jermaine had laid out a full spread on the wet bar in the basement below, which is where Tracey led them next.

"Hey, man," Jermaine greeted, dapping Shamar when he entered the room.

"You got a nice place, man," Shamar complimented.

"Thank you, sir. Make yourself at home."

Shamar's eyes took in the sixty-inch plasma televi-sion mounted to the far wall and a hundred-gallon aquarium filled with exotic saltwater fish. The leather furnishings and caramel-painted walls gave the room a warm and inviting, yet manly, feel that suggest relax-ation. He slapped hands with Garnell after a quick in-troduction; then he settled on the couch while Jasmine chatted with the girls at the wet bar.

"So you drive trucks long distance?" he asked, look-ing at Jermaine.

"I stay on the road," Jermaine answered with a nod as he sucked down the rest of his beer. "But I love it."

"It pay good?"

"Oh yeah. The pay is sweet. They compensate you real well for all that time you're away from your family. It's just me right now, so it's not that bad." Jermaine shrugged.

"Yeah, man, I like this here," Shamar responded, taking a look around the room. This time, he didn't hide how impressed he was. "You gon' have to tell me how to get on that gig."

"What do you do right now? You got driving experience?"

"I mean, I know how to drive. I got a license, but I ain't never drove no big rig," he said, trying to avoid sharing the fact that he was unemployed.

"No problem. I can put in a good word for you and get you on, whenever you're ready. They provide paid training. You'll be a pro at wheelin' them wheels in no time." Jermaine chuckled. "What about you, Garnell? What you do for a livin'?"

Garnell choked a bit on his beer, which he had sworn to Deja he only drank occasionally and socially after she showed her disapproval. "I . . . uh . . . I work for Pfizer," he lied, remembering that he had just seen their commercial only minutes before. "Most people only recognize them for end-user consumer products, but they have a whole pharmaceutical department that a lot of people don't know about," he said knowingly before taking a swig of his beer.

Damn, Shamar thought, feeling small and unaccomplished. *I need to get my shit together. These muthafuckas working for corporations and shit, and I'm sittin' on my ass fucking with a damn Wii.* He cut his eyes over at Jasmine, who was piling spaghetti on his plate. *I bet that's why her manipulative ass wanted me to come to this party so damn bad. To make me look like a piece of shit in front of these job-havin' niggas. Wait 'til I tell my momma this shit.* All of a sudden, he felt anger rising up inside him, but he hid it as best he could. *I'ma deal with her ass when we get home. Naw, fuck that. I'ma cussing her ass out soon as we get in the car.*

"Here you go, baby." Jasmine handed him a plate with the pasta, a few hot wings, and a handful of chips and dip. "What you want to drink?"

"It don't matter," he answered, close to a snarl, but Jasmine had been too distracted by Tracey and Deja standing in the corner, whooping about something one of them had said, to take notice. She returned seconds later with a bottle of beer, handed it to him, and chased back over to her friends. His attitude calmed a bit, once the men started discussing the game and who they thought would go to the Super Bowl that season. Amid the food, beer, conversation, and the game, it didn't take Shamar long to loosen up and enjoy himself.

The ladies decided to take their conversation to the kitchen.

"Girl, this house is off the chain!" Deja commented, winding noodles around her fork and stuffing them in her mouth. "You better marry that joker."

"Think I won't if he ask me? I sho will," Tracey laughed, slapping a high five with Jasmine.

"All this house and you ain't givin' up no pussy?" Jasmine questioned in disbelief.

"I mean I feed him somethin' to eat every now and then, but ain't no dick pushing up in here until his ass make me a Mrs.," Tracey answered. "That's who you need to be concerned with right there," she added, pointing her fork to Deja. "She the one droppin' the drawers for the church boy."

"I am not!" Deja denied, playfully slapping her girl-friend on the arm.

"Girl, you know you fuckin' that man undercover," Tracey teased.

"Why I can't be like you? You claim you ain't ridin' no horses, so why I gotta be on the saddle?" The ladies burst into laughter. "I'm tryin'a live saved, just like y'all are, but with all this cussin' y'all doing, I don't know if y'all heifers tryin'a live right or tryin'a bust hell wide open."

"Whatever, girl. Even Peter cussed in the Bible, and he was a disciple," Tracey replied, still laughing. "So what's the deal? Can a brother put it down or what?"

"I told you, we not rolling like that," Deja repeated for her friends.

"Girl, ain't no way you up under that man just about every night of the week and he ain't getting no pussy," Jasmine said.

"Everybody ain't nasty like y'all!" Deja laughed.

"Ain't nothing nasty about it," Jasmine retorted. "We all need to bust a nut every now and then."

"Well, last I checked, I ain't got no nuts." Deja filled her mouth with more spaghetti.

"Yeah, but you know that kitty cat be wantin' to purr sometimes. Stop tryin'a act like you some kinda virgin," Tracey threw in. "'Cause I'ma tell y'all this—Jermaine got a golden tongue!" She giggled as she began to dance around the kitchen, rocking her hips and weaving her legs, doing what she called "the Tootsie Roll."

"There is more to life than sex, you know," Deja said, rolling her eyes.

"Like what? Bills? A job that get on your nerves?" Jasmine said, pouring herself a glass of red wine. "I'll take some good dick any day of the week."

"And again, Jasmine, you're married, so you don't even count. You not sinnin' every time you open your legs up to Shamar. I, on the other hand, would be."

"All you gotta do is repent," Tracey replied. "That's what I do, 'cause Jermaine be having me speakin' in tongues, and it's just too good to let go." She laughed. Although she felt oral sex wasn't on the same level of fornication as intercourse, she couldn't deny the sense of guilt she felt each time she opened her legs to Jermaine's mouth. She was careful to repent after each pleasure-filled session. "Girl, go on and get you some! The Lord'll forgive you."

All the talk about sex got Deja's insides churning. She had been fighting off the urge to sleep with Garnell for weeks now, but it was getting more and more difficult. There were a couple of times that she and Garnell had gotten wrapped up in a couple of heavy kissing and touching sessions, but she still found the strength to resist—even after Garnell had sucked on her nipples while his fingers found their way inside her panties. Every guy with whom Deja had been intimate before had been quite clumsy with his hands, but Garnell delicately and expertly used his thumb and middle finger to separate her lower lips. Then he used his index finger to tickle her clit right into an orgasm. The only thing that stopped Deja from mounting him that night was the lack of a condom. Garnell cussed himself out all the way home.

Now, reminiscing on how good it felt, and listening to her best girlfriends talk smack, Deja considered getting herself a good licking and sticking before the night was over. Even as she pondered the thought, flexing the muscles of her pussy, she started asking God to forgive her for what she was planning to do.

On the drive home, she turned in her seat, better to face Garnell, and rested a hand on his thigh.

"You have a good time tonight?" she asked.

"Yeah, I did." Garnell placed a hand over Deja's and kept the other on the wheel. "How about you?"

"I always have a good time with my girls." Deja smiled and paused. "But it coulda been better."

"Oh yeah? How?" he asked, shifting his eyes over at Deja for just a second before focusing back on the highway in front of him.

"If you would have met me in one of the bathrooms and let me get a little bit of this, right here." She slid her hand up to his crotch and squeezed.

"Mmm," Garnell moaned. "You shoulda come and got me—sent me a text message or something."

"Yeah. I didn't think of that."

"Well, the night ain't over. You can still get you some if you want it," he replied, covering her hand with his again and encouraging her to squeeze a second time.

"I don't know. The moment might be gone," she teased.

"You feel that?" he asked, causing his manhood to leap up in her hands.

Deja grinned.

"We can recapture the moment."

"We'll see," Deja responded, easing her hand away from his lap and smiling deviously.

When the couple arrived at Deja's home, Garnell wasted no time in planting kisses on her neck and roaming her body with his hands. She accepted his lust-filled affection.

"Hold on a minute, baby," she whispered. "Give me a few minutes to change clothes."

Garnell grabbed a handful of her ass, pressed his hips into her and moaned, "All right, baby."

"Why don't you turn on some music or something," she suggested, slipping out of his hands. "I'll be right back."

Garnell kept himself entertained for the next fifteen minutes until Deja reappeared; she was wearing a pastel yellow chemise with a matching thong. The color made her skin glow radiantly, along with the shy smile she gave him, as she descended the stairs. She had pinned her hair up, but she left tendrils to cascade at her ears.

"You look gorgeous," Garnell commented standing to his feet. "You look like a centerfold model."

For the moment, Deja didn't care about fornication, promiscuity, or anything else. *We all sin and fall short of the glory of God,* she said to herself. *And God promised to forgive us if we confess our sins, and He will cleanse us from all unrighteousness. So, Lord, I'm sorry, but I got to have me some of this!*

Garnell took her into his arms, and they began a slow seductive bump-and-grind dance to Robin Thicke's "Teach U a Lesson" as he filled her lips and neck with kisses.

"Oh yes," Jasmine moaned. "Mmm, baby." Her hands caressed Garnell's head as he took his kisses down to her breasts, leading her to the couch to lay her down. Her pussy was overheated and ready to explode as she moaned, unzipping his pants, but Garnell eased back.

"Un-uh. You made me wait all this time time; I'ma take my time with this shit tonight," he teased. "You know how many times you done sent me home with a hard dick?" Deja grinned at his banter. "Yeah, I'ma have you beggin' for this dick. I'm gonna have fun with this shit," he whispered in her ear, allowing the head of his dick to graze over her pussy. That one movement was as if he had pressed a magic button of some sort as Deja quickly spread her legs. "Yeah . . . you want this dick, don't you, baby?"

"You know I do," Deja answered, fluttering her eyes closed.

He pressed his head against her clit a second time, making her arch her back upward.

"I'ma fuck the hell outta you tonight."

"That's what I want you to do," she cooed, letting go of all inhibitions. "Rock this pussy like a king. Fuck me 'til I can't take no more," she whispered, lifting her hips up to meet his, although he hadn't entered her body yet.

"Oh, I'ma do that," he promised. "Let me see what this pussy taste like first. I bet it's sweet like candy, ain't it?"

"You know it is. It tastes just like cherries," she said, placing her hands on his head and pushing him downward.

"Look at you, with your hot ass." He resisted her nudging. "I told you, you begging tonight. You been teasing me for two months, but tonight it's payback time." He filled his mouth with her left breast, then her right. "Everything you want, you gonna beg me for."

He lowered his kisses to her belly, remembering a lesson he had learned many years before: If a man has a big dick and is capable of sexually satisfying women, nothing else would be required of him. No paying bills or trying to be impressive. He didn't have to work or suffer any out-of-pocket expenses. Basically, the only thing required was to give it to her good in the morning, when she arrived home from work, and put her to sleep at night.

Oh, this gonna be a night to remember right here, Garnell told himself.

The next morning, Deja peeled her eyes open and glanced at the clock, which read a quarter past nine in the morning.

"Oh Lord!" she gasped, realizing she'd overslept, which she hadn't done in years. She tried to spring out of bed, but Garnell caught her wrist and pulled her toward him.

"Good morning, baby," he said with a smile, pushing off the covers with his feet and exposing his erect manhood. "Why don't you take the day off and spend it right here with your man." Deja grinned at the sight of his smooth skin and hard dick. "Call in sick," he coached.

She thought about it for a good fifteen seconds; then she picked up the cordless phone beside her bed.

"Hey, Marilyn," she said, sniffling. "I'm not gonna make it in today. I came down with something last night and ... um ..." She coughed as she struggled not to lie. "I can hardly get myself out of bed this morning," she stated, smiling at Garnell. "I'll try to make it in tomorrow; hopefully, I'll be feeling better. Thanks."

"I doubt you can feel any better." Garnell chuckled. "'Cause last night was phenomenal."

"I can at least try," Deja replied, climbing back into bed and mounting herself on her joystick. Then she rode him like a motorcycle.

It was after twelve when they finally got out of bed. After washing each other's bodies in the shower, their lustful passion took over. Garnell bent Deja at the waist under the running water and entered her from behind. She gripped the edge of the tub and worked her hips backward as she called out his name, increasing his ego.

Yeah, I'm moving up in this muthafucka, Garnell told himself.

Once they were dressed, they sat down in her kitchen to enjoy a lunch of grilled chicken panini, Mediterranean salads, and fresh fruits, which were sided with sweet tea that Deja had ordered in from a local deli. Once again, she was paying for their meals.

As they filled their bellies, Deja couldn't help but smile. "Thank you for a wonderful evening, Garnell."

"The pleasure was all mine, sweetheart. Thank you. I also want to thank you for comin' into my life and for treatin' me so well. I thank the Lord constantly for putting you in my path, and I hope and pray that this isn't the end."

His bullshit words were like sweet music to her ears.

When Garnell left the kitchen to go to the bathroom, Deja grabbed her cell phone and texted her friends: *The cat is purring!*

Chapter Ten

"So, did you have a chance to talk to Jermaine about the truck-driving job?" Jasmine asked as soon as Shamar got out of bed and padded downstairs. She poured him a cup of coffee, set it on the kitchen table, and then began making him a plate of pancakes, eggs, and sausage.

Shamar didn't answer right away, but he cut his eyes at his wife while he gulped down a mouthful of brew. "Yeah, I wanted to talk to you about that."

"What'd he say?" Jasmine beamed, optimistic about the opportunity.

"First of all, I don't appreciate how you tried to embarrass me in front of your friends."

"What do you mean?" Jasmine asked, sprinkling a few drops of water onto her griddle to test the heat. With brows crinkled in confusion, she studied Shamar's face.

"You know exactly what I mean. Keep our business in our house, Jasmine."

"What business?"

"How you gonna sit up there and tell them niggas I ain't working nowhere."

"I didn't tell them that. What are you talking about?" Jasmine denied.

"Got that muthafucka asking me where the hell I work and shit," he sneered.

"Whatever. That's just you and your own insecurities," Jasmine said, rolling her eyes and turning her back to Shamar to tend to the food.

"Why the hell else would he ask me where I work at, all out of the blue? You just tried to set me up to look triflin'," he accused.

"Shamar, you sat right up there and asked him about hooking you up with a job, so don't try to turn it around on me."

"I ain't say shit to nobody about no job," he argued, not remembering how the conversation between him and Jermaine had begun.

"I was standing right there, Shamar! You was the one that was looking all starry-eyed with your jaw dragging on the floor, like we live in the damn projects and you ain't never seen a nice house before," Jasmine retorted.

"Yeah, whatever. Don't be telling people shit about me," he mumbled as Jasmine slammed his breakfast down in front of him.

"Your ass better make sure you call him," she ended, leaving him in the kitchen alone. "I'm going upstairs to get ready for work."

While Jasmine showered, she prayed that God would motivate Shamar enough to follow through with the job opportunity that had fallen in his lap. *Work on him, Lord. Work on him. Don't let him blow this chance. I need him to take this job for him and for us.*

When she emerged downstairs, heading for the door, she found Shamar seated in the living room with a game controller in his hand. She shook her head, picked up her keys, and uttered a quick "bye" over her shoulder. On her drive to work, she phoned Deja.

"What's up, girl?" she asked once Deja answered.

"Girl, Garnell knocked the dust off this pussy last night," Deja started off saying, still in high spirits. "And what didn't fall off last night, he took care of this morning!" She laughed.

"You finally gave it up, huh? Girl, I told Tracey you were gonna give it up the first chance you got. I saw it in your face. Anyhow, how was it, girl? Tell me about it!"

"Hold on a minute. Let me get Tracey on the phone so I ain't got to tell this story but one time." Thirty seconds later, she returned to the line with Tracey's voice attached. "Anyway, ladies, I heard you ain't supposed to tell your girls about how good your man is because eventually they'll want to test the waters, but you know I'm not good at keepin' secrets. It was the bomb!" She snickered.

"That's what I'm talkin' 'bout, girl. And you claim to be a good ole Christian girl. You're a closet church ho! That's what you are," Jasmine quipped. "Was it worth the price of the sin?"

"Why you gotta say it like that?"

"It is what it is. I ain't gonna sugarcoat it."

"Call it what you wanna. I said my prayers before I went to sleep." She giggled. "At least I gave it to a Christian man worthy of havin' it."

"The devil is in church, too, Deja; you know that. Hell, I just started going to church on the regular, and even I know that much," Tracey stated.

"Funny how you weren't saying none of that last night. The way I see it, your concerns need to be on that cross-country truck-drivin' boyfriend you got instead of up in my business. Yeah, I heard about those truck stops and lot lizards."

"'Lot lizards'? What's a 'lot lizard'?" Jasmine asked.

"A term for a 'truck stop ho,'" Deja answered informatively.

"My man don't do that kinda shit. He's too busy tryin' to get back to this—you know what I'm sayin'?"

"Whatever. You ain't even giving him nothin' to get back to," Jasmine answered.

"How did we get on me?" Tracey replied. "We s'posed to be talking about Deja droppin' it like it's hot. Was it big, girl?"

"See, you gettin' too personal now."

"How? You the one calling me, telling me he was the bomb and whatnot," Tracey argued. "Just tell us, girl. Was it big and long, or short and thin?"

"Would you knock it off?"

"He got any friends?" Tracey asked.

"Why? I thought you had a man who had a golden tongue, and Jasmine's married. What you need his friend for?"

"I'm just asking," Tracey responded.

"Since you wanna get personal, how big is Jermaine's?"

"Long, strong, big, and fat! But I told y'all he ain't pushing nothing up in here. For now, I'ma just use my imagination while he use his hand."

"Wow," Jasmine commented. "That's cold."

"No ring, no thing," Tracey cracked. "Anyway, did he go downtown, Deja?"

"Yes, he did, and, girrrrrl, umph, umph, umph!"

"Y'all 'bout to make me drive back home and make Shamar drop them drawers."

"Speaking of Shamar—is Jermaine gonna hook him up with a job?" Tracey asked.

"I sure hope so. He had the nerve to be upset this morning, talking about I tried to embarrass him in front of y'all. He embarrassed himself by not having a job," Jasmine answered, rolling her eyes even though her friends couldn't see her. "I just prayed about it and left it alone."

"I'ma tell Jermaine to call him this evening, then," Tracey offered.

"Okay, cool. Let me call y'all back later. Someone is calling me," Jasmine said.

She quickly bid good-bye to her girls; then she clicked over to her other line to answer a call from a number she didn't recognize. "Hello?"

"Hi, Jasmine, this is Eureen Francis from church."

What in the world? Jasmine immediately thought. "Oh. Hi, how you doing?"

"I got your number off a note that your daughter had wrote to my daughters inviting them to a birthday party in a few weeks," Eureen stated. "And I wanted to talk to you to get the details."

"Oh, okay."

While Jasmine did promise Summer a birthday party, she was not aware that Summer had been inviting people on her own. Caught off guard, she felt forced to share the details, although she would have never thought to invite Eureen's children.

"Well, the party is Saturday, the twenty-fourth, at two o'clock, at my house. It's going to be a pool party and sleepover, but we—"

"Ooh, that sound like fun! So they gon' need a bathing suit?" Eureen asked, cutting Jasmine off and not giving her a chance to *un*invite her. "They gon' love that."

Jasmine let out a nervous laugh.

"So they should pack them an overnight bag and stuff?"

"Uh, well, we hadn't had a chance to finalize the guest list, so I'm not even sure how many girls are spending the night, so—"

"Well, then, I'm glad I called you today, so my girls can be one of the first ones to let you know they gon' come." Eureen grinned through the phone. "I'ma just need your address so I can know where to bring 'em."

I'ma get that girl. Jasmine cringed, thinking about her daughter. "I'll have Summer give your daughters a formal invitation with all the information on it, on Sunday."

"Oh, all right, then. That sounds good. Thank you so much for inviting them."

"Mmm-hmm," Jasmine commented because she couldn't bring herself to say "you're welcome." No sooner had she hung up, when her phone rang again.

"Baby," Shamar started his conversation. "My man Jermaine just called me, and I got an interview at four o'clock at the truck place," he announced.

"Really! That's great, baby!"

"Yeah. I'm 'bout to do this!" Shamar claimed. "I'm 'bout to, you know, step up and, you know, be there for you and the girls like I shoulda been doing a long time ago."

"I'm proud of you, baby," Jasmine said sincerely.

"Thank you. I'ma call him in a few minutes so we can get together for lunch so I can ask him some questions and stuff."

"That's a great idea."

"You know, if I get this job, though, I'ma be on the road all the time, and I ain't gonna be home to help with the girls and stuff," he informed her. "That might take y'all a little bit of gettin' used to."

We already used to that mess from you runnin' to your momma's house, Jasmine privately said to herself. "We probably will need to get adjusted to it, and you know the girls are gonna miss you if you stay gone too long," she said, being careful only to encourage him.

"Just let 'em know I'm out working. They should be able to understand that," Shamar suggested, feeling like he was adding something valuable. "We should go out and celebrate when you get home tonight."

"Let's wait until you get the job first, baby." Jasmine chuckled, and then reconsidered. "But I'm sure that you will get it," she quickly added, wishing she wouldn't have said the first part. "So where you wanna go tonight?"

"Don't matter. Just somewhere."

"It has to be somewhere we can take the kids, so let's keep it simple," Jasmine suggested.

"Right. Okay. I'ma call you later on and let you know how it goes."

"Okay, babe. I love you."

"Love you too."

Jasmine hung up the phone and thanked God in advance for her husband's new career, but she really thanked Him that night as she, Shamar, and the girls sat in a booth at Pizza Hut, enjoying a simple celebration for his new job.

Chapter Eleven

Jermaine pulled into a truck stop in St. Louis, Missouri, ensured his doors were locked, and moved to the back of his cab, which was his home when he was on the road. He lay back, butt naked, on his makeshift bed and turned on a porn movie. He stroked his manhood with one hand while he called Tracey's number on his cell with the other.

"Hey, baby," she answered.

"Mmm, I wish I was there with you right now," he stated.

"You do? Why is that?" Tracey followed his lead, immediately catching his sexy tone.

"So I could feed you some of this big dick right here I got in my hand."

"Oooh," she cooed in response. "I am kinda hungry too."

"Are you?"

"Yeah. I ain't ate nothing all day. I could use a nice big juicy piece of meat in my mouth," she replied, teasing.

"What you got on?" Jermaine questioned, breathing heavily.

"That pink thong you like, and that's all."

"For real?" He traveled his hand up and down his dick a bit faster.

"Yep. I just got finished rubbing baby oil all over my body too. My titties are nice and shiny, like you like 'em."

"Rub them nipples for me, baby," Jermaine coached.

"If I rub 'em, I'ma have to suck 'em myself, since you ain't here. They standing up too, baby, wishing you was here to put your mouth on 'em."

"You got my permission to lick 'em, baby. Go 'head," Jermaine whispered. "Stick that finger in your pussy for me too, baby," he added, motivated by the woman he saw touching herself on the television screen.

"Mmm, that feels so good," Tracey cooed, although she was sitting on her couch with her feet propped up on the coffee table, attempting to paint her toenails.

"Is it wet, baby?"

"It's dripping, Jermaine. I got juice running all down in my ass."

"Oh shit! Can I lick it up? Open them legs up so I can lick that cream," Jermaine grunted out.

"Yeah. Eat that pussy, boy. Mmm! Lick that plate clean," she coaxed, responding to his breathing. "Unnn! Ssss! Unnn! Eat that pussy, Jermaine."

Jermaine pumped his dick harder and faster, wishing Tracey was there to straddle his face.

"Slide that big dick in this pussy. Slide in on—"

Suddenly the conversation was cut off, as Tracey had not charged her phone that day, and the battery was drained. With a shrug, Tracey flipped the phone closed, tossed it on the couch, and continued beautifying her toes.

On the other hand, the abrupt ending jolted Jermaine out of his phone sex fantasy. He was disappointed, and with a rock hard dick. He continued to stroke it for a few more minutes, trying to rebuild his momentum, but he needed some sound effects. He reached for the remote and turned up the volume on the TV, listening to the woman who was now taking two lovers at once. He closed his eyes and pumped for another minute or two after filling his hand with baby oil, but he grew frustrated.

"Fuck this," he commented, sitting up and quickly getting dressed. "I need me some pussy." He emerged from the back of the truck, exited at the driver's door, and walked across the parking lot to a diner. Once inside, he took a booth, ordered a burger and fries, and waited for anything in a skirt to come walking by. When she did, Jermaine wasted no time in taking advantage of the opportunity.

"How you doing there, lady?" he called when she came in and took a seat at the counter. "You ain't got to eat by yourself; there's plenty room over here." He patted the seat beside him and slid over a few inches.

The woman was dressed in a black catsuit, with a wide red belt around her waist, a pair of high-heeled boots decorated with silver buckles, and a head covered by stiff, synthetic braids. She sashayed over, as invited, and took a seat. "Thank you, 'cause I sho hate eatin' by myself. It's good to have some company sometimes, ain't it?" She smiled.

Not that he cared, but just to keep things flowing well, Jermaine asked, "What's your name, sweetheart?"

"You can call me Dee-Dee 'cause I'm delicious," she answered, running her hand way up Jermaine's thigh to his crotch. "Oh, you packing too, ain't you, Daddy?" she asked, aggressively grabbing hold of his dick beneath the table. "I sho would like to take a ride on that soul pole."

"Well, it's your lucky night, 'cause I'm giving out free rides," Jermaine responded. "You ain't got but half of it in your hand. You think you can take all that?"

"I'll put something on you so good that it'll make you call your momma and thank her for making you a boy."

"Is that right?" he asked, slyly grinning.

They ate their meals quickly and downed a couple of beers. No sooner than they got back to his truck, Jermaine had access to all the pussy he could take for the night. Delicious practically tore Jermaine's pants off his body and began giving him a blow job so incredible, Jermaine couldn't help but holler like a child getting his ass whupped.

"Say my name," she demanded.

"Ahh! Oh, baby, that's delicious! Shit!" Delicious worked her tongue around his dick like she was eating a soft-serve ice-cream cone; then she dove down like she was eating a hot dog. Between the two motions, plus the suction she created on her upstroke, Jermaine was jerking and kicking.

"Suck that dick, Delicious! Suck that dick! Get you some more!" he panted out, thrusting his hips forward in quick succession.

Before he came, Delicious stopped and got on her knees, inviting him to enter her from the back.

"Come and get this pussy, big daddy. Blow my muthafuckin' back out," she called.

"Damn, girl!" Jermaine scrambled to get off his back and onto his knees. "You got this dick rock hard and I'ma give it to you good," he promised.

"You better not hold shit back," Delicious warned.

"I'ma lick this 'fore I stick it, though, 'cause it's looking too good for me not to get a taste."

"Put that tongue on me, baby! Lick this delicious pussy."

Jermaine dipped his head and did what he knew he was extremely gifted at, erupting all kinds of moans from Delicious. Her sounds confirmed to him once again that he was the ultimate master at eating pussy. Gripping tightly to the sheets and trying to maintain control, she was practically in a full Chinese split. She was straddled over Jermaine's face; then she spun around for a sixty-nine. It was a matter of minutes before they both exploded in waves of pleasure. After resting for a bit, they went at it again. This time, wrapped in a condom, Jermaine felt the inside of a woman's body, and Delicious delivered on the promise of her name.

The next morning, she woke him up by taking him into her mouth and sucking him into an erection. It was the best morning Jermaine had had in a long time.

"Mmm," he moaned, enjoying his wake-up call. "Shit, girl," he whispered. "You gon' make me take your number and come back."

That's exactly what Delicious wanted to hear. "You can get that," she answered through her sucking.

Jermaine picked up his ringing phone, connecting with Tracey's voice, but it didn't stop Delicious from sucking his dick. "Keep turnin' that dick out, baby. You fuckin' my shit up," he whispered with a smirk, ensuring that his hand was over the mouthpiece. "Hey, baby," he moaned to Tracey.

"How you doing this morning?" Tracey asked.

"Fantastic," he panted. "You gonna finish up with what we started last night? You left me with my dick hard."

"I gotta get ready to go to work, baby. I just wanted to say good morning."

"You sure I can't get no sunrise lovin'?" Jermaine asked, struggling to keep from moaning out loud.

"I'll make it up to you tonight. I promise," she replied.

"All right, then. I'll give you a call a little bit later." He ended the call and lay back, letting Delicious have her way. "Yeah, give me your number, 'cause you sho know how to suck and fuck a dick."

***

Things were looking up for the Murphy family. Shamar had successfully started driving school and enjoyed both the thrill of cranking up big rigs and the feeling of earning a real paycheck. This week, he would be leaving for a long-distance run, which meant spending fourteen days and nights away from his family. He had made a big deal of it before he left, and was a bit frustrated that his family didn't see it as such.

The day of his trip, he called his daughters to him to have "a little talk." Jasmine rolled her eyes and headed to the kitchen to prepare dinner.

"I just wanted to let you girls know that I might not be home as much because I'm starting a new job."

"You got a job?" Winter said in awe.

"Yes, I did. Are you surprised?"

"Yes, because we didn't think you were ever gonna go to work. Did we, Summer?"

"Nope," his oldest daughter agreed. "We thought you was gonna be like the man in *Daddy Day Care,* when the daddy stayed home all the time and played with the kids instead of going to work."

Shamar chuckled, trying to hide the shame he felt from hearing his girls say that. "Naw. I got a job because that's how a man takes care of his family."

"So how was you taking care of us before now, if you ain't have no job? You let Mommy do it, since you didn't have one?" Winter innocently asked.

"No!" he denied, grabbing her and digging in her stomach with tickles. Summer jumped in and got her share of tickles as well. After a minute or two of tussling, he restarted his conversation. "With my new job, I might not be home every night because I will be driving a long way away."

This time, Summer was first to comment. "It's okay, Daddy. It will be just like all the times that you go to Grandma's house and you be over there for a long time, so it won't be that bad. We probably won't miss you all that much."

Her words pierced his heart and made him realize how foolish he'd been just lounging around the house and leaving for days on end whenever the going got rough. He was really at a loss for words, but he felt like he should say something. "Well, I'm gonna miss y'all and your momma," he shared. "I love y'all."

"We love you too," the girls said in unison before skipping away.

Jasmine had been listening from the kitchen and fought to hold in her laughter. *That's exactly what he needed to hear,* she thought. *He done ran outta here too much; they have gotten used to it. That mess don't faze them anymore.*

Because it was his last night at home before hitting the road, Shamar thought it would be a good idea for them to sit down and have dinner together as a family. It was a joke to her, but Jasmine set the table with the "good plates," which Shamar requested. Instead of putting everyone's food on their plates at the stove, like she normally did, she put serving dishes on the table. The soulful aroma of fried pork chops, cabbage, baked macaroni and cheese, and candied yams wafted up from the table. She peeked in around the corner into the living room, shocked to see that Shamar was actually watching the news instead of playing a video game.

"Dinner's ready," she announced. "Can you call the girls down?"

"Yeah," he agreed.

Two minutes later, the four of them were seated at the table, holding hands and saying the blessing over the food.

Shamar's expression seemed solemn to Jasmine.

He acts like he's going to jail tomorrow or something, she smirked inwardly.

"How's your food?" she asked to break the silence.

"It's good, babe."

"You nervous about tomorrow?"

"No. Just not excited about leaving my ladies here alone."

"We stay here by ourself all the time, Daddy. We will be okay," Summer shot out. "But me and Winter are gonna pray for you while we at church."

"Thank you, sweetheart," he said, giving a feeble smile to the girls. "I'm sorry that I'm gonna miss your birthday party," he said.

"Don't worry about it, Daddy. We will just e-mail you some pictures like we did last year when you had to fix something at Grandma's house."

Feeling another wave of shame, Shamar glanced over at Jasmine, who pretended to be preoccupied with rearranging food on her plate. She didn't make eye contact with him. He didn't say another word about his leaving.

Full and satisfied, Jasmine and Shamar washed the dishes and cleaned the kitchen together while the girls took baths.

"I feel like a new man, babe," he shared, reaching into the cabinet to put away a stack of plates. "I don't feel that good about leaving y'all here, but I feel like I'm taking my family to the next level." He eased up behind his wife and circled his arms around her waist. "Thank you for believing in me," he whispered, planting a kiss on her cheek.

"That's what a wife does, baby."

That night, they made passionate love like the world was coming to an end. In the morning, Jasmine got up early to see her husband to the door.

"Be safe." She waved as he backed out of the drive-way. "Love you!"

Jasmine closed the door, feeling grateful, as she had every morning since Shamar had gotten the call for his job. She giggled a bit as she picked up a notepad with the details of the birthday party, thinking about her suggestion to e-mail Shamar pictures of the event.

"Guess she told him."

Chapter Twelve

"Eureen, we need to talk." Monroe dropped his keys on the dresser in his bedroom and headed to the bathroom without stopping his stride. Eureen looked up from her Bible and let her eyes follow her husband. He returned a few minutes later after washing his hands. His message was curt and uncaring.

"I want you out of here." He stuffed his hands in his pockets, stood sure-footedly, and stared Eureen directly in the eyes.

"Wh-what?" she stammered. "What do you mean?"

"I mean just what I said. You need to leave."

"You mean like break up?" Eureen's eyes began to water as she sought clarification.

"Yep," Monroe replied without batting an eye, although he wanted to burst into laughter at the curly wig she wore.

For several seconds, Eureen stared in disbelief at her husband's stoic face. "You puttin' me out on the street!" she shrieked. "Where am I supposed to go?"

"I'm putting you in one of my rental properties. You don't have to worry about the mortgage or utilities." Monroe felt that the offer was fair; he could have offered her nothing. Plus he figured if he took care of her living expenses, she would be less likely to sue him for child support and alimony.

"But why, Monroe? I thought we were doing fine, or at least better since you've been coming to church sometimes."

"Look. I'm not going to go back and forth with you. I'm being straightforward and honest. I want you out of my house by Friday. Here are the keys to the rental property." He pulled his hand out of his pocket and tossed a set of keys on the bed. "It's the five-bedroom over on LaSalle. Take the kids with you, and I'll give you money to support them." He stuck his hand in the inside pocket of his jacket and pulled out an envelope, which held banking information in her name and a Visa debit card. "There's some money to get you some furniture and stuff, and I'll deposit something in your account every month for the kids." He dropped it on the bed; then he turned on his heels to leave. "Get to packing. I'll be back Saturday."

In a total state of confusion, Eureen sat paralyzed, her Bible still in her lap. She wanted to pray, but the words wouldn't come to her mind. All she could do was gasp for air. After a few minutes, she stood from her chair, walked to the bed, and picked up the envelope. Inside was a deposit slip for an account Monroe had established for her, totaling $20,000. That did provide a tiny bit of relief, but it didn't stop the tears. Her heart ached tremendously.

Feeling a myriad of emotions, she tilted her head back and stared up at the ceiling, letting hot tears run into her ears. "What am I gonna tell the kids?" she said out loud. "I can't believe he is doing this to me!" she wailed. "What am I s'posed to do, Lord?"

"Momma, we still going to Summer and Winter's house on Friday?" her seven-year-old daughter, Jametria, asked from her bedroom door.

"Yeah, babe," she answered without looking.

"Why you crying?"

"Nothing," Eureen replied, wiping her eyes with her hand. "I'm fine. I just got something in my eye and it hurt a little bit."

"Oh. Can we still go to Walmart so I can pick out my gift and get my sleeping bag and new pajamas and stuff?"

Eureen started to say no, but then she thought, *Shopping would do me some good right about now.* "Yeah, go put your shoes on and tell your sisters to come on."

Only two of Eureen's four girls wanted to go on the outing until she announced that the trip would include a stop at Outback Steakhouse. It was there that she told the girls that they would be moving. As she expected, they bombarded her with a ton of questions, for which she really didn't have the answers. "God will see us through," she promised. It was the only thing she knew to say.

"So where is this house at?" Mezzi asked.

"On LaSalle. We are gonna stop by there on the way home."

"You got the key already?" asked Tiona, her thirteen-year-old.

"Yeah," Eureen answered, sniffing. She felt tears beginning to trickle down her face again as she drew circles in her garlic mashed potatoes with a fork.

"Why is Daddy doing this, Ma?" the oldest asked. But noticing their mother's tears flowing more rapidly, the girls fell silent and tried as best they could to enjoy the rest of their meals.

Having finished dinner, they visited the property, inspecting each room carefully. The younger girls oohed and aahed at several of the features of the home; the older girls seemed more indifferent. As for Eureen, she had mixed feelings. She had to admit that things hadn't been going that well for her and Monroe for a long time, but she really believed that his recent church attendance was the beginning of a turnaround. *Maybe this break will be good for us,* she thought, trying to convince herself as she walked around an empty master bedroom suite. *Absence makes the heart grow fonder. . . . Is that in the Bible?*

The week went by quickly, and it was Friday before Eureen and the girls knew it. Because she wasn't taking anything from her marital home, leaving it was physically easy; but emotionally, it was hell. If Eureen wasn't crying, she was praying. If she wasn't praying, she was packing. If she wasn't packing, she was trying to explain to the girls, as best she could, why they were leaving—without saying, "Because your daddy don't want us no more."

She called her job, requesting time off, and then took the older girls out of school for two days, which they spent shopping in order to furnish the home with the $20,000 that Monroe had given her. Do-it-yourself paint jobs covered the walls prior to her furniture being delivered in an attempt to cover Eureen's pain. Monroe hadn't so much as called her; and when she attempted to reach him just to discuss things, he refused to answer and ignored her messages.

At least I got somewhere to lay my head, she thought as she walked through her home, which now looked like she had been there for at least two years. She tried to find a reason to smile; and by the time Friday came around, she liked the décor of her new home, but she hated that she had to be there.

Garnell had spent just about every night at Deja's house since Tracey and Jermaine's dinner party. And just about every night, he had been buried deep between Deja's legs, getting all the pussy he wanted. It was becoming increasingly difficult to hide his nonexistent career from her. Every morning, he had to rise early, put on a suit, and pretend to go to work.

"Maybe I can meet you for lunch today?" Deja suggested.

"Naw. I mean, I'ma be in sales meetings all day today, baby. I don't want you to drive all that way and I can't even come out of the meeting," he lied, knowing that he wouldn't always be able to be in a so-called meeting.

"Well, just give me the number to your office and I'll call before I drive up."

"Just call my cell, babe. I'm not always at my desk. It be so much going on in there. I be all over the building sometimes." He leaned over the bed and kissed her lips. "We can go to dinner tonight, though."

Deja smiled. "I'd like that."

Garnell said good-bye, got in his car, and drove first to his uncle's home, where he changed into a dingy gray uniform. Then he headed downtown to the SPCA, where he'd been hired to clean cages. He didn't particularly like it, but it provided enough cash to keep Wilbur at bay. And if he had anything to do with it, he'd be moving in with Deja soon.

He thought back to a conversation he and Deja shared just a few nights before as she lay on his chest. "So you still staying with your uncle, huh?"

"For the moment. Yep, I'm staying with my uncle Willie until he can get hisself together. Ever since that fire, he ain't been able to get through all the red tape that the insurance company been putting him through," he answered, forgetting that he'd previously told Deja that Wilbur had no homeowner's insurance, when he made up the lie about the fire. Luckily, it was a detail that Deja didn't remember.

"Why couldn't you just give him some money to tie him over?"

"Well, I did that for a few months, but it was getting more and more expensive and challenging for me to pay all the expenses for two homes, with no end in sight. The insurance company should have been able to cut him a check in less than thirty days, but now here it is going on a year."

Although Deja wasn't looking at him, he kept a straight face, remained calm, and appeared influential. He wasn't ready to come clean with the truth, beginning with his recent release from prison, his confinement to drug rehab, that cocaine had fucked up his life, and that Uncle Willie put a time frame on his stay. Then, on top of that, he had a wife and kids on the other side of the country.

It's just too risky. I can't take that gamble right now. I've gotta lock her in; then I'll tell her what I want her to know. For now, I'm gonna get all the free pussy I can and keep putting this dick on her like a soldier. On second thought, I'll ease in a little at a time and see how she responds. If she dumps me, at least I got a good night's fuck, a good night's sleep, and a good night's dinner out of the deal, he'd thought at first.

However, the more he lay with her, he knew his chances of coming clean without negative repercussions increased. This was especially so, since he had put it on her so good when she asked for it, and when she didn't.

Before he clocked in for the day, he took a minute to call Deja.

"Hey, baby. I just wanted to call you before I head in here with these stiff-necked executives," he lied. "Ain't no telling how long I'ma be in this conference room today. Just wanted to hear your voice before I got started."

"Aw. That's so sweet," Deja answered. "You tryin'a act like you love me or something," she teased.

When he heard the word "love" used, he knew he was in. *She tryin'a send me a message and I hear her loud and clear.*

"You have me thinking about you all day, girl."

"I'm thinking of you too, Garnell." She giggled with happiness.

"All right. Well, I gotta get in here, so I'll see you tonight."

"Okay, sweetie, have a good day."

"You too."

Even after covering himself for the day, Garnell knew he couldn't get away with lying forever. He was going to have to tell her.

He spent his entire day thinking through the conversation, wondering if he should tell her before or after dinner, before or after sex, before or after he got his next paycheck, or before or after his time ran out at Wilbur's house. He decided, now that she'd mentioned "love," he would tell her before Wilbur's patience wore out—just in case, he needed to drop Deja and find him another woman to prey upon.

At the end of his shift, he went to his uncle's home, showered, and changed back into slacks and a dress shirt; then he headed to Deja's. When he arrived, Deja was waiting on him, looking as gorgeous as ever. She was dressed in a stunning one-shouldered white knit dress, which she'd picked up from *bebe's*. She had her hair pulled back in a sleek bun and accentuated her facial features with large white-gold earrings. The soft scent of jasmine drifted from her skin.

"You look like a movie star," he commented with a huge smile. "I was thinking we were going to dinner, but you gonna make me skip the small stuff and get to dessert!" Garnell took Deja in his arms, cupped his hands around her butt, and pressed forward. "You got me hard already," he mumbled in her ear.

Deja turned in his arms so that Garnell was now pressing his dick into her butt, which she pushed out to meet him. "You like it?" she asked. She then bent at the waist and touched her toes.

"All right now, you better stop," Garnell warned, gripping her waist and bumping forward.

"What are you talking about?" Deja replied, holding her position and wiggling against him.

"See, I know what you want." Garnell slipped a hand beneath her dress, surprised and delighted to find that she wasn't wearing panties. He began fingering her pussy and unbuckled his belt with his other hand. "Uh-huh. This is what you want right there," he mumbled, moving her forward a bit so that she could brace herself against the coffee table. He pushed the head of his dick between her legs, and Deja let out a moan. "Yeah. That's what you want. I'ma give you what you want." He gripped her hips and entered her body. "Aahhhh," he sighed, finding a smooth and rhythmic groove. "Mmm, this pussy is good, Deja."

"Is it?"

"Yes, baby! Shit!" he cried, looking over at their reflection in a wall mirror, which turned him on even more. "Aw, this some good pussy!"

"Yeah, put it on me. Put it on me, Daddy. Make me take all that dick," Deja coached.

"Oh, you want it all?" Garnell sped up his stroke. "You want all this?"

"Yeah, baby!" Deja's eyes were closed tightly. She was thoroughly enjoying every thrust that Garnell gave her. She tightened her walls around him multiple times, causing Garnell's knees to buckle.

He kept his eyes fixed on their mirrored image, and it didn't take long for Garnell to explode. Holding his last thrust deep inside Deja, he nearly collapsed on top of her.

"Damn, that was good," he panted, moving his hands from her hips to her titties and squeezing. "You know how to make a nigga feel welcome at the end of his workday."

Deja smiled at the compliment while Garnell carefully pulled out of her, trying not to drip any fluids on her clothes. "Umph!" he commented a final time as he staggered to the half bath downstairs.

While he cleaned up, Deja scooted upstairs and did some cleaning up as well; then she met Garnell a few minutes later, keys in hand, ready to leave for dinner. She and Garnell held hands throughout the evening, fed each other from their plates, and snuck in kisses every few minutes. By the time dinner was over, Garnell felt confident enough to tell Deja the truth.

Her ass all in love now, and she sho lovin' this dick. She might be mad for a minute, but when that pussy heat back up, she gonna remember what I can do for her.

They drove back to her home, with his hand resting on her thigh all the way.

"You still interested in dessert?" she asked once they got inside, seductively licking her lips.

"You know how I prefer dessert over anything else," Garnell replied, dropping his eyes from her face to her breasts.

"I'll be right back then," she replied.

He knew she would return in something sexy, so he figured he'd get his dick sucked, eat her pussy until she came at least three times, let her ride on his pogo stick, eat her pussy again, until she couldn't take it anymore, and then hit her with the news.

Just like he planned, he had Deja shrieking, shivering, cussing, kicking, and grabbing handfuls of air. She was completely turned out.

"I ain't never had it this good, baby," she told him. "Never!"

Garnell chuckled, tucking his magic stick back into his boxers. Then he gathered her into his arms and circled his finger on her skin. Other than the satisfied moans that escaped Deja's lips, the room was quiet for three full minutes before he broke the silence with the truth.

"Deja, there are a few things I need to tell you," he stated, sighing audibly.

Deja's heart leaped a bit. *Oh hell, here we go. He's probably about to tell me he's married, or he got AIDS, or he sleep with men or something.*

"Would you be disappointed if I reveal the truth about something in my past?"

"Should I be?" she asked nervously.

"That depends on whether or not you're an understanding woman and believe in redemption."

"I do believe in redemption, baby. Isn't that what the love of Christ is about? There is nothing more redeeming than that; while we were yet sinners, Christ died for us," she replied. A lengthy pause followed her statement. "What is it about your past you'd like to tell me, baby?"

He dropped his head as he began explaining. "You know, I feel guilty because I lied to you about certain things, but please don't hold that against me. Please don't."

"What is it you lied about?" she asked.

I knew this was too good to be true. How could I be so damn vulnerable? Why couldn't I have met someone without any issues? Hell, I hope I ain't got nothing . . . including a baby, she thought ruefully.

Garnell sighed loudly before he started. "I don't really have a job with Pfizer, but I do have a job."

"Okay?" Deja prompted, waiting for the real shoe to drop.

"I really work at the SPCA, which was the only job I could find after I was released from prison for possession with intent to distribute and sent to a drug rehab program not too long ago." He paused for a moment, waiting for Deja's reaction. "I felt that you'd reject me without givin' me a chance if I told you before now." Feigning shame, he kept his head lowered.

"So you're not married, or in a relationship with someone else, or bisexual?"

"What? Hell naw, I ain't bisexual!" he answered, making sure he skipped over the married part. "I ain't never been attracted to no man!"

"So you did some jail time and you work at the SPCA?" she clarified.

"Yeah. I apologize for lyin' to you, but I just didn't wanna screw up my chances of—"

"You still use drugs?" she asked, cutting him off.

"No," he answered honestly. "Ever since I got saved, I stopped gettin' high. Now all I'm addicted to is you," Garnell added, hoping to get rid of some of the tension. It worked like a charm; he could tell from Deja's blushing.

"It's okay, baby." She gave him a reassuring kiss. "We're gonna work it out, baby. It's okay."

Garnell glanced at his watch, thinking it would be best for him not to spend the night. He didn't want Deja to feel used or think that he was being insincere about his sharing of the truth. He leaned down and kissed her forehead.

"Listen, sweetheart, thank you for understandin' and not holdin' my past against me. You've got a heart of gold, and God will always bless you and all that you do. I wish I'd met you years earlier, but guess what? That wasn't part of God's plan. It just seems like you're the right woman, and I still don't have my shit together." He sighed for effect. "I would just end up losin' you. Timin' is everything, sweetheart, and I'm sure that the Lord has a perfect relationship for you, but for where I am right now . . ." Garnell fell silent and shook his head. "Let me get out of here," he mumbled, shifting a bit to move Deja away, but she resisted. Instead, she pressed her lips against his in a long, meaningful kiss and smiled.

"God knows what He's doing, Garnell. And His timing is perfect. The Word says that if any man be in Christ, he is a new creature and old things have passed away, and all things are made new. And I think this is a new beginning for the both of us."

Garnell wiped a fake tear from his eye and nodded. "You're right, babe. I guess I need to forgive myself for my past."

"Yes, you do." With a sly grin, she ran her hand up his leg to his crotch. "You think you can hang another round?"

Chapter Thirteen

"So Eureen and her kids are coming over here," Tracey inquired, phrasing it more as a statement. Her nose was turned up as she peered through the window.

"Yeah, thanks to Summer!" Jasmine yelled loud enough for her daughter to hear, which caused her to come running through the patio door and into the kitchen.

"You called me, Mommy," she said, panting.

"Yeah, baby. You enjoying your party?"

"Yes! Is it almost time to get in the pool?"

"Not yet. We're gonna wait until a few more people get here first," Jasmine responded, piling hot dogs on a plate to put out on the grill.

"Okay!" Summer wrapped her arms around her mother's waist for a few seconds; then she darted back outside.

"How long she supposed to stay?" Deja asked.

"I don't know. I didn't tell any of the parents they had to leave, although everybody else had enough sense to drop their little rug rats off and fly down the street." Jasmine laughed. "You here and you don't even have kids," she added, swatting at Deja with a dish towel. "Y'all just be nice."

"Ooh, here she comes," Tracey broadcasted.

"Be nice," Jasmine warned a second time.

"Lawd, ha' mercy, look at that head!" Tracey commented about Eureen's wig.

"Shut up!" Jasmine ordered just before opening the door for her company. "Hey! Come on in. The girls are in the backyard," she said to Eureen's daughters. "Hey, Eureen."

"Hi," Eureen said, feeling a bit uncomfortable, but at the same time feeling privileged, like she had gained access to some private club.

"Come on in. We were just talking in the kitchen while the girls play outside."

"Hi, Tracey. Hi, Deja," Eureen said, entering the kitchen. "How y'all doing?" She took a seat on a bar stool and glanced around the room. "Jasmine, you have a beautiful home." She stood to her feet and looked at a grouping of family photos in the hallway.

"Thank you."

Eureen fought back tears as she looked at each photo of smiling faces in a number of locations. Some of the pictures were professionally taken; others, arranged in a collage, were more candid. All of them displayed a strong family unit. For a moment, she wondered what Monroe was doing. It had been two weeks since he'd forced her out of the house. Although he kept his word about keeping money in her bank account, it hurt her that he hadn't cared enough to call to see how she or the kids were.

She had given up on calling him. It was clear that he wasn't taking her calls. She'd called every night for the first week, and she had left message after message of whatever she could think of to say. Some of the messages were apologies, although she didn't know if she needed to be apologizing in the first place. Some messages were her begging him to come over to talk things over, and some were just to say sarcastically that they were fine and there was no need for him to worry. Every one of them had gone unanswered.

"Who does your hair, Eureen? I see you been gettin' it hooked up lately," Tracey called from the kitchen.

Eureen smudged away a tear before returning to the kitchen. "Oh, uh . . . my daughter does it for me." She blinked her eyes rapidly, pretending to struggle with an eyelash.

"I do hair on the side. You oughta let me hook you up," Tracey offered.

"Seriously? I been wantin' to get some microbraids but didn't know anybody who does 'em. Do you do 'em?"

"Girl, yeah. I can get you straight."

"I could use a makeover." Eureen sighed. "Especially since it looks like I'm going to be single real soon," she spilled.

"What?" Deja commented. "You and your husband are splitting up? What happened?"

The tears began again as Eureen slowly shook her head. "I can't even really tell you."

"Girl, marriage is made of ups and downs," Jasmine offered. "I'm sure whatever it is will blow over soon. I be halfway feeling like divorcing my husband at least once a month."

"I don't think it's gonna be that easy." An octave change took over Eureen's voice.

"But ain't nothing too hard for God," Deja interjected.

"I know, but I just can't help being discouraged because—"

Eureen was cut off by one of her daughters, Mimi, bursting inside. "Ms. Jasmine, can we get something to drink out of the cooler?"

"What are you supposed to say?" Eureen chastised.

"Excuse me," the child replied to the whole group as she focused on her mother's narrowed eyes.

"It's okay, sweetie. You can have some."

"Thank you!" Mimi bounced away as quickly as she'd come. "She said yeah!" she shouted to the other girls.

"Anyway," Eureen started again. "He asked me to leave the house." A long silence followed as none of the women knew what to say. "He owns a lot of rental properties. . . ."

"He? Don't you mean y'all?" Tracey shot in. "Y'all married, right?"

"Yeah, but he got a ton of stuff in his name only because he's a broker. He has properties all over the city that he got without me."

"Shit, if it's his, it's yours!" Jasmine countered. "He was married to you when he got 'em, right?"

"Yeah, but . . ."

"But, hell! That's half your shit too! I wish Shamar would come in here, talking about something is *his!* By the time I got finish goin' off on him, he'd be saying 'we' so much that y'all would think his ass learned how to speak French!"

All the ladies, including Eureen, burst into laughter. When it died down, Eureen started to speak again.

"He just came home one day and told me to get out and take the kids. The good thing about it is since he owns the property, I don't have to worry about the mortgage and he's taking care of the utilities."

"Well, at least he supporting you and the kids financially." Deja scooped a handful of chips from a bowl and placed them on a napkin for herself. "A whole lotta men wouldn't do that much."

"I know. I'm grateful for that, but it still hurts."

"Girl, if I was you, I'd fix myself up diva-fly and walk right up to that joker and be like *bam!*" Tracey hollered, quickly squatting to the floor and getting back up again. *"Bam!"* she repeated, dropping a second time.

"Oww!" This time, she shook her behind at the ladies. "Look what you missin', nigga! Look what you can't get no more!"

"Tracey, you so stupid!" Deja screamed in laughter, nearly falling out of her chair.

Tracey paraded about the kitchen, swinging her hips from side to side. She did more sexually provocative movements. "I'd make that joker miss me! Y'all see how Jermaine do when he get home! Shoo! What? You better ask somebody! Girl, when you want me to hook up your hair?"

Before Eureen left that evening, she felt like she had three new friends, and she had a hair appointment with Tracey—at the very least to have her wig applied correctly, if nothing else.

"Thank y'all so much for letting me vent. I know we haven't always got along, but I appreciate y'all listening to me today. And thanks, Jasmine, for inviting the girls."

"You're welcome." Jasmine hugged her and saw her to the door. "Now that's a mess!" she commented to Deja and Tracey once she'd shut the door. The ladies laughed among themselves.

"She done come a long way, though," Tracey commented. "Whew!"

Deja stayed a few more minutes; then she grabbed her purse. "Well, Sistas, I got a date with my man, so I gotta go!" she said with a grin.

"What are you two getting into tonight?"

"I'm supposed to be meeting his uncle, and then we're gonna swing by my parents'."

"What! He's meeting your parents?" Jasmine asked.
"Yep!"

"Your daddy gonna eat him alive," Tracey quipped before forking cake into her mouth.

"He'll be all right. Matter of fact, both of them will be. I'll see y'all later."

"All right, girl."

Deja jumped in her car and phoned Garnell. "You ready, babe?" she asked once he picked up.

"Yeah, my uncle is trippin', though. I just wanna give you a heads-up."

Deja pulled up in the driveway and tapped the horn. In just a few seconds, Garnell came out of the house, followed by a drunken, red-eyed, dark-complexioned man, who she assumed was Uncle Wilbur. He was visibly upset, spitting out obscenities behind Garnell.

"I know you've been out smokin' that shit, boy! I'll kill you if you had those fuckin' crackheads in my car! You ain't neva gonna learn, are you? I try to be nice to your crackhead ass and let you use my car; but got-damn it, I had to put out an APB on it! I told the police to arrest your black ass on sight when they find you! You leave here lyin', talkin' 'bout you're goin' to church, but I knew you were lyin'! The truth ain't in you, Garnell! I want you outta my got-damn house, right fuckin' now! You hear me, boy! And I don't know where you're goin', but you damn sho gonna leave here!"

"Oh my," Deja stated to herself. "This has got to be tough on Garnell."

Uncle Wilbur finally ran out of breath, allowing Garnell to speak.

"I wanted you to meet the woman I'm seeing, Uncle Willie."

As Deja exited her vehicle and approached Uncle Wilbur, he gave her an angry stare, but he extended his hand.

"Hi, Uncle Willie," she politely greeted.

Wilbur composed himself as best he could. "Hey, how you doin'? So y'all met in church, huh?"

"Yes, we did. The Lord is good, Uncle Willie. Yes, He is." Smelling his alcoholic breath, Deja added, "He's able to do incredible things for imperfect people, Uncle Willie."

Wilbur frowned. "What the hell that mean—"

"It means that in spite of what sin a person has committed, God will forgive that individual and convert him into righteousness," Garnell interrupted. "You see, Uncle Willie, man will never forgive you, but God and His Son, Jesus Christ, always will."

"Sounds like that same shit you were talkin' on all those letters you wrote from prison. That's probably why you keep doin' the same stupid shit, knowin' you'll get forgiven!"

Garnell nodded, grateful that he had already shared his past with Deja. "Let's get outta here, baby. Satan doesn't like anything good. I almost forgot, he's the prince of evil."

Walking away, Deja smiled at Wilbur Sutton.

"Will you join us one Sunday in church, Uncle Willie?" Garnell asked.

He frowned. "You won't be askin' that shit in a few weeks, because the real devil in me is gonna surface and put your ass out of this house." He watched them drive away with a confused look.

How the hell does a crackhead like him score such fine women? Maybe she's one of those functional crackheads who keeps herself up. As much as this boy lie and deceive people, if she ain't a crackhead, he's gonna take her straight to the gutter! He ain't no good. He's the biggest liar and con man in town.

"What on God's earth could a woman with class want with a damn bum like him? All he'll do is fuck her over. Once a crackhead, always a crackhead," he mumbled aloud, and then went back in the house.

"So that's Uncle Willie, huh?"

Garnell nodded slowly, his lips pressed inward showing his frustration. "Yep. That's my daddy's oldest brother. My good ole uncle Willie."

"Well, to be honest with you, babe, he ain't got nothin' on my daddy."

As Deja and Garnell entered her parents' home, holding hands, her niece and nephew ran to greet her.

"Hey, Aunt D!" they both screamed, throwing their arms around her waist.

"Is this supposed to be the Mr. Right you've been longing to meet?" Deja's father, Michael McClendon, asked, approaching the couple with solid, determined steps.

"I certainly hope so," Deja replied, smiling at Garnell and then at her dad. "Dad, this is Garnell. Garnell, this is my daddy." She wrapped her arms around her father's neck and squeezed.

"How do you do, sir?" Garnell greeted, respectfully extending his hand for a shake.

Michael was muscular and six feet four; he was dark brown complexioned and bald. He had a bit of a prison record himself, which was why Deja had been so excusing of Garnell's criminal past.

"How long you been knowin' my daughter?" Michael asked without saying hello.

I know you fucked my daughter last night, punk, Michael was thinking, tightening his grip and maintaining a hard look. *If you hurt her or bullshit her, I'll fuckin' kill you, punk!*

Garnell found it difficult to look the man in the eye.

Deja's mother rounded the corner, showing off a hearty smile. "Hey, baby," she said, greeting her daughter with a hug. "And how you doing, young man? I'm Audra McClendon."

"I'm fine. Thank you. How about yourself?"

"I'm good, sweetheart. I hope you hungry," Audra said, smiling. "I cooked up a storm today, if I do say so myself."

"I haven't eaten all day," Deja replied; then she looked at Garnell. "How about you?"

"I'd love a plate of your mother's good ole soul food." Intimidated by Michael's mean stare, he was actually ready to leave, but he went along with things for Deja's sake.

Deja and her mother excused themselves to the kitchen, leaving a cynical Michael to talk to Garnell alone. "Let me holla at you in my backyard a few minutes."

Garnell nervously followed him, thinking, *Why the fuck does he want me to go in the backyard with him? Maybe he's about to kick my ass because he knows I'm fucking the hell outta his daughter. Damn, I don't like this kinda shit!*

"I ain't one to beat around the bush." Michael made his view clear. "So I'm gonna get to the point. If you ever, and I mean *ever,* do anything to hurt my daughter, I will kill you. Do you understand me?" His eyes grew larger and his stare was intense.

Shaking like a leaf on a tree, Garnell fearfully replied, stuttering, "I'm n—not that t—type of man, sir."

"That's the same thing the last muthafucka said!" Michael replied, frowning. "I beat the dog shit out of his black ass, and guess what else? The muthafucka been missing in action ever since. Get the picture?"

"I—I . . . yes, sir, I u-understand, but you don't have to worry about me doin' anything stupid like that," he stammered.

"Good, 'cause like I said, I'll fuckin' kill you."

"Mr. McClendon, my parents didn't raise me to—"

"Save your words. You might need that extra breath one day," Michael finished for Garnell as he poked him in the chest; then he turned to make his way back inside the house.

Taking a few minutes to regain his composure, Garnell then made his way inside and sat nervously on the sofa.

The baked chicken, with dressing and gravy, collard greens, macaroni and cheese, and corn pudding was delicious; but due to Michael's hard stares, Garnell found it difficult to enjoy his meal. Garnell didn't rush her, but Deja couldn't have been any more ready to go.

"You all right?" she asked, leaning over to peck Garnell on the cheek when they were alone in her car.

"Yeah, I'm fine," he tried to assure her, but she saw how intimidated her dad had made him.

"What did he say to you outside?" she probed.

"Oh, you know what he said."

"No, I don't . . . for real. What did he say?"

"He ready to kick my ass if I ever do anything to you, but I ain't got nothing to worry about," he answered, looking at the window, wishing he'd had the nerve to stand up to Deja's father. *I shoulda broke city on his ass,* he thought, but he would never share it with anyone.

"Babe, I don't like the way your uncle treats you," Deja commented, causing Garnell to leave his imaginary fight with Michael.

"I don't much like it myself, Deja, but I gotta do what I gotta do, until I can do something different."

"You *can* do something different," she said, focusing her eyes on the road as she drove.

"I know. I'm working on it as best I can, baby."

"I know you are; and because of that, I want to help you." She paused for a few seconds. "You can move in with me."

"Deja, I can't. . . ."

"Yes, you can! I don't want you over there getting cussed out every day and having to put up with a bunch of BS. Your uncle ain't never heard that you're not supposed to kick a man while he's down?"

"I'm sure he has." Garnell kept his answer short as he grinned inside. He kept silent and let Deja seal her own deal.

"You spend the night at my house a lot, anyway, and you can't possibly be getting any real rest over there. I have two extra bedrooms, which ain't doing nothing but looking pretty, so you might as well come on—although I really would rather have you in my bed." She smiled.

"You sure you all right with that? You know church folks gonna talk."

"Oh please! Like they don't have sin in their lives. They got *something* that they doing wrong 'cause ain't nobody gettin' it right a hundred percent of the time, so they need to let me worry about my soul while they worry about their own."

Four days later, Garnell was comfortably moved in, just like he'd planned.

Chapter Fourteen

Jermaine had been on the road for a month and was on his way home. He felt guilty about having cheated on Tracey. By now, it was not just one woman, but a number of women. In his mind, he couldn't help it. It was Tracey who was playing this stupid game of not having sex and only being open to him pleasing her, but not wanting to give nothing in return. In Jermaine's opinion, she pushed him out there. Nonetheless, he still felt bad about it because he did have sincere feelings for Tracey. To make himself feel better, he decided to get her a ring, although he was gun-shy about getting married a second time.

He hadn't told Tracey that he was on his way home; he wanted to surprise her. As he drove, he started planning a romantic evening that would end with a proposal. *Maybe I can get some pussy out of this deal tonight,* he hoped. He stopped by Victoria's Secret and purchased two negligees, a few bottles of perfume, bodywashes, lotions, body sprays, and several pairs of sexy panties. He went to the nearby florist for a bouquet of roses, a box of chocolates, and a card expressing sentiments of love.

After a quick stop at the grocery store, Jermaine headed home, ready to prepare his best cooked meal of smothered steak with sautéed onion, baked potatoes rubbed with olive oil and kosher salt, and garden salads. He chilled a bottle of Pinot Noir wine to serve with dinner; then he made a buttery peach cobbler to be served with French vanilla ice cream. It was his goal to spoil Tracey ridiculously that weekend to make up for all the women he'd recently slept with on the road, behind her back, although he would never confess it. And really, Jermaine did feel remorse. "But hell, I got needs too," he mumbled, dialing Tracey's number.

"Hey, baby," he started off the conversation. "What you doing?"

"I'm just finishing up some braids." Tracey handed Eureen a mirror as she continued fluffing curled tendrils. Tracey had the phone wedged between her ear and her shoulder.

"Oh, okay. So you been on your feet all day, huh?"

"Pretty much."

"You tired?" he asked.

"A little bit. I wish you were here to cook me some hot dogs and rub my feet," Tracey answered, snickering. "You can go to the bathroom and look at it," she said to Eureen.

"How 'bout I come pick you up?" he offered.

"That would be great," came through in an unenthusiastic yawn. Tracey didn't feel like role playing, pretending, phone sexing, or anything else.

"You don't sound too excited about seeing me."

"That's because you're in Texas somewhere, and I don't feel like getting excited about something I can't have 'til next weekend."

"Girl, this looks fantastic!" Whipping her head left and right, Eureen returned from the bathroom.

"You like it?" Tracey replied. "Let me call you back, baby."

"All right." Jermaine disconnected the call, showered and shaved, brushed his teeth, and pulled on a pair of black slacks and a burgundy dress shirt. He slapped on some cologne and smiled at himself. A few quick brush strokes groomed his hair; then he spent ten minutes in the mirror, practicing his proposal, which he was bound to forget.

Before he left the house, Jermaine loaded a set of self-made mixed artist CDs in the changer and let the music fill the room. As a last-minute thought, he dashed to the kitchen, placed some fresh fruit and cheese on a small plate, collected the wineglasses and the wine, and set them on the table in the living room. All that was left to be done was for him to light the candles and pop the question.

After cleaning up loose strands of hair from her dining room, Tracey took a hot shower, wrapped her hair in a towel, and put on her favorite pink fluffy bathrobe. Not expecting any company, she ignored the doorbell when it rang, not bothering to even tiptoe to the door to see who it was. She had a strict but simple rule about showing up at her home unannounced: "Don't do it." The doorbell rang three more times and went unanswered before her cell phone finally rang. Seeing it was Jermaine's number, she picked up.

"You at home?" he asked, sounding partially confused.

"Mmm-hmm."

"Why you not answering the door?" he asked suspiciously.

"I wasn't expecting nobody," she answered, jumping to her feet and padding to the door to look out the peephole.

"Well, I'm out here ringing your doorbell." Before he finished his sentence, Tracey swung the door open, but she still talked to Jermaine through her phone.

"Can I call you back? My man just got here."

Jermaine let out a chuckle, although he wasn't 100 percent sure that he should.

His eyes darted around her apartment for signs of another man. Seeing nothing suspicious, he temporarily dismissed the thought. "Yeah, you do that, 'cause I got the sexiest woman alive standing right in front of me." He snapped his phone closed; then he pushed the door closed behind him. He spoke to Tracey directly. "Hey, sexy!" He gathered her in his arms and pressed his lips against hers.

She reciprocated the action and allowed her robe to fall open. "Mmm! What you doing here? I thought you were in Texas 'til next week."

"I had to come see my baby." He kissed her again. "How you think I can stay away from all this?" he mumbled, dipping his head to her breasts. "I missed you so much."

"I missed you too, baby," she replied, arching her back toward him.

Amid his moans and floating hands, he walked Tracey backward to the couch and laid her down. Already knowing that Tracey wasn't going to allow him inside, he didn't even press this time; and because he'd been well taken care of on the road, he didn't mind so much. He enjoyed what she would let him have access to, and made sure she was fully satisfied.

"Get dressed. I got something for you," Jermaine said, stroking her face.

"What is it?" Tracey's mind was blown at the moment; she didn't feel like moving.

"It's a special treat for my queen." He tugged at her arm. "Go 'head. We need to leave."

Tracey sighed as she lifted herself from the couch. "Whew! You wrong for making me get up after that. I can hardly even walk right now." She giggled as she stood to her feet and sauntered to her bedroom.

Jermaine sat on the couch, again wondering if another man was somewhere in the house. He peered down the hall to make sure Tracey was in the bedroom; then he got up and started searching the house, beginning with the kitchen. Seeing no one initially, he checked a small closet and found nothing. He looked in ridiculous places, like in the cabinet under the sink.

"Just in case," he uttered, glancing underneath the dining-room table. He checked the bathroom, peering behind the shower curtain and in the linen closet. "You need help getting dressed," he called out, walking to her bedroom more so to finish his inspection than to help her with her clothes.

"Not really, but you can come in here," Tracey answered from her walk-in closet.

Before joining her, Jermaine glanced under her bed and found nothing but shoes. Satisfied that no one else was lurking, he sat on her bed and waited for her to emerge.

"Is this good?" Tracey was dressed in a skintight pair of jeans, a plain white baby T-shirt with a red heart on the front, large gold hoop earrings, and a pair of black stiletto pumps.

"Damn, you look good girl!" Jermaine licked his lips. "That's perfect." He nodded. "We're just going to the house."

They arrived at Jermaine's home twenty minutes later, where Jermaine asked her to sit in the car for just a minute while he ran inside to light candles and turn on the oven to begin warming their meals. Then he rushed back out to escort her to dinner.

"Keep your eyes closed," he instructed, leading her inside to the living room. When she did open her eyes, a huge grin covered her face as she absorbed the ambience. "Here you are." He handed her a glass of wine.

"This is so nice, Jermaine!" she shrieked. "Oh my goodness."

"This is for you, baby," Jermaine whispered. "Because I love you," he admitted. "Have a seat." Jermaine fed her fresh strawberries, grapes, and cheese cubes, staring into her eyes and thinking about the ring in his pocket. "Let's dance."

Tracey took another sip from her glass, placed it on the table, and then stood to be embraced by her man. He pulled her close while Luther Vandross's "If Only for One Night" filled the room. Teddy Pendergrass followed with "You're My Latest, My Greatest Inspiration," and Jermaine sang some of the lyrics in her ear, feeling her relax in his arms. By the time the song ended, Jermaine couldn't have felt more certain about what he wanted to say.

"Tracey, I know we haven't dated very long, even though we've known each other practically our whole lives. I meant what I said earlier. I love you." His eyes focused intently on hers. "I want you to be my wife."

"That's sweet, Jermaine. I love you too," Tracey commented, not fully understanding what he was saying until he dropped to his knee.

"I want you to be my wife, Tracey," he repeated, fumbling to get the ring out of his pocket. Once he did, he held it up for her to see.

Tracey's hands flew to her face in a gasp. "Jermaine!"

"Will you marry me?" he asked traditionally.

"Yes! Yes, baby! Yes, I will!" She extended her hand, allowing Jermaine to slide the ring on her finger; then she lifted her hand to her face in the dim light to take a closer look at it. "It's beautiful!" She dropped to her knees and threw her arms around his neck. "I love you, Jermaine." Her kisses started as pecks, but they became longer and more passionate as she joined her lips to his flesh.

Feeling a rise in his manhood, but remembering dinner was in the oven, Jermaine pushed back just a bit. "Let's eat dinner first, baby. I fixed you a special meal." He grabbed her hands and helped her stand to her feet, then boosted himself up. After a delicious dinner, Jermaine ran Tracey a hot bath. While she soaked, he brought her the boxes from the lingerie store for her to open. While she appreciated and loved the sleepwear, Tracey was far more intrigued with her hand.

"I'm engaged," she repeated, over and over, for the rest of the evening. Right before she fell asleep that night, with a huge smile on her face, and wrapped in Jermaine's arms, she whispered a prayer:

"Thank you, Lord, for sending this man my way. He is so incredible and I have never had someone to love me like this. And I didn't even have to do it to him. Lord, you know I've never felt truly loved, so please show me how to love, and how to appreciate and be grateful to someone who loves and cares for me. I need Jermaine in my life; you know I do, Lord—not for his possessions or the comfort he can provide me with, but because he can keep me on the right track and be positive."

The following Monday morning, before departing for another cross-country road trip, Jermaine handed Tracey the keys to his Lexus, the keys to his house, along with the alarm remote, and a pocketful of cash.

"My place is closer to your job, so just stay here while I'm gone. Besides, it'safer with the alarm system," he told her. "I need my fiancée to be comfortable and safe while I'm on the road."

"How you figure I'm not comfortable in my own house?" Tracey asked, although she loved his house and all its amenities. Not to mention she loved the way the Lexus handled and the looks she got whenever she drove it.

"I know you are, baby, but I want you to live like a queen," he told her. "You're my queen and this is what you deserve."

Tracey accepted the keys and the cash, kissed her man good-bye for a few weeks; then she later took herself shopping. By the end of the week, she'd become completely comfortable with calling his home her own. After she got settled, she called a day spa to come over and do a private party for her, Deja, Jasmine, and even included Eureen. Tracey and Eureen had established a greater level of friendship from Tracey helping her manage her hair.

The four ladies sat at ease in the den with Sangrias in their hands and their feet being worked on while they watched *Say Yes to the Dress,* a reality-based show of brides-to-be in search of the perfect wedding gown. They had watched three back-to-back episodes when Jasmine was ready to change the channel.

"Ain't something else on?" she asked. "What we watching this mess for?"

"Because it's a good show to watch with your girl-friends," Tracey answered. "Just chill."

"Turn to *Desperate Housewives,*" Deja demanded, reaching for the TV remote trying to catch an encore episode of the previous show.

"No!" Tracey nearly spilled her drink, diving for the remote. "Let's just watch one more," she stated. "Y'all need refills?"

Eureen and Jasmine raised their glasses, which Tracey collected in one hand and jetted upstairs. A few minutes later, she returned with not only their glasses filled, but also with a huge three-carat diamond on her left hand.

"I hope you ladies aren't doing anything in say, oh, three or four months from now," Tracey said, sashaying in front of the ladies with her left hand over her forehead. "I might have special plans for you."

"Move so I can see her dress!" Deja shrieked, "It's beautiful!"

"Not more beautiful than this!" Tracey shot her hand up, and all three ladies, plus the women who were waiting on them all, screamed.

"Oh my goodness, Tracey," Eureen said, scrambling to get to her feet, almost kicking over the woman who was giving her a pedicure.

"Jermaine proposed?" Jasmine asked in delighted shock.

"Yes, ladies! He proposed!"

"When?" Deja asked.

"Last weekend when he was here," she gushed.

"And you didn't tell us?" Jasmine shot back.

"I'm telling y'all now. Why y'all think I'm over here and he gone out of town?"

"I can't do nothing with you, Miss Thang!" Eureen teased.

"That's Mrs. Thang to you, diva," she retorted.

For the next two hours, the ladies shrieked, screamed, and hollered over how Jermaine proposed and Tracey's initial thoughts of wedding plans.

"So you really knew what you were doing with not givin' him the milk, huh, girl?" Jasmine quipped.

"I told you." Tracey flashed a bright smile. "Y'all keep on playin' the ho."

Those words felt like a punch in Deja's stomach.

"Girl, please!" Deja snapped. "You done slept with every Tom, Dick, and Harry from here to Kalamazoo, and you finally keep your drawers halfway on one time, and then wanna call somebody a ho."

"Damn, don't take it so personal—I'm only playing," Tracey replied.

"Well, who the hell you playing with? Both Jasmine and Eureen are married. That leaves me, and I don't appreciate your comment."

"Just chill. You're only offended because you know you screwing that man when you ain't got no business; then you had the nerve to move him into your house."

Deja could feel her face beginning to burn in anger. "I know you ain't judging! You show me in the Bible where it say letting somebody eat your pussy don't count as sex! And then show me how it's all right for you, all of a sudden, to be shackin', 'cause I don't care what you got on your finger. Your ass still ain't married!"

Tracey wasn't ready to admit to herself or anyone else that she was having premarital sex. She held on tightly to her thought that since she'd yet to let Jermaine insert his dick in her walls, they technically hadn't had sex yet.

"It sho look like to me that Mary and Joseph was living together or something when she was engaged to him, 'cause he was 'bout to put her out when he found out she was pregnant," Tracey shot back, giving her interpretation of what she understood the Bible to say.

"You know what? I'm not sitting here listening to no more of this mess. You got some damn nerve calling somebody a ho, when you opening your legs every chance you get. And if you think you got some kinda pass to heaven 'cause you ain't getting no dick, you only lying to yourself, 'cause you gonna bust hell wide open, anyway." The scowl on Deja's face dared Tracey to say another word. She stormed up the stairs from the basement with her purse slung over her shoulder.

"Get the fuck out then," Tracey said flatly to the wind Deja left behind. "You know where the door is."

As soon as Deja got in her car, she called Garnell, needing to vent.

"Don't worry about her, baby," Garnell said. "She's just excited about that ring on her finger. It's probably fake," he commented, trying to make her feel better.

"I just can't believe her! Who the hell she think she is?" Deja went on. "She been halfway saved two damn days in a row and think she doing something special. As soon as she doesn't get her way, I guarantee you that she gonna cuss Jermaine out and try to fight him. You can take a person out of the ghetto, but you can't take the ghetto out of that person." She paused for a few seconds, trying to calm down, but she found it difficult. "Ain't no decent man gonna put up with Tracey's nasty-ass attitude. Her pussy ain't that damn good where a man would overlook all that!"

"Baby, you need to chill. It ain't that serious. She's wrong for saying what she said, but let it go. I had a long, hard day, and I want to see you when you get home, but I don't want you all upset, 'cause that's gonna cause discord in our home, and Tracey don't deserve that much power," Garnell stated calmly. "And don't forget that people can change. All things are possible through faith in Christ. Maybe all she needed was a decent man to influence her in a positive way. If it's a part of the Good Lord's plan, then it'll work out. The Lord works in mysterious ways. He's capable of strengthening the weak and breakin' down the strong and mighty. I mean, look at me and you."

Deja sighed. "You're right, babe. She just really pissed me off with that mess."

"I know she did, but it's all right. Forget her. Don't let her upset you, 'cause I'ma need me somma that brown sugar when you get here."

Chapter Fifteen

Jasmine was pleased with the positive changes happening in her home now that Shamar was gainfully employed. He was home a lot less, but at least he was working and not sitting up at his mother's house, she reasoned. And every other Friday, his paycheck was directly deposited into their joint checking account for Jasmine to handle the bills. The one thing she didn't like was that his absence gave Cyreese more of an excuse to spy on her and the girls. Every time Jasmine turned around, Cyreese was popping over, unannounced, staying over late into the evening, answering her telephone, and chatting with her neighbors. And what had really ticked Jasmine off was Cyreese had been caught twice attempting to steam open and look at their bills, one of them being her corporate American Express credit card statement. It took everything she had not to cuss her mother-in-law out as she kindly snatched the envelopes out of Cyreese's hands. Completely startled by Jasmine's sudden appearance, Cyreese had nearly jumped out of her skin. However, she couldn't say anything, knowing that she'd been caught red-handed.

"I believe those are addressed to me and my husband. If you feel the need to open some mail, I'm sure there is some in your own mailbox with your name on it."

Cyreese backed down for a couple of weeks after that, but she was soon back to her meddling self, reporting to Shamar anything that she thought looked suspicious.

"Baby, I'm just telling you what I seen," Cyreese shared with her son after forcing a two-night stay in his home with his wife and kids. "Look like to me, the bills was outta control."

"Which ones, Momma? You don't know what you was looking at?"

"Well, the light bill was sky-high, like about three-something. Don't make no sense to be burning all them lights. I was tryin'a look at that 'Merican 'Spress you told me to see after, but she came in the kitchen tryin'a see what I was doing, and I had to put it down right quick," Cyreese commented.

"So you didn't see it?"

"Naw. I was s'posed to been cookin' the girls a decent meal for a change. Not no bowl of cold-ass generic cereal or some lumpy instant oatmeal. What kinda mess is that to feed them girls? Toasty O's and shit. And her English-muffin-and-cream-cheese-eatin' ass thinking she doing a good job raising them. Don't nobody want no damn nooks and crannies. I had to spend my last few food stamps to buy some bacon and eggs and orange juice for them girls," she added. "What the hell she doing with the damn money if them girls ain't even got no good brefiss food. Brefiss the cheapest meal you can buy!"

"You shouldn't have to spend your money to feed the girls, Momma," Shamar answered, becoming concerned.

"Well, I rather go without, myself, than to see them girls go to school hungry every morning. Matta fact, Summer don't look like she developin' like she oughta be. And how could she? Eating microwave dinners every night."

"Jasmine not cooking?"

"When she got time to cook between working them crazy hours and spending time at the church and with her hypocritin', wine-drinking friends? I told you I had to pretty much run that child's birthday party by my damn self while she stayed her ass in the house gossiping with them bitches she call friends. You couldn't have picked a sorrier-ass excuse for a woman for a wife. Then you sittin' up there sending her money like she don't have a job. Don't be no damn fool! Keep sending your wife your whole paycheck every week, 'cause you know she'll put you out as soon as things aren't goin' her way, and your ass will be sittin' on the streets! I want you to send me a couple hundred dollars out of each check so I can put it away for you and make sure them girls gettin' a proper meal. Never let your right hand know what your left hand is doin'. You work too damn hard to give a woman all of your money, even if it's your wife. You're the one who's drivin' through snow and ice, stayin' away from home a month at a time, and you're the man of the house! You should be controllin' things, not her. That wife of yours likes control, and likes to buy shit that'll have her in debt!"

"You're right, Momma. You right," Shamar replied. "I'm gonna have a long talk with her when I get home, 'cause things gotta change. I'm tired of sendin' my whole check home every week and not have money left to buy me a pair of Jordans or some CDs. I wanted to buy you a gift, but couldn't 'cause I had sent her all my money."

"That was stupid! You've gotta be smart. I didn't raise my son to be a damn fool!"

"I know, Momma, I know. I'm gonna holla at her when I get to the house; and if she don't like what I'm sayin', then I'll just move back in with you and save my money."

"Good thinkin', Shamar. That's good, sound thinkin'."

Cyreese's words planted deep seeds in Shamar's head. The time he had behind the wheel traveling from state to state allowed him too much time to think about what his mother had fed him across the phone lines. He'd always known Jasmine to be a great mother to the girls, but he wondered if his absence from the home allowed her too much freedom to act single and childless, instead of married with children. While it was hot and fresh on his mind, he called Jasmine. He barely let her get a hello out before he started his interrogation.

"What did the girls have for breakfast this morning?"

"Wow! No hello or nothing, huh?"

"Just answer the question, Jasmine," he ordered.

"What the hell is wrong with you? They had cereal." She shrugged. "Why?"

"Do you think cereal is the best thing for growing girls?"

"The FDA or somebody thinks so. I ate cereal and I turned out just fine. Why are you calling me while I'm at work asking about some stupid cereal?" She was becoming irritated. "I got work to do."

"Yeah, I wanted to talk to you about that. You need to stop working so many hours. You always at the damn job, the church, or running the streets with your friends," Shamar barked, repeating the warped information he'd been given.

It was at that point that Jasmine realized Cyreese was up to her antics. "I can't believe you calling me with some garbage that your momma done filled your head up with."

"My momma ain't got nothing to do with this, Jasmine. I'm talking about the kind of parent you being."

"What! Who you think you talkin' to?"

"You heard me. What you doing with all the money, if my kids ain't even got food to eat?"

"They do have food to eat, Shamar! I don't know what the hell your momma been telling you, but she need to stay up outta our house and outta our business!"

"How you gonna tell me—"

Unwilling to hear another word, Jasmine pushed the off key on her phone. "I can't believe that wench," Jasmine uttered in anger, keeping her voice low only because she was at work. "I got a good mind to call her and cuss her out." The only thing that stopped her was she wanted to go out with her girls that night and Cyreese had already agreed to babysit. Not wanting to miss a night of gossip and drinks with the girls, Jasmine kept her thoughts to herself. "At least for the time being," she mumbled.

Eureen missed Monroe. She had spent the past two months praying and crying over her dissipated marriage, trying to figure out what had really gone wrong. Other than the lack of sex, she didn't feel they really had any problems that they couldn't have worked through. And what was more frustrating was she had no explanation she could offer to her children on why they were in the predicament that they were in.

Monroe had never been too communicative in the first place, and had always worked long hours, but his daughters did miss his presence in the house.

"Mommy, when is Daddy gonna come live with us?" Michelle asked. The nine-year-old had not yet come to terms with the fact that her parents were now split up.

"Have you been praying about it?" she asked her daughter, looking up from the pan of pork chops she was frying on the stove.

Michelle nodded a yes.

"Well, I have too. I don't know when Daddy's coming; but I think if we keep praying about it, he will real soon." She poked a fork into a few potatoes, which were boiling in a large pot.

"Can we visit him? I like my new room, but I miss my old room too."

The thought made Eureen think for a few minutes. "I don't know. I'm cooking right now." She sighed audibly. "I don't really feel like answering a bunch of questions, Michelle. Did you tell your daddy that you wanted to visit him?"

"Yes," she answered, twisting her fingers around each other.

"What did he say?"

"He said he was gonna come get us and take us shopping and to Chuck E. Cheese's."

"What did he say about you coming to visit?"

"He said he been real busy working; and when he off work, we be at church, so he didn't know."

"Mmm-hmm," Eureen moaned. She knew Monroe was not trying to fit the girls into his schedule. "Well, we'll see."

Michelle skipped away to watch TV with her younger sister, Jametria, while the other girls consumed themselves with cell phone conversations and homework. Monroe had offered them the mobile devices as a consolation prize, along with iPods and new wardrobes from their favorite stores. His bribes had been effective. With the girls having their own phones, they could call him directly from their own numbers, minimizing his chances of talking to Eureen.

"Come eat, y'all," Eureen called, putting plates on the table for her younger girls. She padded to her bedroom, thinking about driving by her old house and attempting to talk to her husband.

He ain't gave me no divorce papers to sign, so there's still a chance. Maybe I should go by there and try to talk with him. I'm sure if we just sat down and just listened to each other, we might get back together.

By the time Eureen showered, refreshed the curls in her braids, applied her makeup and fragrance, then slipped into an outfit Tracey had helped her pick to minimize her bulges, it was a little bit before ten. The drive to the house would take her forty-five minutes, and she assumed Monroe would be home by then.

Just as she suspected, Monroe was home, but she was disappointed that it seemed that he was entertaining guests. There were three luxury cars parked in the driveway. Lights illuminating the den indicated where Monroe and his guests were. Just as if she still lived there, Eureen walked up to the door, slid her key in the lock, and attempted to turn it. It wouldn't give way. She jiggled the key a bit more, not believing that he would have changed the locks, but that was exactly what Monroe had done. Tears fueled by rejection and a bit of anger burned in her eyes as she circled the house to creep toward one of the many windows from where she could hear music, laughter, and loud chatter. Wedging herself between the shrubbery and the house, she peered through the slightly opened vertical blinds and sheer curtains.

"Oh my god!" she gasped, clearly witnessing several naked men and women, including Monroe, having sex with one another while dressed in costumes, sniffing cocaine, smoking crack, and drinking alcohol. Monroe was on his back, with a man straddled across his face, while a woman was straddled across his hips.

"No! Heavens no! Oh my God," Eureen whispered; then she began to vomit before pulling herself away. The scene was like a bad car wreck, too terrible to look at, but she couldn't pull away for another fifteen seconds as tears streamed down her face. "Help me, Lord. Give me strength, Father. Please, Lord, help me."

She could hardly see the road as she drove back home, feeling numb, confused, betrayed, embarrassed, and devalued. Even so, she whispered, "Thank you, Lord, thank you. Thank you for revealing that to me. I ask for your protection, Lord, because I don't know how long he's been into that, and I just ask that you please let me be well." All the way back to her home, she cried and prayed for Monroe's deliverance, although she didn't pray for her marriage.

Eureen got home safely, peeked in at her daughters, and retreated to her bedroom. She didn't bother to peel out of her clothes, but turned on some worship music and collapsed on her bed, grateful that Monroe had never lain there or tainted the bed she now slept in with his homosexual acts.

"So it wasn't ever me," she whispered to herself. "He just wanted a man." She couldn't do anything else but cry out to the Lord for her own emotional healing and for wisdom on how to best handle the situation as far as her children were concerned.

"I'll confront him about it when I see him," she prayed out loud, staring at the ceiling. "I need to tell him that you love him and he needs to quit slaving for Satan. And because you love him, I still love him, and I'm still in love with him." She paused. "He's gotta be willing to get some counseling and rehabilitation, though. He'd be okay then, and then maybe he'll allow you to work in his life. I know you will forgive Monroe if he repents."

She shut her eyes tightly, but popped them open, haunted by what she saw replaying behind her lids. "Maybe he was just high off that stuff they were smoking and putting up their noses, and didn't know what he was doing. He didn't become successful and wealthy being stupid; therefore it has to be the drugs and alcohol causing him to do such nasty and vulgar things. I love him with all my heart, Lord, and a person doesn't just give up on someone she truly loves. Lord, you didn't give up on me with all the mistakes I've made. You forgive us of all sin, and I will show your love by forgiving my husband."

At some point, unable to get the images she'd seen out of her head, she drifted into a deep sleep, dreaming that Monroe was giving testimony in a huge auditorium filled with tens of thousands of people about how he'd turned his life around and was now on fire for the Lord.

Waking up the next day, Eureen wanted to be able to talk to someone, but she knew that what she'd found out couldn't be shared with Tracey, Deja, and Jasmine. Not only was it too personal and embarrassing, Eureen thought it best that she stopped hanging with them so much because she thought they were too wordly and secular.

Since the breakup of her marriage, Eureen had committed an hour to prayer every day, and two hours in the Word so that she was able to hear more clearly from God. Since she'd decided that, she found that Tracey, Jasmine, and Deja's profanity, drinking, and fornication were too much of a negative and sinful environment for her to constantly be around.

And not only that, she could already hear in her mind what they would collectively have to say: *"Girl, you mean to tell me your man fuckin' men? Your man suckin' dicks and he ain't eatin' your pussy? He actin' like he got a pussy? Fuck that shit. I'd blow that muth-afucka's brains out! He want a pole in his ass? I'd take a gun and fuck his ass with the barrel; and right when that nigga start comin', I'd pull the damn trigger! I'd give a whole new meaning to 'shit for brains'!"*

"No, Lord! My business ain't nobody's business. This right here gotta stay between me and you!" she said. "I pray for your wisdom and instruction on what to do."

It had been a little over a month since that horrific night that Eureen had found out about Monroe's alternative lifestyle, and she felt like the Lord was leading her to pay him a visit. She drove back to her old home, planning to talk to and pray with Monroe. It was a Tuesday morning, right before eleven, which was definitely a time when Monroe would normally be at work. When she saw his vehicle parked in the driveway, she was inspired to move forward.

More than a minute had passed since she'd rung the doorbell, and discouragement was just about to set in. Right before Eureen could retreat to the car, the front door cracked, revealing a grossly disheveled Monroe.

"What the hell you want?" he snarled. His eyes were red and puffy. His skin seemed to sag, and he hadn't shaved for several days. His breath reeked of alcohol, and he was looked tired and worn-the-hell-out. He looked to have just rolled out of bed, dressed only in his boxers and a dingy T-shirt. He seemed to have lost a tremendous amount of weight. Even so, he was the best thing Eureen had laid eyes on all week.

"Thank you, Lord," she said, looking into his eyes while tears formed in her own. "Thank you, Father God. Thank you for keeping him safe," she whispered. She thought quickly about the white man's penis inside Monroe's mouth but rebuked the devil, who she felt was trying to hinder her mission, and moved on.

"Monroe, I need to talk to you. Can you let me in?"

"What the hell for?" Monroe mumbled. "Something wrong with the girls?" He turned away from the door, leaving it open for her to enter.

"No. I just wanted to see you," she said, partially smiling, taking notice of Monroe's weight loss. "I'm sorry for not calling you before comin' by, but I had such an impression on my spirit to come over and make sure you were all right." She closed the door; then she cautiously approached her husband and embraced him. "I love you, Monroe. I really do. I'm certain that you know I love you for you, and not because of your wealth. You can't buy your way to heaven; you've gotta earn that privilege by living right here on earth. The Lord put us in each other's path for a reason—I'm convinced of that—and that reason is love, understanding, trust, and ultimately marriage. He wants you to repent and learn how to produce love."

"'Produce love'?" he grunted, unenthused, but accepting her embrace. "Haven't heard that word since fuckin' high school."

"What do you mean? I tell you that I love you all the time, and God loves you too," she repeated.

"Hell, you probably don't even know what the word means, just like I don't." He paused for a few seconds, loosely draping his arm around his wife. "To tell you the truth, the only thing I love is my bank account and my assets. I never knew my real parents, so I didn't get any love from them. I heard through the grapevine that my daddy left my mama when I was born and got himself killed in the streets, and my mama ran off with a man and moved to Chicago. That's when I was put in a foster home. I was a got-damn foster child, who had a dream of becomin' rich."

"You don't have to explain," Eureen said softly, knowing that he was influenced by alcohol. She knew all about his upbringing. "I'm here for you, baby."

"I try to leave the past buried; that works for me," he slurred, pressing his drunken lips to hers and beginning to take off his clothes right there in the living room, which triggered disconcerted thoughts in Eureen's mind.

I can't do this, she thought, her mind flashing back to the scene of his lewd sexual acts. *I want to please him and give him what he wants, but not after seeing what I saw. I can't do that to myself. He'll just have to be angry at me.*

"Baby," she said as he tugged her toward the couch. "Mother Nature is in the midst." She cringed internally at lying about her period being on, but she had to do what she had to do to protect herself.

"What!" he snapped. "What the fuck you come over here for?" He had already begun stroking his manhood to speed his erection.

"Please don't be angry, Monroe. Please understand. . . ."

"Understand what? You gotta mouth, don't you? What's wrong with your suckin' then, since you came over here?"

"Monroe, please don't do this, baby. I just wanted to talk to you and—"

"Fuck that! Are you tellin' me you can't give me no pussy and you don't want to suck my dick either? You think that fuckin' house is free and your bills and shit don't cost nothin'?"

Tears began to burn in Eureen's eyes. She didn't want to confess to Monroe that she knew what he was into. He continued his tirade.

"You think all that got-damn money I put in an account for you every month falls off a money tree? And you don't wanna suck my muthafuckin' dick? You're wrong as two left shoes! Got-damn it, you're fuckin' wrong! With all that stuff I give you, I should get pussy and head whenever I want it. Plenty of bitches would love to be in your shoes, but you're too fuckin' stupid to realize that! I'm cancelin' your contract, bitch. That's what I'm gonna do!"

"Monroe, you don't mean that," she replied, smudging away her tears in her refusal to let him upset her. "You love me. I know you do," she claimed.

"I don't mean it, my ass! You've gotta be the craziest bitch in the world to think I'm gonna put up with some shit like this!" he yelled, leaping to his feet and storming to the door to hold it open for her exit. As he reached for the doorknob, Monroe abruptly ran out of breath and grabbed his chest. His eyes widened, and suddenly he looked wild and scared. He opened his mouth to try to ask Eureen to help him, but nothing came out besides a strained puff of air. His eyes fluttered shut as his legs weakened and he collapsed to the floor.

"Monroe!" Eureen gasped, immediately running to his aid. "Monroe, say something!" she begged. "Talk to me!" Eureen patted his face in an attempt to get a response but failing. Monroe lay silent and unconscious, causing Eureen to become hysterical. "God, please help me! I need you, Lord. Please help me," she cried, leaving his side to grab her cell phone and call for help.

Chapter Sixteen

Cyreese couldn't hide the large grin on her face when she opened an envelope from Shamar and pulled out five $100 bills. "That boy know better than to be sending money in the mail like this," she mumbled with a cigarette perched between her lips. "But I'm sho glad he did." She folded the cash and stuffed it inside her bra; then she reached for the phone to call her "baby." She was proud of her son's new employment history and felt that it added to his manhood; however, that didn't stop her from treating him like a spoiled little boy, calling him each day to make sure he was safe on the road.

"You all right, shug?" she cooed as if Shamar was in his elementary years.

"Yeah, Ma, I'm good—just rolling on this highway. You get that money I sent you?"

"Yes, I did. Thank you, baby. You keepin' yourself all right? How you eatin'?"

"Eh," he drew out. "They got a coupla good restaurants out here. Nothing like what you cook me, though."

"I'll fix you somna eat when you get back here," she offered.

"That sounds good, Momma. I got you something too," Shamar answered, thinking about some stolen goods he had stashed in his truck.

"Oooh! What you got for your momma?"

"It's a surprise. You gonna have to wait 'til I get home," Shamar replied.

"All right. Well, when you gonna be here?" she asked, now out of her greed rather than concern.

"I'll be there next weekend. You gonna love it too!"

Shamar had hauled everything from cow manure to airplane parts. It had only taken him a couple of runs to notice the carelessness of both shippers and receivers and their goods. Frequently, on both ends, employees would miscount, or sometimes not even bother to count whatever was being loaded or dropped off. Shamar began to use this to his advantage.

Through watching and listening intently, he began trafficking and selling stolen goods and had lined his pockets well with money he'd gained from laptops, GPS systems, several other electronic devices, plasma televisions, and even groceries and meats. With the money he was making through his illegal sales, he didn't even mind sending Jasmine his full paycheck; but, of course, he couldn't tell Cyreese that. He just let her think he was sending most of his earnings to her, and allowing Jasmine to get only a small portion.

Shamar ended the call with his mother; then he scrolled through the Rolodex in his mind of his buying contacts who were located in the states he'd be passing through. They were always ready to make deals and to purchase whatever he'd been able to steal at prices or at barters he could not refuse. The previous month he'd sold sixteen HP desktops, along with flat-screen monitors, and bought all kinds of items from professional thieves who had boosted from Walmart, Home Depot, and department stores at prices far below wholesale.

He phoned his contact in Greenville, Mississippi, ready to wheel and deal.

"What's up, Drefus?"

"What's up, my truck-drivin' ambassador? Same shit, different day?"

"You got that shit right."

"What you got for me?"

"Computers, nigga. I got twenty-five new Dell computers for you right now. Can you handle 'em or should I pass 'em on to the next man lookin' for a good deal?"

"Does a zebra have stripes?"

"That's what I'm talkin' 'bout, my nigga, that's what I'm talkin' 'bout. Meet me at the truck stop on Highway 82 by the port in thirty."

"Fo' sho."

After the connection broke, Shamar phoned another buyer in California. "What up, Diablo?"

"Hey, my friend, where are you, holmes? Mexico, El Paso, Zaragoza, Juárez, with my homies? The Sierras, the Carolinas? Where are you, holmes?"

"Cruisin' through Mississippi, lettin' it do what it do. A thousand miles ahead of me, pullin' twenty tons behind me. You know how I get down, Diablo."

"Ain't that the truth, holmes? I still waitin' for you to bring me a truckload of good shit, you know what I mean?"

"I feel you, Diablo. Tell you what? I ain't got a truckload for you, but I got some plasmas and surround-sound shit still in the box."

"Bring 'em on. I told you I buy everythin' from horses to hair weave. Everythin' sells."

"I'll touch down in Cali within twenty-six hours and I'll call you then. I need top dollars for this shit, Diablo, so don't try to jew me down like you normally do."

"I'll take care of you, holmes, I said I got you."

"I'll holla at you," Shamar said, ending the call, and then seeing Jasmine's number pop up on the call-waiting caller ID. There was a time when he would have ignored her call, but they were seeing better days in their marriage.

"Hi, honey," she cordially greeted.

"Hey, baby," he answered smoothly.

Now that he was working a real job and his entire paycheck was hitting their joint bank account every single payday, the arguments between Shamar and his wife had ceased. With Jasmine no longer footing the bills alone, she had nothing to balk about.

"How's my sexy wife doing?"

"I'm missing my man right now."

"I'm missin' you too, baby. You keepin' that ass tight for me?"

"You know I am." She giggled.

"What about them titties?"

"I wish you were here to suck on them, baby. They missing your lips," she moaned.

"Oh shit, you getting my dick hard."

"What you gonna do with that hard dick?"

"What you want me to do with it, baby?" Shamar gave his manhood a squeeze, keeping his other hand on the steering wheel.

"I want you to bring it home to me so I can run my tongue all over it and suck it 'til it pop," Jasmine answered in a sultry voice. "Can you do that for me?"

"Girl, I can't wait to feed you somma this dick."

"That's what I like, baby! You got my pussy tightenin', and shit."

"Is it wet, baby?"

"It's dripping, Shamar. Drippin' with honey, waiting for you to lick it all up."

"Shit, girl! You 'bout to make a nigga pull on the side of the road and work this thing out."

"Why don't you save it for me, Daddy, so I can ride it like you like it?"

"How is that, baby?"

"Nice and slow, baby, with a full hip rotation on the stick," Jasmine whispered.

"Where you at?" Shamar asked, pulling his dick out of his pants and handling it.

"Laying across the bed in my pink butterfly thong, needing some dick."

"Touch that pussy for me, baby. Tickle that clit."

"Mmm," she moaned in response.

"Yeah, just like that, girl." Shamar was practically panting; he was happy to see a rest stop just a mile up the road. He couldn't pull over quick enough to finish having phone sex with his wife.

They continued talking each other into full orgasms before they ended that portion of their conversation with heavy panting and sticky hands.

"Damn, you the bomb, baby," Jasmine complimented. "Even over the phone."

"You too, baby," Shamar reciprocated. "I got something special for you when I get home too," he added, thinking about the iPad and a diamond-encrusted watch he had gotten from one of his thieving buddies.

"Well, I got something for you too, baby," she purred, referring to herself.

"Yeah, make sure you save me a little bit of that," he responded possessively.

Shamar was feeling like a man.

Chapter Seventeen

During the next two months, Jermaine had sex with sixteen different women a month, averaging four a week. He hadn't been home since he'd proposed to Tracey. He was now on his way, filled with the hope that Tracey wouldn't come up with some excuse to continue to withhold her body from him.

Then his phone rang, bringing him back to reality.

"Jermaine, this is Alexis," the voice said, speaking calmly.

"Alexis who?" he asked, barely having kept up with the list of women he'd involved himself with.

The woman immediately took offense. "What the fuck you mean? Alexis who? You wasn't saying that shit when you had your dick all in my mouth," the woman spat out at him.

"I don't fuckin' know you, bitch!" Jermaine retaliated.

"Well, you 'bout to, 'cause, nigga, I'm pregnant and I'm 'bout to take your ass for every damn dime you got, since you don't fuckin' know nobody!"

At that, Alexis ended the call, but Jermaine called right back.

"I don't know who the hell you done fucked, but that baby you got in your belly ain't mines!" he declared. "I didn't nut in you. I pulled out!"

"What are you? Fuckin' thirteen?" Alexis screamed. "So the fuck what you pulled out! What the hell that mean? Get your grown, crusty, sour-dick ass in some sex education classes! That is if your ass can afford it after I'm through with you!"

Alexis ended the call again, leaving Jermaine angry and in denial.

"That ain't my baby," he said out loud, trying to convince himself. "Ain't no way that's my damn baby."

He tried to think on other things and even cranked up the music in his truck and began to sing, but he couldn't get the call out of his mind. A pregnancy by any other woman than Tracey would ruin his relationship with her. He replayed Alexis's allegations in his head, over and over, especially the part of him needing to take sex education classes.

"What the fuck was I thinking, not using a rubber," he chastised himself. "How stupid could I fucking be! Stupid ass! As cheap as a damn condom is!" He banged against the steering wheel, cursing at himself and his irresponsible actions.

The vibration of his cell phone in his pocket paused his misery for only a flash of a second. Once he saw Tracey's number, he felt his stomach drop. He couldn't even bring himself to answer the phone right then. Instead, he sighed heavily and slid the phone back into his pocket; then he rubbed his temples with his free hand.

Not more than a week passed when he received a similar call from Alexis's twin sister, Heather. "It ain't mines," he insisted. "Y'all two bitches tryin' put babies on me 'cause I got a job and make good money. That's why I didn't shoot inside y'all! Leave me the fuck alone and figure out who the real daddy is!"

Heather and Alexis together had worked Jermaine over, blowing his mind in a ménage a trois, which was when his thoughts of using a condom for the entire escapade went right out the window. With his dick inside one of them, and the other's pussy up under his nose, he hadn't been able to think straight. He remembered Alexis fondling his balls, not allowing him to come until he begged her to, extending his pleasure for nearly two hours before his first explosion. He had dozed off but woke a short time later to Heather suckling on his dick like a hungry animal feeding off its mother, bringing him back to a full erection.

Both ladies lay on their backs with their legs spread wide, allowing him to feast on two pussies at once. Then they flipped him on his back, and for the first time, Jermaine had his dick and his balls washed over at the same time. It made him feel like a king. Heather had even licked his ass while he came again, which sent him into a deep slumber. When he came to again, they worked him over a final time, making him feel things he'd never felt. He gave them both money and asked if they would mind him stopping through whenever he was nearby. With giggles fueled by the cash they'd been given, the women agreed. He made a special effort to coast through their town in Nevada whenever he left home, even if it was a bit out of the way.

"Those bitches think they're slick! They probably been lookin' for somebody to take care of their asses for long time and out of the blue come me, Mr. Stupid!" he yelled at himself. "I don't know why I ain't wear no rubbers screwin' those sluts!"

He calmed his thoughts for a moment with another theory. "They probably just looking for fake abortion money. Bitches lie about being pregnant all the time," he told himself out loud.

While he was still reasoning things out, Alexis called. Jermaine inhaled deeply, then puffed the breath through his puckered lips before answering. He was determined to stay calm.

"Hello," he answered, trying to show no signs of being upset.

"You came to your damn sense yet?" Alexis snapped. "'Cause I need maternity clothes."

What! I know she ain't expectin' me to buy her no damn clothes!

"Listen Alexis, I don't want to argue today. If you need a couple hundred dollars to take care of things, I got that," he offered, attempting to stay cordial.

"Oh, I'm gonna need more than a couple hundred. I'ma need at least a thousand dollars a month for the next eighteen years 'cause I don't believe in no damn abortions," she said without raising her voice.

"What! Bitch, you gonna hafta find my ass first," he spat out.

"Um, nigga, you stay at 15398 Alabaster Court, Lancaster, California 93534."

Jermaine's stomach sank. He hadn't been prepared for that. When he'd woke up from his encounter with the ladies, he felt assured that his wallet, which he'd never meant to leave accessible in the first place, hadn't been gone through because every dollar that he had was in place. But it was clear to him now that Alexis had gotten the information off his driver's license and was sure to share it with her partner in crime.

"You can run, but you can't hide, deadbeat muthafucka." With a click, she was gone.

Jermaine drove the next 400 miles in complete silence, wondering how he was going to best handle the mess he had suddenly found himself in. He tried to place blame on Tracey.

"If she had been having sex with me in the first place, I wouldn'ta needed to sleep around," he mumbled. Deep down, however, he knew he couldn't blame anyone but himself.

Next he tried to figure out how he could possibly pay for two babies at once, not to mention keep them from his soon-to-be-wife.

"Wait a minute. Them babies probably ain't even mine. I know I ain't the only man they done dropped they drawers for. They probably ridin' every dick in their state. Why the fuck am I sittin' here worrying about these Jerry Springer–ass bitches. Shit, I ain't got nothin' to worry about. Them bitches don't know who their babies' daddy is."

With that thought, he dismissed the whole notion of whores, babies, child support, maternity clothes, and empty threats.

Two, long depressing days of testing diagnosed Monroe as HIV positive. According to the doctors, he did not have much longer to live, being that the disease was in its last stages. Unfortunately, his illness had gone untreated. The testing disclosed the disease had dominated Monroe's blood cells beginning at least two years earlier. Because of the severity of his condition, Monroe was ordered to keep on a mask to protect others and also to remain in the AIDS ward and receive treatment that would enable him to live a bit longer. His doctor was blunt in predicting that Monroe's death was no more than a month away.

"We can offer some level of treatment that will extend his life for a short period, and in order to do that, we'll need to keep him here," the doctor spoke to Eureen.

"Fuck that!" Monroe yelled. "I ain't stayin' up in this muthafucka! If I'm gonna die, then got-damn it, I wanna go out havin' some fuckin' fun. Why lay up in this muthafucka and die! Why can't y'all muthafuckas fly some medicine up in here from Africa, or Japan, or the fuckin' Middle East to cure this shit! If a muthafucka was white, y'all racist muthafuckas wouldn't have a problem with that! My money spend just like y'alls, but y'all muthafuckas want me to lay up in here and rot! Ain't that a bitch!"

"Calm down, sweetheart," Eureen suggested, embarrassed at Monroe's language in front of Pastor Gardner, whom she had called to pray for her husband.

"No, fuck that! Can't you see what's happenin'? They tryin'a kill me up in here, and I ain't going out like no muthafuckin' dummy!"

"Can y'all please leave for a few minutes while I talk to him alone . . . please?" Eureen requested, seeing Monroe was out of control and acting unreasonably.

"Listen, Monroe," she said softly. "The doctor's recommendation is for your own good, so please do as they suggest and quit resisting, using all that foolish and harsh talk. Then maybe—"

"Maybe what?" he snapped. "Maybe I'll live five or six hours longer? Hospitals are nothin' but fuckin' businesses, Eureen! The longer these muthafuckas keep me here and keep runnin' these expensive-ass tests, the more of my money they get! This is bullshit!"

She sighed, shook her head, and replied solemnly, "Monroe, you've gotta realize that there are some things money can't buy."

Uninvited, the nurses and doctors abruptly reentered the room, despite Monroe's agitation.

"Get the fuck outta here! I'm gonna die, any-fuckin'-way, so fuck all of y'all, and fuck the world too! Get the fuck outta here, and leave me the fuck alone! That goes for you too, Eureen!"

Per his request, Eureen left the room, shaking her head and wiping away tears.

Pastor Gardner stood in the hallway, leaning against the wall.

"He's quite miserable, huh?" he asked.

Eureen could only nod initially, but somehow she formed a few words several seconds later. "He really needs prayer, Pastor. He's in bad shape."

"Well, you know the Bible says sometimes a man needs to be turned over to the devil for the destruction of his flesh, so that his spirit might be saved," David said, trying to comfort his parishioner.

On the contrary, she took offense, gasping and grabbing at her chest.

"What are you tryin'a say, Pastor! That God gave him AIDS to save him?"

"Well, what I am saying is that you've been praying for Brother Francis for a long time and—"

"So you think he's being punished, and that he deserves it?" Eureen snapped.

"Sister Francis, sin has its own consequences," he started to say, but Eureen stopped him again.

"You know what, Pastor? I asked you to come because I thought I could count on you to stand in the gap for Monroe and me, but I see you are here to condemn and to judge!"

"Not at all, Sister Fra—"

"Just leave!" Eureen ordered. "Leave now! I'll pray for my own husband!"

She turned her back to David and stormed away, not quite sure where she was going. She knew, however, that she didn't want to be in her pastor's presence any longer.

Chapter Eighteen

Garnell's felony convictions prevented him from finding a decent job. Feeling like he was stuck at his minimum-wage job shoveling animal feces led him to experience agitation and stress, although Deja took care of most of the household expenses. He often didn't get home until hours after he'd gotten off, and sometimes was drunk.

"Garnell, don't do this," Deja pleaded with him one evening. "Don't make things worse by making foolish choices."

"What do you mean?" he slurred, a bit tipsy from stopping at a bar after work and throwing back several beers.

"I mean, I know it's tough tryin'a get on your feet, but I'm here for you like I've always been, making sure you don't want for nothing. It's not fair to me that you are turning your back on me and God to nurse a bottle, Garnell."

"Well, I need more than a minimum-wage job, Deja!" he exploded, pounding a fist against the wall. "Here I am tryin'a be a man and I can't even pay my lady's rent for her so she can go buy herself something nice with her paycheck!" he bellowed. "How the hell you think that make me feel?"

Deja didn't know how to respond. She'd always been able to find and keep a job. Even more so, she managed her money well and didn't know what it meant to struggle with bills. She paused in thought before responding.

"Garnell, I know there are other brothers out there who are trying to make it, and they don't even have a roof over their heads. They don't have a woman who loves them and is in their corner every step of the way."

"Yeah, whatever," he dismissed, collapsing onto the sofa. "I'm tired of everybody being on my back and down my damn throat."

Deja sighed. "I don't mean to be down your throat, babe. I'm only trying to help."

"Well, help by fixing me something to eat," he barked.

Deja shook her head, rose to her feet, then padded to the kitchen, trying to control her frustration. While she prepared a plate of baked turkey wings, rice and gravy, and green beans, she called a friend who happened to work on the recruiting staff on her job. She hoped she could help Garnell secure a position, but she was informed that the company did not hire felons.

She watched in silence as Garnell wolfed down his food; then he stomped upstairs, showered, and went straight to bed, leaving Deja hot and horny for the fourth consecutive night. Even when she tried sliding beneath the covers and attempting to cover his manhood with her mouth, he grunted and turned away from her before she could wrap her lips around him. This time, she did show her frustration by snatching all the covers from their bed and storming to the living-room couch to sleep.

The following day, after being denied employment on three separate interviews because of his unfavorable background check, an irate Garnell returned home and voiced his anger.

"After they find out about my felonies, they treat me like I raped one of their kids or something! I paid my dues for my wrongdoing, and I just don't think it's right for them to hold my past against me! I'm trying to do the right thing in life, but it seems like they want you to go out and steal or sell dope, so they can lock you back up again!"

"The only thing we can do, babe, is be optimistic and keep praying about it. We've got to have faith. The Lord knows your situation, your past, and your present mind-set, and I'm certain that soon he'll bless you with a good job," Deja replied sensibly.

"But when are my prayers gonna be answered? I need a job, like yesterday!"

"God doesn't move when we want Him to move. He moves when He sees it appropriate to. He's not going to give us what we want, when we want it; but I can guarantee you, He'll be on time."

"I hear what you're saying, sweetheart, but it's been rejection after rejection not only by the white man, but my own people as well! It seems like a black man would give you a break by giving you a chance to prove yourself, but some of 'em act worse than the white man!"

"Complaining won't do any good, babe. All we can do is keep praying about it and keep being optimistic and not let it frustrate you."

Deja silenced herself a few moments and went into deep thought. "Maybe the reason you haven't been blessed with a job is because we're not living right, according to God's Word or His will. We sit on the third pew from the pulpit every Sunday in church, but we're fornicating every night. Do you get my drift?"

"Yeah, you're right."

"People all over the church are gossiping about us, and you're not having any luck with a job, but we still fail to do what we know is right. God is more than likely cutting our blessings short until we decide to please Him, and not ourselves. We're supposed to be examples; but instead we're fornicating, doing the devil's will," Deja said. Then she silenced herself a few moments and let him absorb what she had said.

"I know what you're getting at, Deja, but I just ain't ready to get married yet, and I couldn't care less about what those damn hypocrites think in church because ninety percent of 'em got dirt inside their closets."

"But what does that have to do with getting married?"

"I just ain't ready yet, sweetheart." He gulped, thinking about the one wife he already had in South Carolina.

"So you'd rather keep following the devil, huh?"

"I didn't say that."

"That's what you're implying, Garnell."

"You're twisting it, Deja. Stop it. What the hell do I look like getting married and I don't even have a good job? All that'll do is give those damn hypocrites something else to talk about because then they'll be saying you're taking care of me."

"They're probably already saying that, don't you think?"

"I swear, I can't win for losing."

"You can win if you do things the right way. Pastor Gardner always says that when a man is right, his world will be right."

"Those preachers think they know everything!"

"To me, it's obvious," she said, pressuring for a commitment. "But tell me, Garnell, when exactly *will* you be ready to get married?"

"When I find a good job and save up about ten thousand dollars, then I'll be ready. I ain't stupid, Deja. I know your friends don't like me because they think I'm freeloading off you and using you! Neither of them thinks I'm good enough for you. I can tell by the look they give me. And besides, how do you think your father will respond to your marrying a broke-ass man?"

"I'm not trying to please man; I'm trying to please God."

"Listen, Deja, I'll always belong to you, okay? Nothing could ever change that, but just bear with me until I find a good job and get on my feet. Then you'll know I won't have a problem marrying you. And actually, it's just like you're my wife, anyhow; that's what I refer to you as."

Deja shook her head disapprovingly and walked away, feeling like God would be pleased and bless them if they just did the right thing.

That night, after praying for forgiveness of her sins, Deja then went into a sincere prayer for Garnell's employment status. Surprisingly, the following day, she received a call from her friend in human resources enlightening her on an available position. Her friend even faxed an application to her home for Garnell to complete, which he immediately did and faxed back. Deja thanked God that the human resources manager was more understanding than most, due to her own husband being an ex-felon, so she never submitted the background check. It wasn't long before he was called for an interview and soon began training as an installation tech with AT&T.

The day that he came home from his first full day of work, Deja started planning a wedding.

Chapter Nineteen

Eureen was completely exhausted from staying at Monroe's side over the past few weeks and trying to comfort her daughters' devastation from seeing their father wither away, and then having to deal with their emotions regarding what would be the root cause of his death.

"Daddy's gay?" her oldest had asked.

Eureen didn't quite know how to answer. She didn't want to say yes, although she had clearly seen him involved in homosexual activity, and she didn't want to say no and insult her daughter's intelligence. In a split second, she came up with a middle-of-the-road answer.

"I'm not sure how your daddy contracted HIV, sweetheart," she replied. She felt this was honest enough. Outside of that, she let the girls draw their own conclusions.

Eureen tiptoed into Monroe's room, where he lay, close to lifeless, staring at the ceiling, seemingly in deep thought. Eureen sat next to him and held his hand; she looked into his eyes.

"You're still the love of my life, you know," she whispered.

Monroe stared silently at his wife as a tear escaped the corner of his eye. He coughed twice, leaving a glob of spit just outside his lips. Eureen lovingly wiped it away with a tissue.

"Listen, baby," he said weakly. "I've never been much for church and living right, and I don't even know how to pray, but do you think it's possible that a man like me can get to heaven?"

As if his life depended on her answer, Monroe earnestly looked at the woman he'd treated so badly. The only thing he had not done was put his hands on her.

"All things are possible through faith in Christ, Monroe, if you accept the Lord Jesus Christ as your savior and ask Him for forgiveness."

"I'll accept Him. Honestly, I will. I'll do anything; I'll beg for forgiveness or whatever I gotta do. Come on, baby, teach me how to talk to Him."

"Okay," she gratefully said. "Address Him as Heavenly Father, the Creator of all, and ask all of your requests in the name of the Son of God, Jesus."

"If I'm talkin' directly to God, then why do I have to ask my request in Jesus' name?"

"Simple. Jesus, the Son of Almighty God, sacrificed His life by dying for our sins; therefore, we should acknowledge that by asking everything in His name."

"Oh." Monroe paused, trying to get his thoughts together. "You know, baby, I think you're an angel sent from heaven to watch over me."

"You never can tell." Eureen patted his hand and continued. "Close your eyes and I'll pray first; then you can share your heart with the Lord. You ready?"

"I was ready yesterday."

After a lengthy, humble prayer, Eureen kissed Monroe's forehead; then she spoke softly.

"Only God can judge you, Monroe. He's the only one who can determine your destiny being heaven or hell on Judgment Day, despite your sins. Now close your eyes and talk with Him, asking Him to forgive you for your sins, asking Him to renew your heart, mind, and soul, and asking Him to let His will be done."

"I just told you I ain't never prayed before and—"

She cut him off. "Tell you what? Pretend you're pray-ing to God for one of those big deals in real estate to close. Talk to Him like He's your friend, but speak re-spectfully and with earnestness, acknowledging Him as God Almighty, the most powerful being on earth and in heaven. You've got to acknowledge God and Jesus for your prayers to be heard and answered."

Incredibly weak but humble, Monroe eased out of bed, fell to his knees, closed his eyes to talk to God, at-tempting to get an extension of a few more years on his life.

"Heavenly Father, in Jesus' name, please forgive me for not knowin' you or never tryin' to get to know you. Forgive me for my sins and arrogance, Heavenly Father, and renew my heart, mind, and soul. Mold me the way you see fit, Heavenly Father, in Jesus' name, cleanse my heart and forgive me." He got emotional and began crying. "I'm sorry for all the wrong I did in my life. Heavenly Father, please forgive me in Jesus' name! I'm sorry for not believin' in you prior to my illness, Heavenly Father, but I didn't know any better! The devil had his clutches on me, Heavenly Father, and I just couldn't break loose. Please forgive me in Jesus' name. Please forgive me, Father! Money was my god, I admit that, but please forgive me! Please spare my life, Heavenly Father, in your son Jesus Christ's name. Please spare me and see to it that I make it to heaven! I'm sorry for talkin' down to poor people, and I'm also sorry for committin' bisexual acts. I'm sorry, Heavenly Father. I didn't know any better.

"I also wanna thank you for puttin' Eureen in my life, Heavenly Father. In Jesus' name, I thank you. She cares about me and loves me. Please forgive me for treatin' her so bad and for talkin' to her so harsh. In

Jesus' name, please forgive me. I now understand that she's a blessing. She's been tryin' to sway me toward you since day one, but I kept rejectin' you, Father. I'm sorry! I was too blinded by my ego and my money to realize that you put her in my path for a reason. I wish I'da known you earlier, Heavenly Father; then I wouldn't be in this life-threatening situation, and maybe the devil wouldn't have such a strong hold on me. Convert me, Heavenly Father. In Jesus' name, convert me! If you hear me, Heavenly Father, in Jesus' name, please forgive me for all the wrong I've done, for all the people I've swindled for personal gain, and allow me to enter into the gates of heaven. In Jesus' name, Heavenly Father, I beg you to forgive me. Heavenly Father, have mercy on me and let your will be done. In Jesus' name, let your will be done. Heavenly Father, I ain't ready to die!"

His cries weakened into a whisper.

Kneeling beside him, Eureen kissed his cheek and squeezed her hands around his in consolation.

After whimpering for several minutes, Monroe climbed back into bed, with his wife's assistance, and lay blank-faced, staring at the monitors attached to his body.

The only thing she was tryin' to get me to do was change from my old ways and allow God to do me, instead of me doin' me. Out of all the straight and decent men in the world, she loved me, even though we're like day and night, total opposites. Obviously, she loves and cares for me. If she didn't, she wouldn't be here, especially after all the bad things I've said to her. All she ever wanted was my time and to help convert me from bad to good. She deserves a good, wealthy life. I wonder if she'll remarry me, knowin' I'm about to die any minute.

"Eureen," he whispered, disrupting her prayer.

"Yes, sweetheart."

"Do you love me?"

She eased up and looked into his eyes.

"Yes, Monroe, I love you. I always have loved you, and I'll love you no matter what." She kissed him repeatedly on the forehead, giving him the affection she felt like he needed.

"I love you too, baby," he humbly said. "I'm sorry for the way I treated you, and—"

"Shh," she whispered, putting a finger across his lips. "That was the old Monroe; this is the new and improved Monroe, right?"

He produced a weak smile. "You're a godsend." Again he coughed, and his face contorted into a pained expression. "I ain't gonna be here too much longer, Eureen."

"Hold on as long as you can, honey."

"I gotta get some stuff in order," he said, gazing at her. "I ain't done you right all these years, but I'ma fix it as good as I can with what I got left. If you will have me, I want to renew my vows before I close my eyes."

He instructed Eureen to call Kevin, his attorney, as well as his secret lover of eight years, and have him report to the hospital right away for the purpose of paperwork preparation to sign 100 percent of his assets to his wife.

"You think your pastor will come and officiate a little ceremony for us?"

"I don't want him nowhere around here," Eureen replied curtly. "We need to find somebody else." She was still angry with Pastor Gardner for what she felt like he'd said. "Matter of fact, why do we need anybody at all? We already married. Let's just renew our vows in front of God. That is who matters in the first place—not

these jacklegged, hypocritin' men who try to live holier
than thou!"

Monroe nodded slightly. "That's fine, if that's what
you want to do." Monroe instructed his wife on where
to access his credit cards, telling her to purchase a new
bridal ring set. "Get you something real nice," he sput-
tered.

Eureen was reluctant to leave his bedside, assum-
ing she might return to find him already transitioned,
but she pulled herself away, rushing out to the store.
Eureen desperately wanted her daughters to be a part
of her vow renewal, but not under these tragic circumstances. They had a hard time looking at their father in
such a horrid condition.

She tried to hurry; but when Eureen got to the jewelry store, the vast array of choices that were presented
to her, along with the fact that money was no object,
caused her to take more than two hours to select a set
of rings, change into a white spring dress and shoes,
and then whip her car into a space in the hospital's
parking lot. Wind whirred in her ears as she rushed
down the hallway and rounded the corner near Monroe's room, running smack into Derrick Kelly.

"Oh!" she gasped as they collided, knocking the small
ring box out of her hand. "Excuse me. I'm so sorry."

"It's all right, Sista." Deacon Kelly rested his hand for
just a hair of a second at Eureen's waist; then he pulled
away to reach for the ring box. "Here you go."

"Thank you, Deacon."

"Call me Derrick," he insisted. "What you got there?"
His eyes drifted down her body as she focused on the
box in her hand.

"Oh, I . . . um . . . we . . ." Before she finished her sentence, she had what she thought was a stroke of genius.
"Derrick, are you ordained to officiate weddings?"

"Who's getting married?" he asked, to best determine what his answer should be.

I know she ain't about to remarry that crumpled-up old-ass bastard lying in that bed, he thought.

"Monroe and I want to renew our vows before he passes over."

"Oh, of course," he answered soothingly before he lied. "Yes, yes, I can do weddings."

"I know this is off-the-cuff, but would you mind doing our vow renewal real quick," Eureen asked, resting a hand on Derrick's shoulder.

"It would be my pleasure. I was just in there with Brother Monroe and he was grinning all over hisself about how much he loved you." He smiled, displaying himself as an angel of light, but his eyes were full of the devil, which Eureen didn't notice.

"Thank you so much for coming to see about him. It means so much."

"I had to come," Derrick responded.

"Pastor Gardner told you?" Eureen asked, thinking that maybe David did care a little bit.

"Naw." Derrick waved his hand. "You know you ain't seen me in church for a while now. I had to get out of there. Just something about the spirit in that place that just wasn't right."

That was all he needed to say, fully swaying Eureen's thinking back to the negative about her pastor.

"I mean, I ain't judgin' or nothing, but Pastor Gardner, just . . . he just . . . Well, I don't wanna say nothing bad about"—he held up two fingers on each hand to emphasize his next words in invisibe quotation marks—"'the man of God,' but . . . uh . . . I'ma just leave that alone, but I had to get up outta there so my spirit wouldn't suffer," he ended.

Truth be told, David had demanded Derrick leave when a rash of women complained of how he was screwing everyone in a skirt, and breaking hearts across the sanctuary.

"Hmph! I know that's right," she huffed, rolling her eyes. "I made a decision to leave there myself!"

That made Derrick grin even harder inside. It was no secret that Eureen, despite her years of former physical shabbiness, was married to a man with deep pockets. The timing was perfect: Monroe practically on his next-to-last breath, and Eureen moving out from the watchful, protective eyes of a spiritual father.

It will be a piece of cake to whip this dick on her and take that fat pussy and her fat wallet, he thought.

Quietly the two of them entered Monroe's room, where he lay seemingly lifeless. Only because the monitor let out a steady and even chirp did Eureen know that he was still among the living. After tiptoeing to his bedside, she gently touched his face.

"Monroe," she called softly.

His eyes fluttered open slowly.

"I ran into Deacon Kelly as I was coming in. He's actually going to do our vows for us." Eureen turned her head toward Derrick and smiled.

Monroe nodded slightly.

"I'm just gonna run to my car and get my little book," Derrick added, referring to a general church manual. He had lifted the book from Pastor's Gardner's office months ago in order to study and make himself seem far more spiritual and holy.

Ten minutes later, Eureen stood by Monroe's side, holding his hand and letting tears trickle down her face as she watched him struggle to breathe. Eureen softly and sincerely repeated the words Derrick read off, and Monroe did the same.

They both slid bands around each other's fingers, with Monroe's being very loose due to his tremendous weight loss. He'd only been able to get Eureen's ring onto the knuckle, midway the length of her finger. He was too weak to push it any farther. With her fingers wrapped around his, Eureen wriggled it the rest of the way.

"You may kiss the bride," Derrick announced, and cringed as Eureen covered Monroe's grayed and crusty lips with her own, then stroked his head.

"I love you, baby," she whispered.

"I love you too, 'Reen."

Thirty-six hours later, Monroe died.

Chapter Twenty

Tracey and Jermaine simply could not keep their hands or minds off one another since Tracey finally let Jermaine into her honey hole three months after he'd proposed. He'd been angry and frustrated when he'd given Tracey a proposal and a ring to match, and Tracey still kept her clothes on and her legs closed.

"Let's just snuggle," she'd said. "I wanna make sure that this is really real and not just sex based," she'd whined.

Jermaine was as angry as a disturbed nest of hornets but complied, since it was all he could do. But now, three months into the engagement, and assured that Jermaine would indeed be her husband, she felt that he deserved the pleasure of her body. Even so, she held back on engaging in wild, back-blowing sex, still wanting to have something to look forward to on their wedding night. She lay on her back and allowed Jermaine, covered in a condom that she insisted he use, to enter her body slowly and carefully, but then pound into her walls until he released. He seemed satisfied enough, but Tracey hadn't expected anything less.

"Mmm, that was so good, baby," he said, lapping at her neck and breasts.

"You like that, huh?" she teased.

"Liked it? How about loved it!" he answered, sliding down her belly to her secret triangle.

That next day, Tracey found herself hot and horny; she rushed home during her hour lunch break for him to fuck her. After work, she sped home for more. They were hooked on one another, and they loved every second of their intimacy.

They made love in front of the fireplace, on the sectional sofa, in the recliner, on the waterbed, and a few times even did it on the washing machine as it tousled a load of clothes. With each session, Tracey let a little more of herself go, giving Jermaine more and more.

"Shit, baby!" he squealed during a release. On his way down, he growled, "You gon' make a nigga take two weeks off from work! Shit!" And Jermaine did just that.

He used his time off to get the feel of what it was like to live under the same roof with Tracey, aiming to find out more about her habits and idiosyncrasies. He wanted to learn how she managed the household: if she kept the house tidy, like he thought a good wife should; if she would prepare him meals; if she would pick up after him. He was convinced that she loved him for him and not because of what she thought she'd get from him financially, like his ex-wife.

Yeah, I think she's the one, he thought one morning as she served him breakfast in bed. The only thing he didn't necessarily care for was she was too tied to her church. He saw evidence of that everywhere.

They were cuddled next to the fireplace about to watch a movie. Jermaine wanted to see *Law Abiding Citizen,* but Tracey insisted on *The Passion of the Christ.*

"This is a good movie right here," she commented, thumbing the remote control to fast-forward the DVD.

Jermaine threw his head back in a heavy sigh.

"What?" Tracey questioned.

"Do we have to watch this?" he commented, rubbing his eyes.

"What's wrong with it?"

"If the movie has all that church stuff and singin' in it, then I don't wanna watch it. I can't stand watchin' that kinda shit."

Tracey jerked her head back quickly. "Excuse me? Suppose I ask you to go to church with me?"

"Sweetheart," he somberly said. "I don't mind going sometimes, but I ain't tryin'a go every Sunday. I don't do churches."

Tracey was almost speechless. "Do you believe in God and in the Son of God, Jesus Christ?"

"Sometimes I do, but most times I don't. I hope that doesn't turn you off, but that's how I am, and I'll tell you why. So many times when I was down and out with no job or a place to lay my head, I prayed to God and asked Him to take care of my needs and wants, but not a damn thing happened. Then I prayed to Jesus, thinkin' He might answer, but He didn't come through either, so I stopped prayin'. Both of 'em left me hangin', babe. They left me fuckin' hangin'! I had to sleep in my car in dangerous areas—hungry, broke, and frustrated. So why should I believe in them now that I got a good job, a pocket filled with money, and a nice house? Tell me, why should I?"

Tracey pressed her lips tightly together in silence and disappointment; then she shook her head.

"I hope you don't look at me any different, because overall, I'm a good person, but I'm just not with the church thing, and I'm damn sho not good at fakin'," he explained.

"I'm sorry for your misfortunes, Jermaine, but the thing you've got to realize is that God doesn't move when we want Him to move. He blesses us when He

sees it as appropriate. Most important, we have to ex-
amine our hearts and mind-set and make certain we're
in step with the Word in order to receive blessings we
request. No offense, sweetheart, but some people pray
to God and their hearts are far from Him. Some people
are spiritually bankrupt, but always claimin' to be
blessed or need a blessing. When we pray, we have to
be sincere and not doubtful. Our faith cannot waver; it
has to be strong. As long as you're connected, you'll be
protected and your blessings will come in abundance."

Jermaine listened, though he really didn't want to
hear it, but at least the movie wasn't playing.

The following night, Jermaine was partially asleep
when Tracey arrived from work, but he woke up prompt-
ly. She had barely spoken two words to him since the discussion about church, but he was sure things had blown
over by now. He craved a good, long fuck and began to
massage his penis into a stiff erection, ready for his fiancée, but Tracey took her sweet time coming to bed.

First, she drew a hot bath and soaked for thirty minutes before she let some of the water out, only to replace it with more hot water. Sipping on a glass of wine,
she relaxed in the bubble bath. Fifteen minutes later,
she pulled herself from the tub, and took another thirty
minutes smoothing on lotion, clipping her toenails,
brushing her teeth, and wrapping her head in an old
greasy scarf. She shed her towel in front of Jermaine,
hanging it on the towel rack; then she sauntered naked
to the dresser and pulled out a pair of faded plaid pajama pants and a T-shirt.

What the hell, Jermaine thought, but he said nothing.

Instead of Tracey climbing into bed with Jermaine,
she went to one of the guest bedrooms, closed the door
behind herself, drew back the covers on the bed, and
sandwiched herself between the flat and fitted sheets.

"I knew I shouldn'ta given it up, Lord," she whispered. "Sex is for marriage, not for engagements." She lay in meditation for several minutes, whispering a few words of prayer every now and then, and wondering what she should do with her relationship with a man who couldn't care less about God.

"I know I ain't perfect, Lord, but I do try to honor and acknowlegdge you. I don't know if I can be married to a man who don't think nothing of you."

"Tracey, what's wrong with you?" Jermaine asked, whisking the bedroom door open and startling her. As he walked over to the bed, Tracey couldn't help but to admire his handsome face and full erection, so she turned her back to him.

"Nothing," she mumbled.

"Well, why are you sleeping in here?"

"'Cause we're not married," she answered sharply as she pulled the covers up to her neck, as if she didn't want Jermaine to see any of her body.

"Damn, Tracey!" He frowned. "I let you live in my damn house, put a ring on your finger, and asked you to marry me, but you wanna hold on to your body while we wait on a sheet of paper?"

"Yep," she shot back.

A sigh escaped Jermaine's lips. "Baby, you can't be serious."

"Why can't I? You were serious about not wanting nothing to do with God," Tracey replied without turning over.

Jermaine stood in silence for a few seconds; then he commented, "To hell with it then!" He didn't feel like going back and forth with her. He left the room, slamming the door behind him.

Tracey lay motionless. She was silent, with the exception of an occasional sniff, for she'd begun crying.

"I should have known better, Lord," she whispered out loud, feeling like she was facing consequences for not keeping her commitment to abstain from intercourse. "Sex is for marriage, not for engagements and dating. I should have lived by your Word. That's what I get," Tracey said, chastising herself. "Please forgive me, Lord. Wash me clean from my sins and show me what to do with this relationship."

Although she could barely see it, she twisted her engagement ring around her finger as she prayed. "Show me a sign if I should continue or not, Lord. I don't care what kind of sign it is, just something that I can figure out if you want me to stay with Jermaine or not."

The words had barely escaped her lips before Jermaine, much more calm now, returned just a few minutes later. Quickly, Tracey smudged her tears into her cheeks with the heels of her hand.

"Tracey, I'm sorry, babe," Jermaine said as he climbed into the bed beside her. He was shirtless, but his erection was confined by a pair of boxers. "I didn't mean to offend you." He wrapped his arm around her and pulled her close. Feeling her resist a bit, he let her know his intentions. "Just let me hold you, baby. We ain't gotta do nothing."

At that, Tracey slowly relaxed into his arms, thinking that this just might be the sign she had just prayed for. Jermaine kissed her forehead, tightened his hug slightly, and held on to her until they both drifted off to sleep.

The next morning, with a stretch and a yawn, Tracey's eyes fluttered open, prompted by the smell of bacon and coffee. A glance to her left revealed that Jermaine had awakened and had slid out of bed undetected. She smiled at the thought of him making breakfast, but still she couldn't shake the fact that he felt like he didn't need the Lord. With her eyes randomly roaming the ceiling, she weighed in her head the pros and cons of continuining her relationship with Jermaine.

He's such a good man, she quietly listed. *He has a great job, pays the bills on time, doesn't mind spoiling me. He ain't got no baby mommas. He got a house to put me in and told me I don't have to work if I don't want to.*

The sparkle of the diamond on Tracey's hand twinkled in the rays of sun that peered through the bedroom curtains. She studied the stone set in white gold for a full minute before twisting it off her hand. Now looking at her finger without the ring, it looked strangely naked.

Hearing Jermaine climb the stairs, she quickly pushed the ring back onto her hand and snuggled down into the pillows, pretending to still be in repose.

Carrying a breakfast-in-bed tray, Jermaine crept toward her, with a smile on his face. "Wake up, sleepyhead," he sang, now standing by the bedside and gently peeling back the covers. "Sleeping Beauty," he cooed to her.

Tracey, again, stretched and yawned, trying to make her act of just waking up appear realistic.

"Good morning," Jermaine greeted.

"Good morning," she replied with a hint of a smile.

"I fixed you breakfast," he said, stating the obvious.

Her smile widened as she looked at the tray holding a plate featuring a vegetable-and-cheese omelet, bacon fried extra crisp, a saucer with four slices of buttered wheat toast, each slice cut in half, a bowl of fresh fruit, some orange juice in a glass carafe etched with flowers, and two mugs of steaming coffee. "Wow. This is what I have to look forward to, huh?"

"This and more," Jermaine commented as he eased the tray over her lap. Then he slid back into bed on the other side. He picked up a fork, used its side to cut into the omelet, stabbed into it, then lifted it to Tracey's mouth.

"Hold on for a second," she asked before bowing her head. "Father God, I thank you for your wonderful mercy and grace, which is made new every morning. Thank you for waking me up in my right mind and with the activity of my limbs. I have to tell you, thank you, Lord, for this beautiful breakfast, which has been prepared for me, and for *always* taking care of and providing for me, even when I didn't recognize that it was you. I could have been hungry this morning, Lord, and unaware of where my next meal would be coming from, but you saw fit to give me daily bread, and I just want to say thank you. I ask that you bless even more the hands that thought enough of me not just to fix me something to eat, but to bring it and serve it to me like a queen. I thank you for all these things. In Jesus' name I pray, amen," she ended.

Just as she finished, she felt she had the sign she needed to go on when Jermaine cracked his lips and whispered, "Amen."

Chapter Twenty-one

Eureen laid a single flower on Monroe's casket; then she stepped back into an emotional circle of sadness, wrapping her arms around as many of her daughters as she could.

Derrick stood at the private graveside in a black suit and minister's collar. He had a somber expression as he led the committal service.

"Merciful Father and Lord of Life, with whom live the spirits of those who depart in the faith, we thank you for the blessings of body and soul that you granted this beloved, departed brother, whose earthly remains we now lay to rest. Even though we are saddened today, we rejoice at your gracious promise to all your servants, living and departed, that we shall rise again at the coming of our Lord, Jesus Christ, who lives and reigns with you and the Holy Spirit, one God, now and forever."

Like an expert preacher, Derrick manipulated his voice, changing octaves and inflection, emphasizing some words more than others, and sometimes bellowing in feigned power.

"For your Word says that we shall not all sleep, but we will be changed in a moment, in the twinkling of an eye, and the mortal shall be clothed with immortality. Then the saying that is written will come true: 'O Death, where is your victory? O Grave, where is your sting?' We now commit the body of our dear brother,

Monroe Francis, to the ground. Earth to earth, ashes to ashes, dust to dust, in the sure and certain hope of the resurrection to eternal life, through Jesus Christ. Comfort his bride and his children in this terrible yet joyous occasion, and we thank you for these things now, in Jesus' name, amen."

Respectfully, he approached Eureen and her girls and hugged each of them. "God bless and keep you, Sister Francis."

"Thank you so much," Eureen replied, sincerely grateful for Derrick's services. "I have something for you," she added, reaching into a small black clutch for a check.

"Oh no, no, no," Derrick refused, gently pushing her hand away, although his eyes were filled with undetected greed. "There is no way I could charge you for this."

"No, I insist. Please take it. Monroe wouldn't have wanted it any other way. He always believed in paying for quality, and I couldn't have asked for a better minister to lead his home going."

Derrick couldn't wrap his fingers around the check quickly enough, but he managed to pause before he did, studying Eureen's face, pretending to struggle with taking the money.

"You're a good woman, Eureen," he whispered, only because he couldn't think of anything else to say besides "Thank you."

"No, thank you. I really appreciate you being there for me and my girls."

"How are you holding up, Sister?" Jasmine asked, resting a hand on Eureen's shoulder from behind.

Jasmine eyed Derrick suspiciously, having heard about his flagrant womanizing throughout Abundant Grace Fellowship. It was only because Derrick knew that Jasmine was married—and he was intimidated by

Shamar's stance and demeanor—that he'd never tried to insert his dick inside Jasmine's panties.

"I'm doing as well as I can," Eureen said, nodding a bit.

"You know we're here for you." Jasmine hugged her friend as both Tracey and Deja approached.

Trying to lighten the mood somewhat, Tracey lifted Eureen's hand and gawked at the five-carat ring, which glistened as if it were the sun itself.

"Mmm! Now *that's* what you call a ring!"

Eureen smiled, although the jewelry did nothing for the pain she felt. "It doesn't replace him, though."

"It's beautiful," Deja commented to be polite, but inside she was beginning to fume with envy.

Why am I the only one without a damn ring? Eureen got a ring out of a dead man, and I ain't got shit, she thought in her frustration. She looked over her shoulder at Garnell, who stood chatting with Derrick.

More so than the ring, Deja couldn't understand why she and Garnell were not yet married. He'd been working the job she'd found for him for almost a month, and Deja saw no signs of them moving forward.

When she shared her thoughts with the girls, they only made excuses for Garnell.

"He probably is saving up to get you something nice," Jasmine had stated optimistically.

Tracey nodded her head in agreement.

"Forget nice! God ain't gonna honor nice. He's gonna honor marriage!" Deja countered.

"Well, I'm just saying . . ." Jasmine had shrugged. "You don't want no ghetto proposal with no ring. Both of y'all too old for that mess."

Seeing how she would get nowhere with her friends, Deja just dropped the subject.

Today, though, her thoughts floated back to the night when she'd broached the subject with Garnell directly.

She led with fried catfish, hush puppies, cole slaw, sweet tea, and peach cobbler for dessert. With a huge smile on his face, Garnell gobbled down his meal, complimenting her after every few bites. With a full belly, he lay back on the bed while Deja straddled him and rode him like he was a rodeo bull.

"Man, I'ma have to work an hour of overtime more often," he said with a satisfied release of air from his lungs. "I told the Lord I was gonna stop cussin', but damn, girl!"

Deja slid off his body, then lay against his chest.

"Whew!" he commented further.

While he still was on a high, Deja deployed her strategy. "Garnell, can I ask you something?"

"You can ask anything you want, girl." He chuckled.

"When do you think we'll get married?" She rushed her question, and then held her breath.

Garnell sighed before answering. That bothered Deja, but she stayed silent, awaiting his response.

"I'm still tryin'a get myself together, baby. I ain't been working that long and I wanna get you something nice to put on your finger."

"I don't care about a ring, babe," she answered sincerely. "All I care about is being your wife and spending the rest of my life with you. I don't care if all you put on my finger is a bread bag tie," she replied.

"What? A bread bag tie? Deja . . ." He paused for a minute. "What kinda man is that gonna make me look like, asking you to be my wife and ain't got no ring to give you? I'm sho not putting no twist tie on your hand for no ring, baby. That's just straight-up trifling. Don't no real man ask a woman to marry him and give her a piece of junk to put on her finger."

"I'm saying, though, the ring is not as important as the marriage, and we should focus on what's important, not something that we can change or buy at any time," Deja explained from her heart.

"Naw, baby. I can't do it that way. If I'ma do it, I'ma do it right."

And right meant getting rid of the wife he already had first, which he had no intention on doing to avoid paying alimony and child support.

Shortly after, Garnell drifted off to sleep, leaving Deja disappointed and fully awake, staring at nothing but darkness.

Now as she made her way back to the car, where Garnell waited for her, Deja tried to hide her negative emotions, but she had a hard time doing so. Tears of anger and frustration rolled down her cheeks as she plopped down in the passenger seat.

"You all right, baby?" Garnell asked, reaching for her hand.

"Not really," she answered honestly.

Garnell assumed the tears were fueled by the sadness of the funeral.

"It'll be all right." He paused momentarily, watching Eureen, her daughters, and other funeral attendees get back into their vehicles. "Where's she having the repast at?"

"Their house," Deja mumbled. "Just follow the limo."

"You sure you feel like going? We can go 'head home, if you want, baby."

"No, I need to be there for my friend." Deja couldn't bear to lift her eyes and look at Garnell at the moment. "If you don't want to stay, you can drop me off if you want and I'll just get Tracey or somebody to bring me home." It was her cover to get out of Garnell's presence at least temporarily.

"No, baby, I'm here for you," he insisted.

Deja sighed and let silence take over for the remainder of the ride.

Eureen had chosen a top-dollar caterer to feed her guests in celebration of Monroe's home-going celebration. While most were used to having fried or baked chicken, potato salad, and green beans after saying good-bye to a loved one, Eureen's guests were served a choice of healthy portions of tender, moist Rock Cornish game hen, roasted to perfection, and covered with a special orange glaze, coupled with Minnesota long-grain wild rice, or whole-roasted beef tenderloin covered with Italian mushroom sauce and served with buttered baby red potatoes, an apple-sage dressing, green vegetables, and French bread rolls. For dessert, there were individual servings of raspberry rosettes, lemon almond macaroon, and fruit and cream scones. Instead of foam and paper plates and plastic forks, the clinking of real silverware against china could be heard throughout the rooms where the guests were gathered.

"You sure didn't hold back any expense," Derrick commented to Eureen as he filled his mouth with meat and potatoes.

"I'd pay twice this if it would bring my husband back," she said, looking down at her plate. "I guess this is like the wedding reception that we never got to have," she said somberly.

"I know this is a crucial time for you, Eureen, and I have been praying for you ever since I found out Monroe had been taken ill."

"Thank you. I sho need a lot of that."

Derrick cleared his throat and focused on Eureen's eyes. "While I was praying the other day that the Lord would give you strength in your heart, He spoke to me and I'm here to let you know I've received a message from the Lord to encourage you and to sway you closer to Him, especially since you don't have a church home anymore."

He paused a minute to allow his words to sink in.

"With that bein' said, I'd like you to come visit my church with me. You don't want to fall out of fellowship with the Lord."

"You're right about that. I'd be glad to come."

Chapter Twenty-two

Winter and Summer darted across the front yard as soon as they saw Shamar pull into the driveway.

"Daddy!" they shrieked in unison.

Shamar had been on the road for three weeks and was happy to be able to sleep in his own bed for the next four nights.

"Daddy, did you bring us something?" Winter asked, peering in the back window. Just as she suspected, there was a large plain cardboard box centered in the seat.

"You know I'ma bring my girls something," he answered, grabbing a girl in each arm and lifting them off the ground. "Where your momma at?"

"She in the house cookin'," the youngest answered. "Can we get that box out of the car?"

"Not right now. Let me go in the house first."

"Please! Please, Daddy!" they both begged. "We wanna see what you brought us!"

"That's the only reason why y'all happy to see me, huh? So you can get new stuff?"

"No. We love you too, Daddy," Winter answered, trying to refute him. "But I hope you brought us some new jeans and an iPod Touch."

"And I hope you did all your homework and chores since I've been gone," Shamar challenged, walking toward the house. He thought that would be enough to silence the girls, as sometimes they had trouble keeping up with both their schoolwork and housework.

Instead, they sang out together, "We did!"

"Mmm-hmm. We'll see. Go play for a little bit. I will show y'all what I brought you in a little while."

Although disappointed, Shamar's daughters ran ahead of him into the house, announcing his arrival; then they disappeared to their bedroom.

"Hey, baby," Shamar whispered, gathering Jasmine in his arms. Then he delivered a long, wet kiss. His hands trailed down her waist and to her butt, where he gave her a firm squeeze.

"Hey, Shamar," she mumbled on the top of his lips.

"I got something for you," he spoke, pressing his hip forward.

"Mmm," she moaned in response. "Where is it?"

Shamar took her hand and positioned it on his manhood. "Right there. You feel that?"

"All I feel is a piece of iron pipe," Jasmine teased. "Is that what you brought for me? Some iron?"

"Mmm-hmm," Shamar answered, backing his wife up the stairs and to their bedroom. "You want it?"

"I want everything you got for me," Jasmine whispered back. "I got something for you too, though." Jasmine led her husband to their large walk-in closet and closed the door. Once inside, she blindfolded him.

"What in the world?" he asked, going along with whatever she had in store for him.

"Welcome to Jasmine's Gentlemen's Club," she replied.

With the press of a remote, 50 Cent's "Candy Shop" suddenly boomed in the enclosed space, transporting Shamar's mind to a strip club.

"Okay!" He grinned in anticipation, feeling his wife's now-naked body grinding against his body. "Damn, girl, what's your name?"

"Candy Cane," she answered, inspired by the music. "You bring some money, big daddy."

"I think I got a little something," Shamar said, beginning to pant as he blindly grabbed for his wallet.

"You wanna lap dance?"

"Hell yeah!" Shamar answered. He let Jasmine strip him of his clothes while he worked the billfold out of his back pocket, just before his pants fell around his ankles. Jasmine worked her body against his and dropped to her knees, taking her husband in her mouth.

"Oh shit!" Shamar moaned. "Do it, Candy Cane," he mumbled. He slowly gyrated his hips, easing in and out of Jasmine's lips. "Yeah, girl, suck that dick."

Jasmine licked and sucked until Shamar was no longer able to stand and lowered himself to the carpeted floor, which Jasmine had already covered with a sheet. Shamar now lay on his back, fully engaged in a fantasy. His hands roamed his wife's body as she planted kisses all over his body.

Lil' Kim's "How Many Licks?" came on, and Jasmine straddled Shamar's face, letting him eat her sweet spot. He gobbled her up like he hadn't eaten a good meal in months. Jasmine was squirming and moaning like a wild woman. It was only minutes before she spilled her juices all over his face, which he greedily lapped up. Still blindfolded, he flipped Jasmine to her back and quickly slid his dick inside her body and thrust rapidly.

"Fuck me, big daddy," she cried, feeding his ego. "Lay that pipe!"

"Yeah!" he commented, encouraging himself. "Take it all. Take all that dick."

"Give it to me, baby. Hit the top!" she begged.

"Oh shit, baby, this some good pussy!" Shamar squealed as he exploded. "Shit!" He collapsed on top of Jasmine with a wide grin on his face. "Whew! I'ma have to come back here more often!"

"Yeah, you do that," Jasmine replied, removing the blindfold from her husband's eyes and opening up the closet door, letting in a bit of light. "That will be a hundred dollars," she joked; but to her surprise, Shamar fingered two $100 bills from his wallet and handed them to his wife.

"You take that and save me a spot in the VIP section next time I come through."

"Fa sho!" Jasmine's eyes widened at the cash, and she wondered for a moment where Shamar had gotten the money. She didn't want to break the mood, though. She made a note to ask him about it later, but for now she turned on the shower and they both stepped inside.

"Ahh!" Shamar released standing under the flow of hot water. "It sure is good to be home and stand in my own bathtub."

"It's good having you home, baby," Jasmine answered, lathering her husband's body with her loofah.

"Mmm, that feels good."

"I'm glad you like it." She continued soaping and caressing Shamar's body as he expressed his enjoyment with a series of relaxing moans.

"Where you get that club shit from, baby? That was hot!" he asked, grinning, trying to hide his suspicions that she'd been hanging out at strip clubs since he'd been gone.

"I gotta make sure I give you something to come home to. Ain't no ho in the streets gonna outdo what I can do for my man," Jasmine answered. "You been gone for three weeks, and I gotta make sure you gonna come back to me, not fall in love with some hoochie out there on the road."

He wasn't sure what to make of her answer, and responded, "You ain't got to worry about that, baby." Shamar pooled a small handful of shampoo in his palm and then rubbed it into his hair. "It's too many diseases and too many bitches lookin' for a baby daddy out there for me to even play them kind of games."

"For real?"

"Yeah, babe. They all over the place," he told her. "But it ain't nobody like my baby. You got that good-good, and keep a nigga comin' in bed, and comin' back for more."

Jasmine giggled as Shamar swatted her behind.

"Wit' your sexy self," he gushed.

Jasmine stepped out of the shower two minutes before Shamar, and took the extra time to peek into his wallet, spotting what she estimated to be at least $2,000. She crinkled her brows, curious about where the extra cash had come from, since Shamar had direct deposit and his full check went to the bank each payday. Hearing the change in the water, she quickly pushed his wallet back under his clothes. They toweled each other off and pulled on some comfort clothes.

"Let me go see what my babies are up to," Shamar commented, heading toward the bedroom door. "Oh yeah, baby, guess who pregnant?"

"Who?" Jasmine sat on the bed, pulling on a pair of socks, without giving the question the effort of thought.

"Your girl Tracey," Shamar informed. "Don't say nothin', though. Let her tell you."

"What!" Jasmine gasped. "How you know, Shamar?"

"Jermaine told me."

"That ol' stank heifer! Tryin'a act like she won't be giving up the goods."

"Well, she gave up something; 'cause when I talked to the dude, he said, 'Man, I done knocked this bitch up.'"

"He called her a *bitch?* How he gonna ask her to marry him and call her a bitch! That's wrong!"

"I don't know, baby; that's just how guys talk. It don't mean nothing."

"You bed'not be out there calling me no bitch," Jasmine warned.

"You know me better than that, baby." Shamar stepped to his wife and kissed her lips. "But you'd be my bitch, though, and the way you was suckin' my dick in that closet . . . shiiiit!" He chuckled.

"Move!" Jasmine playfully shoved her husband out of the way. "I'll be your closet bitch, but you better not be calling me that to none of your friends."

"Shake, sh—sh—shake that ass, girl." He laughed and followed her out of the bedroom. "Summer and Winter, come on and get what Daddy brought for y'all," he called out to his daughters.

"Yay!" they both shrieked, and came tearing down the hallway.

Shamar went out to the car and pulled the box from its backseat; then he brought it inside. Just as the girls had hoped, he had iPads for both of them and several pieces of designer label clothing. Everything from House of Deréon jeans to Baby Phat shoes were pulled out of the box, and the girls grinned like it was Christmas Day. They ran to their rooms to try on and put away their new clothes.

"These for you, baby," Shamar said, pulling out a pair of Dolce & Gabbana black leather boots. Jasmine screamed out loud, having wanted the boots for months. Next he handed her a platinum pair of Versace sunglasses and two Vera Wang business suits.

"Them stores be throwing so much stuff away; it don't make no sense," he lied when Jasmine asked how he was able to purchase so many designer things. "They don't be tellin' people, but once it goes out of season, they give it away in big bags 'cause they can't do nothing with it."

"That's just a waste," Jasmine commented, shaking her head as she pranced around the living room in her new shoes. Then she strutted to the kitchen to answer the ringing phone.

"Hey, Jasmine," Tracey greeted.

"Girl!" Jasmine enthused, but then she remembered that she wasn't supposed to know about Tracey's pregnancy.

"What?"

"Um . . . Shamar just brought me some *bad* boots!" she said, covering her near slipup.

"Oh, he's home? Well, I know what y'all are up to," she replied, snickering. "Let me let you off this phone. I didn't want nothing, anyway."

"You know we done took care of that already, but I'ma call you later." Jasmine placed the phone back on the hook; then she looked at Shamar. "That was Tracey," she said with a smirk.

"You didn't say nothing, did you?"

"No, baby, I didn't. I will wait for her to spill the beans."

"Don't say nothing, Jasmine," Shamar warned.

"I won't," she assured him, sucking her teeth; but secretly, she couldn't wait to ask Tracey about the baby. "But look," she said, shifting to another subject, "where you get all that extra money from?"

"What extra money?" he asked.

"The two hundred dollars you gave me upstairs." Jasmine wasn't going to admit that she'd been in his wallet.

"I got a bonus for finishing up a run a day early," he lied off-the-cuff. "That's why I'm home already."

Jasmine didn't exactly believe Shamar, but she couldn't think of a good reason not to believe him. So she simply answered, "Oh."

"I'm 'bout to go to my momma's house for a minute," he said, standing to his feet. "She want me to look at some tile for her kitchen floor."

"You gotta go right now? You just got home."

"I'd rather go today and free up the weekend to spend with you and the girls than to be over there all day tomorrow." Jasmine sighed and rolled her eyes. "I won't be long, baby. I promise."

"Go 'head, Shamar, 'cause you gonna do that, anyway. I'ma go in here and start cooking."

No sooner had Shamar pulled out of the driveway than Jasmine called Deja.

"Girl, guess whose fast behind, virgin tail, is pregnant?"

"Who? Tracey?"

"Yep! Talking 'bout she ain't givin' up no booty. Don't say nothing, though, 'cause I'm not supposed to know," Jasmine advised.

"How do you know then?"

"I can't tell you all that, but trust me . . . it was from a reliable source," Jasmine replied.

"Momma, you been keeping an eye on the house for me," Shamar asked Cyreese as soon as he entered her house.

"I been tryin' to, but her ass so fast, I can't hardly keep up with her," she answered, turning up her nose. "Running up and down the street every damn chance she gets."

Shamar shook his head.

"I had a feeling," he commented, thinking about the role-playing scenario Jasmine had greeted him with. Never in their marriage had she acted so promiscuously nasty. "I think she fuckin' somebody too, Ma," he said, rubbin' his hand over his head. "You ever seen her with another nigga in my house?"

"Naw. Not yet, anyway, but I wouldn't put it past her. I done drove by there plenty uh times and her car wasn't in the yard."

"Did you look in the garage?"

"Naw. She ain't been parking in the damn garage, so what she gonna start for?"

"I'm just asking." He paused in thought as he pulled his wallet from his pocket.

"I went around there one night, and it was a Mustang-looking car sittin' in front of the house," she fabricated, wanting Shamar to leave Jasmine. "I rang the doorbell a coupla times, but she ain't answer. I don't know who da hell she had up in there."

"I'ma say this, if she givin' another nigga my pussy, that's gonna be her ass!"

He handed ten $100 bills to Cyreese and thanked her for keeping an eye on his wife.

"I need to get in your garage and put some stuff in there," he uttered.

"When you gonna get that other stuff out?"

"I done took care of that already. Where you think that grand came from I just gave you?"

Shamar took the keys from his mother's hands and walked outside to open the garage door. He stashed away some large items, which he planned to sell later that week.

Chapter Twenty-three

It took nearly two weeks, but with Derrick's help, Eureen had moved back into her original home. She traded her marriage furniture for the newer furniture that had been in her temporary home, unable to deal with the thought that Monroe had probably had a multitude of lovers propped up on everything they'd owned. She was sure every surface was contaminated with other people's bodily fluids, so she had the house professionally cleaned and sold or donated anything that could be physically moved.

Having loaded the last of a large box of old linen and clothing onto the back of a Goodwill truck, and sending the driver on his way, Derrick wiped pretend dust from his hands.

"I think that does it," he commented, but it went unheard.

Eureen was preoccupied at her mailbox, reading a letter.

"Oh, thank God!" she gasped, patting her chest. "Thank you, Jesus!" Tears escaped her eyes, although she hadn't meant to release any.

"What is it, sweetheart?" Derrick slipped in the endearment, hoping Eureen wouldn't correct him. He felt he was making progress when she didn't say anything about his word choice.

"It's my test results. They all came back negative—HIV, chlamydia, syphilis, all of 'em," she said gratefully. "God is so good!"

She paused, thinking about the last time she'd had sex with Monroe, trying to get him to love her.

"God is so good," she repeated, still praying that HIV wouldn't show up later, knowing that it could be in incubation for several years before being detected.

"Yes, He is," Derrick agreed aloud.

Good! he thought. *'Cause I ain't tryin'a catch shit from the bitch, and I'm sho gon' pump her full uh this dick. When she get somma this, she gon' be hooked, like a muthafuckin' fish.* He chuckled inwardly.

"That's why I don't mind praisin' Him." Right there on the spot, Derrick began clapping his hands. "Thank ya!" he yelled up at the sky.

Eureen couldn't help but smile as she clapped her hands along with him. She loved the fact that Derrick acknowledged God frequently and loved going to church, which was the exact opposite of Monroe.

You sure work in mysterious ways, Lord, she thought. *You took away Monroe, who didn't even really love me anymore, but you always got a ram in the bush. Derrick is smart, handsome, and has a heart for you, Lord.*

"Thank you!" she yelled after Derrick, grateful for her test results but even more grateful that Derrick was a part of her life.

As they stood in the yard, grinning and yelling words of praise into the air, Jasmine pulled up in front of the house.

"What the hell is his conniving ass doing here?" She stepped out of her truck and walked toward the two of them.

"Hey, Eureen," she called; then she mumbled an insincere greeting to Derrick.

"How you doing, Sister?" Derrick answered back. "Eureen, I'll call and check on you later."

The last thing Derrick wanted to do was hang around Jasmine's fat ass and big titties, which he couldn't have, and get his dick hard for nothing. As he backed out of the yard, he squeezed his dick as he watched Jasmine bend over to pick up the keys she'd accidentally dropped in the yard.

"Good Gadda-Mighty," he mumbled. "I bet that shit is tight too. Let that jacklegged Shamar fuck up one time and I'ma tear that piece of pussy up!" He tapped his horn twice as a good-bye and drove off.

"What is he doing over here?" Jasmine asked, walking Eureen to the front door. "Your behind gonna end up like Tracey, with a baby in your belly." She spilled the news with a grin.

"What do you mean, 'what is he doing over here'?" Eureen asked, taking immediate offense. "He's helped a lot ever since Monroe got sick."

Jasmine rolled her eyes. "I'm just saying, you know that man ain't a lick of good, and he only—"

"Look, Jasmine," Eureen cut her off. "I don't wanna hear it."

Eureen had been poorly treated by her late husband, and had lived many years desperate for love, attention, and affection, that she just wasn't ready to entertain the notion that Derrick Kelly wasn't sincere.

"You don't wanna hear what? I'm just saying—"

"I said, I don't want to hear it," she interrupted again, becoming angry. "I remember how you bitches used to sit back and laugh and talk about me!" she spat out. "Do you honestly think I didn't notice that neither you, Tracey, nor Deja dared to show your faces after Monroe put me out? Y'all was probably laughing at me behind my back then too," she accused. "And how many times did you come see him when he was in the hospital? Even for my sake? Now that I have someone over here tryin'a be a true man and show me some compassion, you wanna have something to say?" she asked incredulously. "Well, guess what? I don't wanna hear shit you gotta say, so climb your uppity ass back in your truck and get the hell off my property."

Eureen walked through her front door and slammed it in Jasmine's face, leaving her stunned and speechless.

Once inside, Eureen blew out a puff of steam through her pouted lips. "Who the hell she think she is! Excuse me, Lord. Forgive me for cussin'. And thank you for letting me see that those women are not even good for me."

For the next two hours, Eureen busied herself looking over several legal documents of property and assets, which she didn't understand for the most part. She worked her way through a folder of reports outlining several rental properties, indications of whether they were occupied or vacant, and the rental amount on each, and the current mortgage. From what she could tell, she was clearly in the black on the properties, with only a few needing tenants. Although bored, she reviewed the names of all the tenants, not really paying any attention to them as they scrolled past her eyes. That was, until she got to one family in particular: Shamar and Jasmine Murphy.

"What? She been renting from me all this time?" Eureen snickered. "I thought they were home owners. Hmph! Straight perpetratin'!" She verified by looking at the address, to be sure it was indeed the Shamar and Jasmine she knew. She laughed out loud to herself when the address matched where she knew Jasmine lived.

"Oh, I'ma fix her little red wagon," she blurted out, fueled by her anger with Jasmine for trying to call Derrick no good, mixed with how she felt the ladies hadn't

supported her as much as they could have during Monroe's sickness and death. She studied the papers more
intently until her daughters began, two at a time, to
stagger in from their friends' houses.

"Ma, we still going out today?" Mezzi asked.

Eureen tried hard to spend more time with her girls
now that they were robbed of their father, thankful
that his assets and insurance were substaantial enough
to allow her to quit her job. She had promised to take
them to the mall to shop that day.

"Yeah, as soon as your sisters get home," she assured
her, putting away the file she'd been looking at, and
now ready to implement a hefty rent increase at the
property where Jasmine and Shamar resided.

She picked up her cell phone and called Monroe's
property manager.

"Hello, Edgar, it's Eureen Francis," she stated. "Listen, can you pull a rent history report for the property
at 2711 Carell Avenue?"

"Sure," he agreed. "Was there a problem with that
particular location?"

"No, no. I'm just curious about those tenants."

"Oh, okay, just give me a few minutes." Eureen could
hear Edgar's fingers tapping on his keyboard. "I think
they are pretty good tenants. I've not really had any
problems with them, but let me look at their records."
A few seconds of silence passed before Edgar spoke
again. "There have been several late pays over the
years, but they've always paid . . . eventually. They've
been there for, let's see, four years now."

"I think I need to increase the rent there," she announced. "What are the guidelines around that? Have
they had a rent increase lately?"

"No, I'm not showing anything since they've been at
the property."

"Good. I need to look at doing an inflation increase," Eureen replied. She discussed a new rent figure with Edgar and ended the call.

Since Monroe's name wasn't reflected in his business name, Eureen was confident that the Murphys would never know she was now their landlord. "There's a new sheriff in town. Let's see who's laughing now."

While at the mall, Eureen ran into Jermaine and Tracey. They sat with smiles on their faces at Hallmark, thumbing through a large wedding invitation book.

"Hey, lovebirds," she called.

"Oh, hey, girl," Tracey responded back with a wave while Jermaine uttered a cordial but simple greeting. "How are you holding up?"

"We're making it," Eureen responded. "It gets rough sometimes, but God is faithful."

"That's good. Well, I'm sho praying for you and the girls." Tracey was lying, because it seemed like the right thing to say to Eureen.

"Thanks. We need that more than anything." There was a two-second pause before Eureen spoke again. "So I hear that a second congratulations is in order." She beamed at her friend.

"Oh, because we set a date?"

"No," Eureen sang out. "I'm talking about the baby!"

Jermaine's heart stopped, but he said nothing. He was still thumbing through the book in front of them.

"The baby? What are you talking about?" Tracey asked with a confused giggle. "You know something I don't even know?"

"You got something you need to tell me, baby," Jermaine asked, rubbing a hand across Tracey's belly, which she quickly swatted away.

"I heard you were pregnant." Eureen wasn't sure if she'd stuck her foot in her mouth or not, due to Tracey's completely confused expression.

"That ain't what these cramps I'm feeling is saying. Where did you get that from?"

"Jasmine told me. Please don't tell me she was making it up."

That fucking bastard! Jermaine cussed in his head. *How the fuck he gonna tell his wife! I told that nigga not to say nothin'. I'ma fuck his ass up when I see him again. I'ma punch him right in his throat! Punk-ass gossiping like a muthafuckin' woman! Shit!*

"I don't know why she thought that. I mean, I know I done gained a few pounds since my baby be spoiling me with steak and lobster and whatnot." She laughed, rubbing Jermaine's shoulder. "But ain't no babies over here! First come love; then come marriage; *then* come the baby in the baby carriage. We still working on the marriage part."

"I heard that!" Eureen snickered with her. "Okay, girl, don't let me hold up your wedding plans. Y'all take care," she finished, and walked off. "Lying heifer!" Eureen mumbled under her breath.

"How in the world is she telling people that I'm pregnant?" Tracey balked with crinkled brows.

"I have no idea, babe. Those are your friends."

"I mean, how she just gonna make that lie up like that? Especially when she could have asked me before she started gossiping."

"Don't worry about it, baby. Maybe Eureen heard her wrong or something," Jermaine answered, trying to change the subject.

"I'm 'bout to call her," Tracey adamantly stated, digging in her purse for her cell phone.

"Naw, baby, don't do that," Jermaine said, grabbing her hand. "I'm tryin'a have a good night and you 'bout to let her wreck our whole evening," Jermaine pointed out, not wanting the women to talk. "You know I ain't

gonna be here much longer, and I don't feel like wasting our time on that stupid mess Jasmine talking about.
Then she gonna have you with your lips all poked out
and upset. I don't feel like that mess tonight. Let's have
a good night."

Tracey sighed. "You're right, baby. I'm not gonna let
her ruin our date night, but I'ma have some words for
her as soon as you get back on the road."

Yeah, and I'ma have some words for Shamar's ass,
Jermaine kept to himself. *How the hell am I gonna get
out of this?* He thought for a minute to pray about it,
but he didn't feel that God would help him.

Looking up at the ceiling for a split second, he continued his negative thoughts. *You ain't been helpin',
so it ain't no need in me even asking you. Every time
I ask you to do anything for me, you act just like you
don't hear me. I'm not even gonna waste my time.*

Chapter Twenty-four

"You sure you're gonna be okay while I'm gone?" Garnell asked, sitting on the edge of the bed and pressing the back of his hand against Deja's forehead.

"Yeah," her voice came muffled through the comforter. "I'm just gonna stay here and sleep." Deja snorted loudly, then sneezed. She yanked the covers over her head for a few seconds to contain her germs.

"Aww, look, my baby is sick," Garnell teased, again feeling her face for signs of a fever. "You still feel a bit warm; here."

Reaching over to the nightstand, he picked up a bottle of cold syrup, measured out a dosage in a small cup, and lifted it to Deja's lips. She gulped the medicine down with a grimace, then chased it down with a swallow of water from a glass Garnell offered her.

He playfully tucked the covers up and around her neck. "I'll be back right after church, okay?"

"I ain't going nowhere," Deja answered, sealing her eyes shut. "Pray for me while you're there."

"I will, baby." Garnell kissed her forehead; then he rose from the bed and brushed invisible lint and wrinkles from his pants. He was dressed in a tan Sean John suit, with a blue banker-striped square-cuffed shirt and coordinating tie. His feet were neatly tied in a pair of Prada calf-leather derby-style shoes, which Deja had used almost a full paycheck to get for his birthday last week. He strolled to the bathroom to check his appearance one last time in a full-length mirror.

Damn, I'm fine! he told himself. He winked, licked his lips, and then left the house, heading for church. Maybe he would be able to score a lunch date, since Deja wasn't with him this Sunday.

He pulled into the church parking lot, scanning for anyone who looked both available and gullible. As his eyes swept the lot and focused on a woman who walked past him, Garnell couldn't help but turn his head, watching the wiggle in her behind. *Mmph, mmph, mmph!* he commented to himself.

"Brother Sutton," Pastor Gardner called, startling him back to reality. "I want to see you in my office after service today," he ordered. Without breaking his stride, he walked past Garnell; then he looked back to confirm his expectation with a solid glare.

Garnell nodded and stuttered that he'd be there. Anticipating what the meeting would be about, he couldn't count how many times he felt his stomach drop during the service. He forgot all about his plans to find a quick hookup. He couldn't focus on the preached Word, trying to come up with excuses and lies for why he was living with a woman, although he had a wife. He rattled his brain as he tried to come up with reasons as to why he hadn't yet moved his family from the East Coast to be with him, especially since he was now gainfully employed. His brows were furrowed for pretty much the entire service, which gave the perception that Pastor Gardner had his full attention, but nothing could have been further from the truth.

Any other Sunday, the service seemed to drag on and on; but this particular day, Pastor Gardner seemed to give the benediction ten minutes after the service had started. Like normal, the parishioners chatted among themselves, clearing the sanctuary at the speed of a mournful funeral walk. Garnell did his share of greetings, hugs, handshakes, and back pats. Then feigning confidence, he took long strides to the pastor's office.

He ain't nothing but a man. He put his pants on one leg at a time, just like I do, and he ain't got no heaven or hell to put me in, Garnell reminded himself.

He tapped on the pastor's office door twice and waited for a response.

"Come on in," David answered.

"How you doin', Pastor?" Garnell asked as he entered.

"Good. Have a seat. I hear that despite you having a family, you're now shacking up with one of the young ladies here," David answered without skipping a beat. The expression on his face demanded an explanation.

"Oh naw. Naw, it ain't nothing like that, Pastor," Garnell stated. "See, when I got here, I was staying at my uncle's house, but he on, like, a fixed-income thing with his rent, man, where he can't have more than a certain amount of income in his house. When I started working at AT&T, that kinda messed his situation up and he was 'bout to get put out," he explained.

"Somebody had told his landlord that I was living there and making good money, and everything, and they was about to put him out. That's when Sister McClendon offered me a room in her home," he said, referring to Deja.

"Mmm-hmm." David nodded.

"She said she was looking for a roommate, and I made it clear that I was married and working on bringing my family out here. And she said she was just looking for some extra income, and nothing more." Garnell paused for a second, looking for a bit of approval and belief. "I know it don't look right, but it ain't nothing. It's all good."

"You know the Word says to let not your good be spoken evil of, and I'm hearing a lot of evil circulating around you and Deja. And what I've heard don't sound nothing like what you just told me."

"You know people talk, sir. And a lot of times, they don't have a clue what they talking about."

"So why haven't you brought your family out here yet?" David interlaced his fingers and rested his elbows atop his desk.

"Well, I'm still tryin'a secure suitable housing for us, but she also tryin'a finish her degree. She got about two more semesters and she said she don't wanna transfer to finish out here."

"Where is she going?"

"University of South Carolina," he answered quickly, not even sure if there was such a school, but he figured all states had a university named after them.

"What is she majoring in?"

"Business," Garnell shot off. "I can call her right now and you can ask her." He patted his pockets, feeling for his cell phone and praying that the pastor wouldn't take him up on the offer.

Lucky for him, David didn't move.

"Mmm-hmm." David's eyes were piercing, not buying a word of it. "The wages of sin are death. You know that, right?"

Garnell swallowed hard with conviction. "Yes, sir, we all sin and fall short of His glory. That's why I daily ask the Lord to guide my footsteps and to forgive me for anything that I've done that has displeased Him."

"We all need to do that," David responded; then he rose to his feet and extended his hand for a shake, giving indication that their conversation was over. "I appreciate you coming in."

"Oh, no doubt, no doubt," Garnell said, jumping to his feet and returning the hand gesture. Internally he sighed in relief. "I don't have nothing to hide. I'll see you later this week at Bible Study."

Now sitting in his car, he smiled to himself. Lying had been simple enough, and in his mind, he didn't owe Deja a damn thing. He wasn't married to her and had made no commitments or promises. He loved the way his life currently was: he hadn't heard a peep from his wife in almost a year; Deja was far too independent to let him pay her mortgage, so it cost him practically nothing to have a roof over his head; he finally had a good job with a decent salary; and he drove a nice car and had an impressive wardrobe.

The only thing that would make it all better was a good high. "One good hit won't hurt shit," he said out loud, chuckling, as he wheeled his vehicle around the corner and headed for a part of town he was all too familiar with, although he hadn't been that way in months.

On his way, he stopped by an ATM machine and withdrew a couple hundred dollars in what he called spending money. Remembering that Deja was home, sick in bed, he pulled out his cell to give her a call.

"Hello," she mumbled, sounding miserable.

"Hey, baby, how you feeling?"

"Awful."

"I know, you sound pretty bad too. Were you sleeping?"

"Yeah. Trying to, anyway." Deja coughed a few times, then snorted.

"Well, I'll let you get back to rest. I just wanted to tell you that Pastor asked me to stay after church today to help the brothers move a couple things. I shouldn't be too long, okay?"

"All right. Bring me some soup from somewhere, please," she requested.

"What kind?"

"Chicken noodle, I guess. Nothing too heavy. And some orange juice too."

"Okay, baby," Garnell agreed. "I won't be too long."

Deja's initial thoughts were something devastatingly tragic had happened to Garnell; she had peeled her eyes open just past eleven at night and he was nowhere to be found.

"Garnell!" she yelled a few times, waiting for him to rush to her side.

When he didn't, she dragged herself from bed and stumbled downstairs, thinking she'd find him asleep on the couch, but she was only disappointed and confused. Her eyes darted around the room, looking for any signs of his presence; then she glanced out the window, looking for his car.

"What the . . ."

The kitchen showed no proof that he'd been in the house; there was no soup, juice, or dirty dishes. At this point, Deja began to panic slightly, reaching for the phone, which hung on the wall, and quickly dialing Garnell's cell.

When there was no answer, she dialed the police.

"I think something has happened to my boyfriend," she started her story; but by the time she finished her explanation of her thoughts, she only felt stupid.

"Ma'am, it sounds like your boyfriend may just be out painting the town red, whooping it up with his friends." To Deja, the female detective's tone seemed cold and lacked compassion, but the officer had seen this type of thing too many times to take it seriously. "If you don't hear from him in forty-eight hours, what you can do is file a missing persons report; but honestly, I think if you check a few downtown hot spots, you might find your answer."

Deja gasped at her abruptness. "You wouldn't be so heartless if it was one of your loved ones!" she barked. "You'd be doing all you could to—"

"Ma'am, unless you find out something more definitive about his absence, just call us back in a couple days. You're also welcome to call the hospitals to see if he's been checked in anywhere. Have a nice night."

Leaning against the wall, still in the kitchen, Deja wasn't sure what to think or do. A cup of hot cocoa warmed her insides, but it didn't calm her nerves. *Where is he?* She had ruled out something happening to him at the church because she figured Pastor Gardner or one of the other brothers would have called, knowing that they'd been living together.

Maybe they called his uncle, instead, she reasoned. She started to dial his number, but thought better of it after looking at the clock and seeing that it was almost midnight.

"Uncle Willie ain't gon' cuss me out tonight," she said out loud, remembering how nasty his disposition was when she met him. "I'll call him in the morning."

Wrapped in a blanket, Deja only found a couple of uncomfortable hours of sleep, stretched out on the couch. When the sun poured into her living room at seven-thirty on Monday morning, she called her boss, letting him know she'd be out sick for the day. Then she began to cry, realizing that Garnell was nowhere to be found; and she knew from her past that when her man disappeared for a night, it meant one of two things: jail or another woman.

The phone rang two hours later, and Deja practically leaped over her coffee table like an Olympic athlete jumping hurdles. To her disappointment, it was Tracey calling. She took the call, anyway, although she didn't feel much like talking.

"Hey, girl, what's wrong with you?" Tracey asked, immediately noticing Deja's depressed tone.

"Garnell didn't come home last night," she shared without hesitation. "Girl, I'm so mad right now! I don't know what to do."

"Did he call and tell you where he was supposed to be?"

"No. Last I heard from him, he was moving stuff at the church. That was about one-thirty yesterday. He s'posed to have been bringing me some soup, and I ain't heard nothing else from him."

"Did you call the cops?"

"Yeah. You know they don't care nothing about a missing black person." Deja paused as she chewed on the inside of her bottom lip. "I don't know what to think. I mean, I know what to think, but I don't wanna think it."

"Did you call his uncle?" Tracey suggested, already drawing the conclusion that Garnell was a cheating dog.

"Not yet, but I'ma go around there in a little while after I get myself together. This cold is kicking my tail right now; I need to rest up first."

"Well, I was just calling to ask you: why is Jasmine running around town telling people that I'm pregnant?" Tracey's question was rhetorical, so she didn't wait for Deja to respond. "I'd like to know where she got that bit of news from."

"Did you ask her?"

"Not yet 'cause Jermaine won't let me. He know I'ma have some words for her ass, and he don't want me to mess up our little bit of time together fussing with her."

"How you know she telling people that in the first place, then?" Deja sniffled.

"'Cause I saw Eureen in the mall and she told me."

"Eureen told you that Jasmine told her that you were pregnant," Deja stated more than asked. "Girl, do you even hear yourself? That's secondhand hearsay. If you ain't pregnant, why are you even worrying yourself about it? I wouldn't pay that mess no mind," Deja advised. "She probably ain't said nothing. Eureen probably got confused about what she heard, since she dealing with the death of her husband still."

"I don't know about all that. Why would Eureen say that?"

"Girl, who knows? Are you pregnant or not?" Deja asked bluntly.

"No!" Tracey denied adamantly. "Girl, you know I don't even roll like that!" she added, still wanting her friends to believe she and Jermaine had not yet had sexual intercourse.

"Tracey, you better give that man some pussy before he get him some from somewhere else!" Deja chuckled.

"If he finding pussy on the streets, he bet' not let me find out about it. And, anyway, if he is screwing around, he ain't worth getting in my pussy in the first place."

"That might be true, but what you think that man is doing when his dick get hard? Ain't but so many hand jobs he gonna wanna give hisself. And if you ain't givin' up no pussy, ain't no way in the world you suckin' his dick."

"You so nasty!" Tracey guffawed, trying to avoid a confession. "Ugh!"

"You can turn up your nose all you want, but don't nothing bring a nigga to his knees like a tongue wrapped around his dick. I been so sick lately that I haven't been able to do Garnell right; plus I'm sick of fornicating, anyway."

"Well, for your sake, I hope he somewhere givin' hisself a hand job, 'cause based on what you just said—he might be dicking another pussy right now."

"You make me sick," Deja replied, wincing. "Like I'm not sick enough!"

"Girl, he ain't doing that; I'm just playing," Tracey responded, smirking. "Anyway, I'ma talk to you later. Call me if you need me to roll out with you to find Garnell."

"Yeah, yeah, yeah," Deja answered, trying again to brush off the thought that Garnell was cheating on her. "I'll keep you posted."

Chapter Twenty-five

"What the hell?" Shamar snapped, glancing over the letter that his wife handed him. His eyes caught sight of a couple of dollar figures, which reiterated what Jasmine had already told him. "How they gonna raise the damn rent two hundred dollars? What the fuck is that about!"

"I don't know, Shamar. They ain't never raised our rent before. Now, out of the clear blue sky, they sent this letter."

"Ain't there some kinda law about how they supposed to raise rent? They can't just do that. Where the hell they think somebody gonna pull out an extra two hundred dollars a month?"

"Yeah, there is a law, but the law only says that if they raising the rent up to ten percent, they gotta give us thirty days' notice; and if it's more than ten percent, they gotta give us sixty days' notice. It's not going up 'til three months from now, so that's like ninety days away," Jasmine rattled off, having already tried to find a legal loophole for not paying the sudden housing-expense increase.

"Well, shit, we better find somewhere else to live. Ain't nobody paying an extra two hundred dollars to live here."

"And how we gonna do that, Shamar, with your credit tore slam out the frame? You can't get a piece of bubble gum with your credit score."

"Just use your Social Security number and apply by yourself," Shamar suggested.

"You know just as good as I do, they gonna check the credit of every grown person we put on the lease."

"So just apply by yourself—just you and the girls. Tell the people that you single or divorced or separated or something. People do that shit all the time."

"They also get put out when the landlord find out it's other people on the lease."

"Just tell them we got back together. I'm on the damn road all the time, anyway; ain't like they gonna really see me coming and going." Shamar refolded the letter and tossed it on the kitchen table. "That shit don't make no sense."

"I really don't wanna move, Shamar. The girls are doing real well in school, and you know how hard it was to get them in there. And I like this house. We been here too long to be moving, and we not buying our own place."

"That school ain't gonna mean a damn thing when we don't have nowhere to live 'cause the rent too damn high."

"Really, it's not too high," Jasmine reasoned. "Even with it going up two hundred dollars, it's gonna be about the same amount that we gonna pay going some-where else. Especially since it ain't never went up since we been living here."

"That's what I'm saying! So the landlord is just being a greedy-ass pig! They ain't got no reason to be goin' up on our rent like this, except to fill their own pockets, and I ain't paying for no man to take an extra ride on my damn back."

"Well, I ain't tryin'a move," Jasmine stated firmly, having given it more thought since she'd seen the letter two days before Shamar had. "I already looked at some other houses in the paper; and for what they want for those raggedy houses, we might as well stay here."

"We can move in with my momma. She got plenty of room, and she wouldn't charge us nothing, anyway." Shamar looked at his wife as if his suggestion was something she'd actually consider.

"You know it ain't no way in hell I'ma move in your momma's house. The only way I would do that is if she dead and gone; and even then, I wouldn't be happy about it. That woman can't stand me." Jasmine stopped short of saying that the feeling was completely mutual. "You need to man up and dig up the rest of the money," she ordered.

"No, I don't either. As the man, all I gotta say is what the plan is gonna be; and if the plan is that we move in with Momma, then you supposed to follow."

"What?" Jasmine's frustration was apparent. "What kind of low-grade crack you been smoking? You must be out of your rabid bit mind if you think I'ma follow you in some half-assed plan that depends on your momma be nice to me. Do I have 'fool' written on my forehead or something?"

"Look, you either gonna pay that extra money yourself, or we ain't staying here. You decide." Shamar stood to his feet and walked out of the room. Just as he did, the phone rang.

"Hello," Jasmine answered.

"Jasmine, I got a bone to pick with you," Tracey stated right off the bat. "Why are you going around and telling people I'm pregnant?"

"That's what Shamar told me Jermaine said, but you gonna have to pick it later 'cause me and Shamar having a discussion right now," Jasmine replied, cutting Tracey off, before yelling up the staircase at her husband. "I know you just didn't walk your ass away while I was talking to you!"

"You don't fucking tell me when I can leave the damn room," Shamar yelled back.

"I'll call you later, Tracey." Jasmine didn't wait for Tracey to agree, but instead immediately ended the call and focused back on Shamar. "Who the hell you think you talking to like that?"

"I'm talking to you, damn it! Ain't nobody else walked up in here, and the girls ain't home. You heard what the fuck I said! You gonna pay it yourself, or we moving out!"

"Well, you can get the fuck out right now!" Jasmine walked up the stairs and stood toe to toe with Shamar, twisting her neck with every word. "You ain't never been much of a man, anyway! Always looking for your stupid-ass momma to bail you outta some shit! You big-baby-ass excuse for a—"

Before Jasmine could get the last word out, Shamar had slapped her so hard that she'd spun in a full circle and landed on the floor.

"I know you ain't fuckin' talking about my momma!" he snarled, towering over her.

Too stunned to speak, Jasmine didn't utter another word.

"Say something else! Go 'head," he challenged. "She done already told me about you hanging in the street and fucking around with some other nigga. I oughta whup your ass right now for that shit!"

"What!" Jasmine blurted out. "Ain't nobody doing nothing, Shamar!" Tears had already begun streaming down her face.

"So you saying my momma lying?" Shamar sneered. "Is that what you saying? Call her a liar then," he said, balling up his fist. "If she lying, say she lying."

Too fearful that Shamar would land a blow, Jasmine scrambled to her feet, but said nothing.

"That's what I thought," he added, grabbing his wallet and keys. "Don't wait up." Shamar headed out the front door on his way to exchange stolen merchandise for cash.

"Lick my pussy some more. I wanna come. Put down that damn pipe and eat me some more," a woman who called herself Juicy demanded as she fingered herself.

High out of his mind, and as naked as a newborn infant, Garnell was too paranoid to respond. Instead, he continuously peeped through the curtains for uninvited guests.

"Shh," he whispered. "I hear something out there." His eyes were huge and abnormal, and his heart was beating three times the usual rate. Scared for no apparent reason, he hid in the closet a few times for several minutes and had once jumped in the tub, hiding behind the shower curtain. "Shh, they're comin'. I hear them," he whispered. "Throw that shit away! Hurry up and get rid of it. They're comin'."

"You stupid, paranoid muthafucka! That's why I hate to get high with muthafuckas like you! Ain't nobody out there!" she yelled, making him even more paranoid.

"Shut up, bitch! I'm tellin' you, I hear them at the door," he growled, standing away from the window, not wanting to be in the path of the bullets he was sure would fly through the window at any minute.

Horny as hell, Juicy gapped her legs open, getting herself off, then took another hit.

"Put that shit down, you dumb bitch! I ain't goin' back to jail because of you!"

He sprinted to the bathtub another time, still naked, closing the shower curtain to hide.

"Scary muthafucka! I don't know why you waste your money to get high and act all scary and shit!" Juicy commented, continuing to inhale from the pipe.

Meanwhile, as she paid a few bills online, Deja discovered that more than $2,000 had been withdrawn from her bank account. It amounted to a few hundred dollars at a time, for every day that Garnell had been gone, which was not five full days. She was sick of crying, but tears of anger burned in Deja's eyes. Her rage finally prompted her to call his uncle Wilbur. Quickly she told him of Garnell's absence and her realization of the missing cash.

"What! That boy done smoked two thousand dollars' worth of crack and still livin'! I'll be damned! I tried to tell you 'bout that no-good muthafucka when you came around here, but you ain't wanna listen to no got-damn body!"

"What am I gonna do? He's just about drained my bank account!" Deja wailed, ignoring Wilbur's last comment. "Do you know how I can find him?"

"What the hell is he doing with access to your money? You stupid or something?"

Deja didn't know what to say, for she did feel rather stupid for having given Garnell an ATM card to her bank account. She said nothing in reply.

"Your computer tell you what ATM that fool last got the money from?" Wilbur snarled.

"Yes. Bank of America on Manchester and Broadway."

"I know the area he's in, and that's a start. I'ma catch that crack-smokin' nigga! Leave the rest up to me."

"What am I supposed to do in the meanwhile?"

"Close your bank accounts and wait it out. The boy is out there on deadly grounds, Deja. That ain't any place for a girl like you. He's dealing with all kinds of scum, thugs, drug dealers, and hoes, but I'm gonna catch him and bring 'im down. That's a promise."

"Do you think he's having sex with prostitutes, Uncle Willie?"

"Do shit stink? He damn sho ain't playin' marbles or blackjack with 'em, and he got-damn sho ain't spendin' money like that with a bunch of niggas! He out there with those hoes gettin' his freak on—that's what his ass is doin'! I'm surprised you fucking wit' his ass, in the first place, when he got a wife and some damn crumb-snatchin' rug rat kids."

She could have sworn her heart had just stopped beating. "What? What wife and kids?" Deja gasped. "He's married?" She couldn't believe her ears, and didn't know what to think. Her mind was completely muddled with everything Garnell had told her about his past. How much of it had been lies?

"You just as stupid as the day is long," Wilbur commented, guffawing. "I bet you believe he some kinda got-damn doctor too, don't you, with your gullible ass!" He laughed even harder.

His teasing and chuckling annoyed her, but Deja sucked it up only because she felt like she needed his help. She didn't know a thing about a crack addict's habits and hangouts.

"I don't care how dangerous it is. I wanna know what are you gonna do, 'cause I need to be in on it too. I need to look in his eyes and confront him," Deja insisted.

Wilbur laughed for another fifteen seconds or so before he answered. "I'll tell you what. Meet me in two hours on the corner of Figueroa and Florence at Burger King, and we'll take it from there." ·

"You're about to drive all the way to L.A.?"

"How else are we gonna catch the muthafucka? Can't call the police, 'cause they don't give a fuck about another crackhead statistic. Matta fact, I'll be around there in a little bit to pick you up. I know how da find 'im."

"Okay. I really appreciate this, Uncle Willie. Thanks."

"Uh-huh," Wilbur responded. "Stupid-ass girl," she heard him mumble as he hung up the phone.

An hour later, both Wilbur and Deja sat in his car parked in the Burger King lot right across from the bank where most of the ATM transactions had taken place. They were plotting, strategizing, and keeping an eye on their surroundings, waiting to spot Garnell, who was sure to emerge to get more money or drugs.

"So, Uncle Willie, Garnell is married?" Deja questioned a second time.

"Just as married as George and Weezie," he answered, referencing the couple from the sitcom *The Jeffersons*.

"How long has he been married?"

"'Bout ten years."

Too numb to be shocked again, Deja continued to ask questions.

"How many kids does he have?" She braced herself for the answer.

"Six, seven, eight?" Wilbur said, overstating the true number of four children. "Hell, I don't know. That boy got kids all over the United States."

"I'm so stupid," she said under her breath; then she stared out the window, turning her head away from Wilbur. She was too ashamed to let him see her face. While she waited, she sent a text message to her father, bringing him into the loop and asking him to meet the two of them.

Right away, Michael dialed his daughter's number, but Deja wasn't ready to talk yet. She did not want to be belittled a second time, although she knew her father would reprimand in love, not in mockery like Wilbur had done. And second, she didn't want to make Wilbur privy to the conversation. Her phone vibrated in her hand, alerting her of her father's text response.

Answer ur damn phone!
I cant rite now daddy—can u plz just come?
On my way.

That made Deja feel a bit better. She knew her dad would jack Garnell up. Her eyes floated up to the sky and followed a series of clouds slowly drifting by. *How in the world did I get here, Lord? Look at me. Sitting here, mixed up with a married crackhead with kids. Why wasn't I able to discern this, Lord?* She pursed her lips and shook her head at herself, thinking long and hard about the course of their fake relationship. *Eight kids? No wonder he ain't gave me no ring. Thank you, Lord.* She sighed, grateful for small blessings. *'Cause that would have really been a mess.*

"So where does his wife live?"

"There that muthafucka go right there!" Wilbur blurted out, whisking the question out of Deja's mind.

"Where?" Deja smudged more tears away before whipping her head in both directions, trying to spot Garnell.

He was pulling up to the same ATM, preparing to withdraw more money.

"You close your accounts?" Wilbur asked.

"Yep." Almost frantic, Deja yanked at the door, ready to sprint across the street and charge toward Garnell, but it was locked and didn't give.

"Hold your horses and slow your ass down," Wilbur chastised. "Soon as he see your ass, he gon' pull off.

Don't be stupid. Oh, I forgot—you already stupid." Wilbur slapped his hand on his thigh in laughter, causing Deja to grimace. "If you closed them accounts, he ain't gonna get no money. All we gotta do is follow his ass to where he been staying and wait 'til he get in his room. That's when you wanna jump out on his ass."

Deja stayed put and updated her dad that Garnell had been spotted; he texted back that he was just minutes away.

"I don't know what the fuck is goin' on!" Garnell spat out, confused at the "insufficient funds" message he received, over and over again, even when he changed the amount of the withdrawal to as low as twenty dollars. "I know it was some more money in this account!"

"I need a fuckin' hit! If you can't get no money, then you may as well drop me off on the corner so I can make some," Juicy demanded of him.

"You're gonna do me like that? You're gonna just leave a nigga hangin' after all I spent?"

"Nigga, please! I ain't tryin' to hear that shit! I've got tricks who spend way more in an hour than you spend in a whole day, nigga, so stop boring me with the bullshit . . . unless you're gonna ask Hurricane for some credit. You've spent a grip of money with him. I know he'll give you credit 'til tomorrow," Juicy suggested, feeling like it was the best option for getting her next hit.

"Suppose he don't. You still gonna jet out on me?"

"He'll give it to you on credit; don't trip," she replied with assurance.

"But what if he don't? You know I didn't come yet, and I need some head."

"Knock it off and let's go to Hurricane's spot. I've been tryin'a give your limp-ass dick some head five days straight, and you can't even get it hard."

"I'll get hard next time, 'cause I'm gonna make damn sho I get mines before I take a hit."

"Yeah, right. You been saying that shit the whole time."

"Watch and see, just watch and see," Garnell promised, wheeling his car to where he could find some drugs on credit.

Watching Garnell pull out of the lot, Willie made a quick, illegal U-turn and followed him from a distance.

Staring angrily in Garnell's direction, Deja felt her blood pressure increasing, but she managed to remain as calm as she could.

A few minutes later, Garnell stopped the car in front of a crack house and knocked on the door.

"Hurricane," Garnell said, "it's your homie Garnell. I need to holla at you."

A tall, thin brother, with a head of loose braids, opened the door. "What's up, cuzz? How much you got this time?"

"That's what I need to holla at you about."

"Hope you ain't about to ask me for credit, 'cause that shit ain't happenin'."

"Man, I've spent 'bout two g's wit' you, and a nigga tapped out right now; but I promise you, man, I'll pay you double tomorrow, soon as the bank open. I put that on my kids, man."

"What you tryin' to get?"

"'Bout a hundred pack or sumthin'," Garnell said, almost begging. "I got you first thing in the morning, man. I get paid tomorrow."

"Let me tell you sumthin', nigga. I've already sent sixteen muthafuckas to their graves for fuckin' with my scrilla, and I won't hesitate to make you number seventeen if you try to fuck me."

"I'm a man of my word, Hurricane. You see what I'm drivin', so that—"

"That shit don't mean a muthafuckin' thang to me, cuzz. If you ain't paid me by nine-thirty, you'll be a dead muthafucka by ten. Take that to the bank."

"I promise, man, you ain't gotta worry about—"

"Save your words, nigga. You might need that last breath, feel me?" he said, shutting Garnell down. He slapped the drugs in his hand.

"I feel you, Hurricane. I do feel you. Thanks, man, I appreciate it."

Entering the motel room, Juicy and Garnell wasted no time undressing.

Juicy took a hit and went to work, sucking and licking his erection; but minutes into it, he stopped her.

"I need a hit, baby, just a small one."

"I knew it! I fuckin' knew your ass was gonna want one. You've got a hard-on, so why can't you jus' lay back and enjoy this good head?"

"Just a little one, baby. I ain't gonna trip. I promise you I ain't."

"Damn!" Juicy complained.

Just outside the motel room, Deja's father handed the keys to his car to his daughter. "Go on home," he ordered.

"But I wanna see—"

"Deja, take my keys. . . . Get in my car . . . and go home!" he bellowed with fatherly authority, which Deja didn't question a second time. "You don't need to be nowhere around what's about to happen. You don't even need to know what's 'bout to happen. The less you know, the better for you. Now go."

Reluctant, but knowing that it was best, Deja obeyed.

Once she pulled away, Michael turned to Wilbur and assured him that he would handle the situation from there.

"I'ma close my eyes on this on," Wilbur said. "Just don't kill 'im."

"When I finish wit' him, he gonna wish I had kilt his punk ass," Michael responded. "I'ma leave some life in 'im, though, only 'cause you asking me to."

At that, Wilbur got in his car and headed back home, expecting to get a call from his nephew in a few hours— granted, that is if Garnell would be able to talk.

Inside, Garnell took a hit, held it in a few seconds, and then exhaled. He jumped to his feet, startled by the door being kicked in. Before he could take half a step, he was staring at the distorted and angry face of Michael McClendon.

Chapter Twenty-six

"Derrick," Eureen greeted with surprise. She smiled as she opened her front door. "Come on in."

"You sure I'm not interrupting anything? I know I'm dropping by unannounced." Derrick was strategically dressed in a pair of black skintight Nike running pants, with a matching long-sleeved shirt, when he arrived at Eureen's house. He'd parked his car two blocks away and sprinted to her front door, breaking a quick sweat, giving the illusion that he'd been out on a run. Because he kept his body in tip-top shape, it wasn't hard for Eureen to believe.

"No, come on in," she offered a second time. Eureen couldn't help but notice his well-defined chest, toned biceps and triceps, flat abs, and, most noticeably, the huge bulge in his pants centered between the top of his thighs. He caught her glance, but he pretended not to see it at all, playing his cards right.

"I just wanted to drop by and see how you were doing. I'm sorry I'm all sweaty and whatnot," he said, gesturing his hands toward himself, wanting her to take another look at what he was packing.

"Oh, don't worry about that." Eureen dismissed it with a wave of her hand. "Let me get you some water. Come on in the kitchen," she invited.

"Sure." He followed her, focusing his eyes on the movement of her hips, becoming aroused. He didn't mind the swelling in his pants; he wanted Eureen to see it, so he let his mind travel to the nastiest thoughts he could conjure at the moment, hoping to get close to a full hard-on. If Eureen expressed offense, he would simply apologize, feign embarrassment, and tell her that she was so beautiful that he found it difficult to control an erection around her. If she said nothing, that would be all the better for his plan of fucking her before the week ended.

He hoped Eureen would be too flattered to be suspicious. He'd already pictured himself driving the vehicles that sat so attractively in the circular driveway, and he had also envisioned himself walking through the mansion, puffing an expensive cigar and sporting the dead man's classy jewelry.

"So how you doing?" she asked, pulling a bottle of water from the refrigerator and handing it to him.

With a cliché ever present on his tongue, he wasted no time on his reply. "Blessed and highly favored." Derrick took a long swig from the plastic bottle. "Too blessed to be stressed, ain't got time for no mess." He chuckled. "I was reading the Word this morning, and it was just mmm-mmm good to my soul."

"Really? What did you read?"

"Proverbs 3:5 through 6. 'Trust in the Lord with all thine heart; and lean not unto thine own understanding. In all thy ways acknowledge him, and he shall direct thy paths.'" He quoted the passage as easily as saying his own name and rolled his hand into a fist to emphasize his words.

"Just that little bit is so powerful, Sista! If we just learn how to trust God and let Him guide our footsteps, we'd be amazed at how He's so willing to bless us!" Derrick's articulation held Eureen captive like a fly caught in a spider's web. The expression on her face gave indication that she was fully engaged, which made Derrick smile inwardly.

"You're so inspiring, Derrick," Eureen commented, confirming what he'd already sensed.

"I just try to live the way God want me to," he responded in false humility.

Yeah, this shit is a piece of cake. I've gotta take cool, calculated steps and not rush things. This thing is much larger than me and can easily crumble if not carried out appropriately. Make her want you. He silently coached himself, gapping his legs a little farther apart and pulsing his manhood. He was careful not to make eye contact for a few seconds. *Don't make her feel like you want her; let her come to you. It works every time. Flex that dick, but captivate her mind with the Word of God.*

They talked only a few minutes more before Derrick headed to the door, careful not to have the slightest amount of physical contact with Eureen.

"I need to get back on my run, Sista. I sho appreciate the water and the fellowship."

"Oh, no problem," Eureen answered, somewhat disappointed that he was leaving so soon. "My pleasure."

"See you Sunday?" Derrick asked, already starting to trot away with a hand wave.

"Yeah. Definitely," she confirmed, standing in the doorway and watching his backside. "Lawd, Lawd, Lawd!" she whispered to herself. "That was a mighty big piece of pipe laid under that ground."

Lustful thoughts circled her mind for the next few seconds, but then her thoughts shifted slightly. *He wasn't as enthused about me as he was that other day. No brotherly or sisterly love hug or holy kiss? Maybe that's a good thing; 'cause from the way he was looking, I mighta gave him some if he woulda made a move. Help me, Lord!*

As Derrick walked back to his car, he confidently thought, *I bet that heifer is playing with her pussy right now. She wanted this dick so bad; I feel the green light coming. I know she was hot as fish grease and ready to write me a check for a million bucks just to fuck her.*

He felt his cell phone buzz at his waist and reached to get it. Thumbing through the keys, he read a text message from Eureen:

I'd like to invite you to a lunch date on Saturday if you're free.

Derrick chuckled out loud. "You's a bad muthafucka, Derrick Kelly," he boasted, and grinned.

He waited two full hours before he answered, to give the impression that he was still out running:

Lunch sounds great, as long as you let me pay.

Although she could now afford to go to any salon in the state, Eureen was at Tracey and Jermaine's place, getting her hair done, when the text came through. It brought an instant smile to her face.

Tracey took immediate notice of her grin. "What got you smiling like that?" she asked as she quickly worked her fingers, weaving thin strands of human hair into a microbraid.

"Nothing." Eureen smirked, sliding her phone back in her purse.

"Yeah, right. That looks like a man smile."

"Girl, the only man who can make me smile is Jesus," Eureen said, trying to throw her off.

"Naw, I seen your Jesus smile and it don't look nothing like that!" Tracey laughed. "You let me find out you done started dating Derrick Kelly."

Eureen was caught off guard by Tracey mentioning Derrick's name; it caused her to take too long to respond.

"Uh-huh! That's what I thought!" Tracey further accused.

"What?"

"What nothing! I saw how he was looking at you at the funeral."

"He was not!" Eureen denied, truly unsure if Derrick had been giving her the eye then or not.

"I heard he be all at your house and stuff."

"Girl, Jasmine need to stop running her mouth! Now, if anybody know that, you know that!" Eureen barked.

"Speaking of, I tried to call her on that hot lie she told, talking 'bout I'm pregnant. She said Shamar told her that Jermaine told her I was pregnant, but her and Shamar sounded like they were fightin', so I couldn't get her like I wanted."

"She was about to have two arguments on her hands, huh?" Eureen pried, still angry at Jasmine's negative comments regarding Derrick being at her house.

"Sho was. And now Shamar done left her."

Eureen gasped, but she smirked internally. "What? That's terrible."

"Yep. He moved in with his momma 'cause their rent got jacked up sky-high."

"They both make good money, though. It seem like they would be halfway all right," Eureen said, egging Tracey on.

"I think they do got the money, but he don't wanna pay it. When I talked to her later, she said it went up, like, two hundred dollars, girl," Tracey continued.

"That's crazy!"

"I know. She said she didn't want to move; and he said if she ain't wanna move, it gonna have to come out of her pocket, or they could all move in with his momma. Jasmine won't tryin'a do that, so Shamar left . . . after he beat her ass!"

Shaking her head, Eureen commented, "That's a mess." She was careful, however, not to say too much more.

"Girl, after she told me all that, I didn't even mention the whole baby thing again."

"Yeah, I can see why."

"So for real, what's the deal with you and Derrick?"

Feeling a bit at ease, Eureen shrugged. "Nothing. He's a nice guy."

"And?"

"And nothing. He's nice. He's made himself available to me and the girls since Monroe died."

"Well, I heard he know how to put it down in the bedroom. They say he be blowing people's backs out and whatnot." Tracey laughed. "What you know about that?"

"Not a thing," she answered honestly.

I could stand a little bit of that, Eureen thought. *It been too long since I had me a piece of dick; and if all that I saw today is all him, I just might have to repent!*

"We haven't done nothing more than have a couple of meaningful conversations. Sex isn't everything," Eureen demurred.

"You right about that. First you've gotta make certain the three *C*'s are there: chemistry, communication, and compatibility. After that, you can then proceed further. Once you get a piece, you do the fourth *C*: cartwheels."

The ladies burst into laughter.

"Well, he looks like he packing a serious weapon," Eureen commented.

"So you done peeped it out, huh?" Tracey probed.

"Not really. It was more like it was standing out, looking like a tree trunk stuffed in his running pants."

"You know, they say that he got some kinda tattoo on it. It supposed to say 'religion' in Chinese. Guess he be talking 'bout 'me love you long time.'"

"You sho know a lot about that man's ding-a-ling!"
Eureen laughed.

"I'm just telling you what I heard," Tracey lied, actually speaking from first-hand experience, as she'd
been one of the many women Derrick had successfully
seduced from the church congregation. You keep on
hanging around him, and I'm sure you're gonna find
out."

"Right now, it ain't nothing more than his presence,
his politeness, his intelligence, and his spirituality."

"And his religion!" Tracey tossed in, but she didn't let
on that she had taken a ride on it plenty of times. "You
better remember that everything that glitters ain't gold.
I advise you to keep your guard up. I once met a minister, and even went as far as fucking him on the regular,
just like we were married . . ." her voice trailed reminiscing about the good sex she and Derrick would have. Just
thinking back about it made her panties wet."Nothing
good came out of the relationship. In fact, it wasn't a
relationship; it was more of a sex thing."

"Really?"

"Yep. I would feel so guilty after we had sex, I'd cry
for days. He told me he loved me and that he planned
to marry me, once he got his finances together. Like
a dummy, I fell for it. The sex, gifts, and money were
good while it lasted; but once again, I got the short end
of the stick. He wasn't a bit thinking about marrying
me, but I was giving it up like we were married, and
that was enough for him. I had to get my self-esteem
back and kick him to the curb, girl. It was hard; but
with the help of the Lord, I did it. You better keep in
mind that just because they go to church doesn't necessarily mean they're in the church. Sometimes the
ones that show up every Sunday morning are the worst
ones," Tracey warned.

"I'd rather have someone who love God at least a little bit than to have somebody who don't want nothing to do with God at all; like Monroe was, until he was about ready to take his last breath." Eureen had no idea that she was describing Jermaine as well and continued talking. "To me, if he at least willing to be in a place where God can speak to him, he can change. When you don't wanna hear nothing God got to say"—she paused and shrugged—"then what in the world can you get out of that mess?"

The ring of the doorbell saved Tracey from having to comment at the moment. "Be right back."

She folded her lips inside her mouth, thinking about what Eureen had said and about Jermaine's refusal to acknowledge God.

I can change him, though. All he has to do is see God in me.

She pulled the door open and greeted the mailman.

"How you doing? I need a signature for this envelope," he spoke routinely, hardly noticing Tracey at all.

"Good, thanks," she answered, scribbling her name on a small slip of paper, then taking the flat package and glancing over it. She saw that it only had the address on it, with no name indicating who it was for. She looked at the return address curiously, but she temporarily dismissed it, tossing it on a sofa table with the rest of the mail and making a mental note to look at it later once she finished Eureen's hair.

Trying her best to avoid returning to the same conversation, Tracey stopped in the kitchen, grabbed a bottle of water for herself and another for Eureen, along with a bag of chips to offer her.

"Thought you might be thirsty. Here you go," she said, rejoining her and restarting on her hair. "It's probably going to be another hour; you wanna watch TV?"

Not waiting for a response, she turned the TV on and tuned to BET, where *King's Ransom* was being featured. She increased the volume.

When Eureen began to giggle at the movie's antics, Tracey let her thoughts float back to Jermaine and his spirituality, which worried her more and more.

If I can just get him to come to church a couple of times, I know you can change him, Lord, and everything will be all right. He's just too good to me to let go. Her eyes floated around the house at its furnishings and the beautiful things Jermaine had provided her with; she thought about how well he treated her, how he took care of her needs, gave her money when and if she needed it—and even when she didn't—and how he constantly showered her with affection, both physically and with gifts.

Lord, you know I ain't never had a man be this good to me, and your Word says all good things are a gift from you. She tried to recall if she had really read that in the Bible, and where was it so that she could study it later. *And look at Paul, Lord. He was the worst of the worst and wasn't thinking nothing about you when you called him out. If you can do that for Paul, I know you can do that for Jermaine.*

Suddenly she felt encouraged and began to smile to herself; then she frowned as she thought of the mess Eureen was about to get herself into by messing around with Derrick Kelly. *Now* that *is something I don't want to have no parts of . . . no more.* But she couldn't help but lick her lips when she thought about how fantastic the sex had been. Secretly, she was suddenly jealous that it would be just a matter of time before Eureen would soon be getting some of Derrick's good 'religion'.

Chapter Twenty-Seven

A full month had passed since Shamar had again left his wife and kids, thinking he was teaching Jasmine a lesson. On the contrary, since he had laid hands to her face, which was truly not negotiable for Jasmine, she'd already made preparations to divorce Shamar. He'd spent the first week of his departure not even trying to contact her or the girls; on the second week, he realized that she was ignoring his calls.

"What the hell?" he mumbled when her phone rang for the umpteenth time, then went to voice mail. "Jasmine! Your ass better answer this phone! You see my number popping up on the screen and you gonna sit up there and not take my calls. But I bet you got your greedy hands stuck out, waiting for my damn paycheck, don't you? If your ass don't call me back, you ain't getting shit!" he yelled, ending the call.

What the fuck wrong with her? Had he not been on the road a thousand miles away, he would have gone to the house and kicked the door in. With the press of his thumb, he phoned his mother, who answered after two rings.

"Ma, can you drive by the house and see what the hell goin' on over there? Jasmine ain't answered the phone all week."

"I done already told you that skank is tippin', but I guess you missing that pussy now, huh? You can get pussy anywhere; she sho taking dick from anywhere while you gone!" Cyreese fabricated.

Her words hurt his eardrums, not wanting to think such a thing of his wife. He had to admit that Jasmine was quite a prize, intellectually as well as physically, and he couldn't bear the thought of her caramel thighs wrapped around another man as he pounded her insides.

"Just go around there and look. If I come home and catch another nigga in my house, somebody gon' die!" he promised.

"You just need to leave her ass alone, Shamar. What you holdin' on for? She ain't doing nothing but spen'in' up your money and whoring in the streets. She done already told you to get gone. What you holdin' on for?" she asked a second time. "If she don't want you, there's plenty women that do! You out here working a good job, takin' care of your family and givin' them all kinda nice stuff, and her stank uppity ass too good to be grateful? To hell with her simple ass! You shoulda left her. Matta fact, she done sent a restraining order around here with your name on it."

"What? When?"

"It came yesterday. That's why I was calling you and telling you to call me back."

"What it say?" Shamar asked, becoming angrier.

"It say you better not take your ass within five hundred feet of her or the house," Cyreese informed him.

"How the hell they gon' tell me I can't go to my own house!" he yelled. In his rage behind the wheel, Shamar's foot became heavier on the gas. "And how she gonna keep me away from my girls like that! She out of her rabid-ass mind!"

"She can't keep them girls from you. What she decide to do with her life is her own damn business, but them girls is yours as much as they is hers. You need to go get 'em and bring 'em here so you can get custody of 'em and make her pay child support," Cyreese suggested.

"You gon' keep 'em for me while I'm on the road?" Shamar asked, slightly entertaining the thought.

"I damn near keep 'em all the time now," she lied again. "You gon' have to give me somethin' for keepin' them and getting 'em to school, and all that. God knows they need a momma who know how to be a momma."

"Let me call you back, Ma. These damn cops tryin'a pull me over," he huffed, taking note of the blue lights of two state police vehicles in his sideview mirror. He transitioned his foot over to the vehicle's brakes. While the truck slowed, his heart sped up from knowing that he was hauling tens of thousands of dollars of various hot goods.

"License and registration, please," the officer demanded.

Shamar stuttered, "Y-yes, sir," and then reached for his back pocket to dig out his wallet. He handed the officer his driver's license between two fingers; then he reached to the overhead visor, where he kept the truck's other paperwork.

"Where you headed?"

"Tennessee," he answered truthfully.

"What you hauling?"

"Honestly, I don't even know." The lie slid easily from Shamar's lips. "They just hitched the trailer onto the cab and told me where to take it."

"Mmm-hmm. So you don't know if you carrying dead bodies or school paper," the officer asked in a deadpan tone.

"No, sir, I don't."

"You mind opening up the back for me?"

Shamar felt his stomach drop, but he tried not to panic. *They don't know what the hell is hot and what is not,* he reminded himself. *Ain't like they got a manifest.*

With that thought, he hopped from the cab, went to the rear of the truck, and opened its doors, revealing pallets of boxes that gave no indication as to what was inside. The pallets were positioned so that a narrow aisleway had been created from the rear to the front of the trailer.

"I'm going to let my partner take a walk through there," the officer informed Shamar, signaling his partner to bring a drug-detecting canine from the back of an SUV. Growling and barking, the dog approached the truck, leaped up to the inside, and wasted no time sniffing its way around, but it returned with no positive results. As it jumped down back onto the pavement, the officer stated, "Be right back. I'm just gonna run some things through the system and see what we come up with. Anything you want to tell me before I do that?"

"N-no. Everything is everything," Shamar stated with a stutter. He was relieved when several minutes later he was simply handed a speeding ticket, which carried a hefty fine.

Once he pulled back onto the highway, he started to call Jasmine again to cuss her out about the restraining order, but he thought he'd better wait until he was safely off the road to avoid another stop, which maybe wouldn't go so smoothly.

Instead, he called one of his contacts, Dino.

"Look, man, I'ma get at you tomorrow. I got some heat on my ass right now, and I don't need no funny stuff."

"Word. Holla at me then. I got some shit lined up already and I can't have my flow fucked up," Dino replied.

"All right." No sooner than Shamar ended the call, he took a call from Jermaine, who dug into him just as quickly as he'd answered the phone.

"What the fuck you say to Jasmine, man?"

"What you talking 'bout, J?"

"Why you tell her that baby shit? She done told the whole damn world, nigga!"

"I ain't told Jasmine shit! I ain't even talked to that bitch in a month."

"Well, how the hell she know 'bout this got-damn baby? Your punk ass run your mouth too got-damn much! She telling people Tracey pregnant, and shit!"

"I don't know what the fuck you talkin' about. Maybe Tracey tellin' people that herself."

"Naw, nigga! This came from you!" Jermaine emphasized. "I'm tryin'a make a life with this woman and here you go fuckin' it up with your mouth! Your ass better hope Tracey don't put two and two together! I'm having a hard enough time dealing with this psycho bitch on the road without you helpin' her out. Shit!"

"Man, I ain't said shit to nobody—"

"Just shut the fuck up, Shamar. If Tracey find out about this pregnant bitch, you betta watch your got-damn back, nigga!" Jermaine threatened Shamar, and then clicked off the line.

"Nigga, you better keep your got-damn dick in your pants," Shamar mumbled, although he knew Jermaine had hung up already. "Blaming me for this bullshit. Ain't nobody tell you to be fuckin' these bitches out here. And if your ass stupid enough to get caught out there, then you get what you get, nigga."

And this was just another issue that he planned to cuss his wife out about when they spoke again.

Chapter Twenty-eight

Just as Derrick had planned, he was sinking his dick into Eureen's pussy at the end of their fourth date. He'd held his ground on the first three, being the perfect God-fearing gentleman, only showing her a slight bit of sexual attraction to start her fire on a slow burn. He even excused himself early one night, pretending not to be able to control himself.

"I'ma have to get up outta here," he'd said. "'Cause you looking so good tonight, I'm not sure if I'ma be able to stay saved tonight if I stay another five minutes." Derrick bit into his bottom lips and let his eyes roam her body; then he quickly looked away. "Lawd, ha' mercy."

Eureen giggled like a schoolgirl when he pecked her on the cheek and he said, "Have a good night, Sista. I gotta go so that I don't bring shame to the name of the Lord."

He'd disappeared in a flash, leaving Eureen feeling like the sexiest, most desirable woman on earth. He continued his same flirtatiously lustful but slyly respectful behavior for their next few encounters, until he recognized the crack in Eureen's flesh that told him it was time to move.

The next time Eureen and Derrick went out, Eureen dressed in a pair of thongs and a matching bra, along with a pair of thigh-high stockings, beneath her clothes. She wore a skirt slightly tighter and shorter than her usual style, paired with a blouse that fit tightly in the waist and enhanced her bustline. She'd become more skilled at walking in heels, and had bought a new pair of stilettos, which featured tiny black bows around the ankles. After a stop at the mall to have her makeup professionally done at a department store's cosmetic counter, she truly felt like a diva by the time she'd met Derrick for dinner that evening.

Eureen looked far different from the woman Monroe had been married to even six months before. Her skin tingled as Derrick placed his hand on the small of her back, escorting her into The Cheesecake Factory. Derrick recognized the smile that slid across her face. They stood as they waited for a table; and standing behind her, he wrapped his arms gently around her waist.

He leaned down a bit and whispered in her ear, "You look so amazing tonight."

"Thank you, Derrick." She blushed.

"No, thank you, because it's truly an honor to be in your presence tonight, and to be able to spend the evening with such an incredible, intriguing, and sexy woman."

Eureen couldn't remember the last time she'd been called sexy; and now that she thought about it, she realized that maybe it was the first time.

Instead of sitting across from her in the booth, Derrick slid beside Eureen and gazed into her eyes. When he leaned in slowly for a kiss, Eureen allowed their lips to meet. When they did, the softness of Derrick's lips enveloping her own created a sizzle that shimmied down her spine and turned into a puddle of cream in her panties. She crossed her legs, trying to hide her delight, but Derrick took notice.

Yeah, that pussy is mine! He cleared his throat and took a sip of water. "Don't be offended, Eureen, but I think it's better for the both of us that I sit over here tonight." He slid away from her, taking his seat on the other side. He commented, "My, my, my. God sho is good."

It wasn't long after dinner that Eureen willingly found herself lying on her back across Derrick's bed, with her legs spread wide open. She still had on her heels, stockings, thongs, and bra, but her skirt and blouse had been discarded. Derrick had dropped his head between her thighs, teasing her pussy with his mouth through her panties. She arched her back and ground her hips into his face, completely turned on by the sound of him sucking on the fabric of her thong, and his tongue teasing the perimeter of her lower lips. *Monroe ain't never break me off like this!* she thought. She grinned inside, pretending to be one of the women she'd seen when she'd sneakily watched a few of Monroe's porn videos. She wiggled her hips trying to mimick as best she could what flashed in her mind from her memory.

"Derrick," Eureen moaned, "ahh, baby!"

"Mmm-hmm," he moaned back; then when he felt like he'd teased her long enough, he moved her panties and absorbed her clit into his lips and circled it with his tongue, sending Eureen into a wild frenzy. Her hands clasped on his head while Derrick worked a miracle on her pussy that had her crying out in pleasure she'd never known.

"Mmm," he moaned again, letting her know he was enjoying every minute of her pussy being in his face. It hadn't even been a full minute before Eureen's body locked, then oozed a hot liquid all over his face. "Ahh-hhhh! Derrick!" she cried, desperately grabbing for the sheets, comforter, pillows, and anything else she could get her hands on.

While she was yet trembling, Derrick eased his way up her body, ran the head of his dick over her clit, causing her to arch her back, then slowly circled his hips, thrusting inside her body an inch at a time.

"Oh, baby, hit that pussy!" she begged, blowing up Derrick's ego.

"Yeah! You like that religion, baby?" he whispered in her ear. "You liking how that feel?"

"Fuck me, Derrick!" she panted, matching his movements, meeting his downstroke with an upstroke. "Work this pussy over! Show me what I been missing!"

Oh yeah, I got this bitch cussin' now. Shit! She gon' fuck around and make me bust a nut.

At her command, Derrick circled his hips a bit faster and thrust more deeply as Eureen tightened her pussy around him. He was surprised that she was easily able to accommodate the full length of his dick; and when he realized he could go as fast and as hard as he wanted, he unleashed on her with a wild fury that had previously put women in the hospital. By now, most women would have been screaming out in pain and begging him to stop, but not Eureen.

"Yeah! Lay that pipe, baby! Give me all that dick!" she coached, encouraging him to thrust harder. "Fuck the hell outta me. Save me with that religion! Get this pussy like you want it."

Without warning, Derrick quickly withdrew, sending Eureen into a gasping withdrawal response, but he flipped her onto her stomach and mounted her back.

"Yessss! Fuck me doggie style, baby!" she screamed. "Oh yeah!" Eureen arched her back like a cat, working her ring of pussy around Derrick's dick while he held her ass apart and pumped furiously. "Sign your name on this shit, Derrick! It's yours, baby! Sign it! Sign your name in cursive."

"Oh shit!" Derrick growled, having never been invited to sign a pussy with his dick. He imagined using his dick to form cursive letters, which forced him to come hard in a matter of seconds. After being frozen in his last thrust for several seconds, he collapsed on Eureen's back, panting for air.

"Shit, baby!" he whispered. "Damn!"

Within minutes, they both drifted off to sleep, but Derrick was delighted when Eureen slurping on his dick awakened him later. She covered its head with her mouth and worked her tongue around his shaft, making him pump his hips forward.

Damn! She know how to suck a dick too? She done flipped on a brother.

Derrick just lay back, enjoying the view of his dick sliding in and out of her mouth; but he stopped short of coming, although he did want to see her swallow. Instead, he coaxed her upward and forward, taking her titties in his mouth one at a time.

"Mmm, I love that shit, baby," he moaned. "That's how you wake a man up in the morning." He pulled her up even more until she sat straddled across his face; then he mumbled, "Let me pay you back, baby."

He pulled her hips down and darted his tongue in and around her pussy, licking and sucking while she squirmed, wiggled, and moaned.

"Derrick! Oh, baby, eat that pussy! Yeah, eat that pussy up!"

He filled his mouth with pussy until she came twice; then she mounted him backward, again giving him a tantalizing view of her ass as she worked him over.

"That's some good fuckin' right there," he cried.

He almost lost his mind when Eureen dipped even lower, first taking his balls in her mouth, but then repeatedly slid her tongue down into his crack and fluttered it over his asshole. This was something she'd caught a glimpse of on the night she had seen Monroe fucking and being fucked by a multitude of people.

"Don't stop, baby," he chanted. "Don't stop!"

While she licked, she used her hand to pump his dick until he popped like an overinflated balloon, spilling cum all over his belly. A slew of cusswords left his lips.

"Damn, girl. I'ma have to take you to dinner more often." He paused for a few seconds to catch his breath. "You done fucked a brother up; do you know that?" Eureen grinned at him, glad that he was pleased. "I mean, you done fucked a brother *up!*"

And when Derrick showed up at Tracey's doorstep later that day, he expected the same level of service. He had been surprised to hear from her a few weeks back, but was more than willing to take her up on her no-strings-attached, for-old-time's-sake offer for a good night's sex session which easily turned into an every night affair since Jermaine was on the road.

Chapter Twenty-nine

Shamar was beside himself with grief and envy not being able to talk to, see, or have sex with his wife, and even more so when he thought that someone else was dipping and licking his puddin'. He had been slapped with the divorce papers so quickly that it made him spin and fall, just as quickly as Jasmine had done that night he'd hit her.

When he was home, he did nothing more than sit on Cyreese's couch and listen to The Temptations' "I Wish It Would Rain."

Witnessing her son's stupidity sickened his mother.

"You're disgustin', Shamar. That girl has moved on with her life and she ain't thinkin' 'bout you, so quit makin' yo'self look like a damn fool!"

"Stay out of my business, Momma," he snapped. "It's all your fault, anyway! I'm still in love with Jasmine, and nothin' can change that—not even you!"

"You gonna mess around and get yo'self in some shit, boy! You know that girl probably got another man for real by now! You gon' end up getting the shit beat out of you; then your ass is gonna be in a damn hospital somewhere!"

"You don't know what you're talkin' 'bout! Jasmine ain't gonna put another man over our kids. She ain't that kind of woman!"

Despite divorce proceedings, as far as he was concerned, Jasmine and his daughters were still a part of him, which he refused to let go.

He ignored his mother and continued calling Jasmine's cell and home phone number with no success of speaking with her.

Four days later, his persistence finally paid off.

"I've been tryin' to call you for four days, baby. Why didn't you answer the phone?"

"What is it, Shamar?" The tone of her voice suggested she wasn't in a humorous mood.

"You ain't still mad at me, are you? Sweetheart, everyone makes mistakes, and I—"

"I'm not your 'sweetheart' or your 'baby,' so save that shit!"

"Aw, girl, you're trippin'," he replied, snickering.

"What do you want, Shamar?"

"I—I just wanted to see you and my girls, that's all. Baby, I really think we should put that shit behind us and move forward. See what I'm sayin'? I 'pologize for the stupid mistakes I made, but I don't deserve to be punished for life, baby."

"Quit calling me 'baby,' because I'm not. I've moved on with my life; and in doing so, I've put you so far out of my mind, it's like you don't even exist anymore."

"So you're sayin' you got somebody else?"

Little did he know, but his mother was eavesdropping.

"That ain't none of your damn business."

"So you're givin' up my pussy, huh?"

"Boy, please. *Hel-lo,* we're divorced, if you forgot. It ain't shit over here with your name on it, except these two kids."

"Who gettin' my pussy, Jasmine? I'll kill the muthafucka who's gettin' my got-damn pussy!" He was on fire.

"Hold on a minute; my friend is trying to call me," she teased, putting him on hold for a few moments.

He assumed she was referring to the man she was now fucking as her "friend"; therefore he changed his demeanor to calm, once she clicked back over.

"Listen, baby, it's all good. I just want to see my girls—that's all."

"Hold on and I'll ask them if they're interested in seeing you—the man who slapped their momma."

Convicted by his guilt, Shamar pounded the wall. He was grateful that she at least talked to him, but that just wasn't enough. Emotions of jealousy haunted him, but he strongly felt that if he was allowed the opportunity to be in her presence, he could iron out the wrinkles and rectify things.

Summer and Winter sprang up with joy upon hearing their father wanted to see them; it had been well over two months since they'd seen and talked to him last.

"Yes, Daddy's coming over! Yes!" they shouted in unison.

Jasmine returned to the phone and told Shamar he could visit the girls for a little while. He wasted no time, grabbing his car keys and leaving out of the house. Making it to the home where he'd resided for so many years, Shamar stood nervously at the front door. He felt funny about having to ring the doorbell, but he no longer had a key.

Little did he know, but Jasmine was observing him through an upstairs bedroom window, staring in disgust. She hesitated about alerting the girls to his presence, wanting to stare at the man she'd loved since junior high school, the man who'd taken her virginity, the man she'd married and took care of for so many years, and the man who'd beat her ass.

I should blow his fucking brains out! Better yet, I should fuck 'im, then cry rape and send his ass to jail!

Finally she heard the chime of the bell, which summoned the girls. They all headed downstairs to open the door.

"Daddy! Daddy! Daddy!" shouted the girls, delighted to see their father.

Winter grabbed his waist, and Summer reached for his neck, but Shamar's focus was on Jasmine.

"Hey, sweetheart," he said to Jasmine, who just rolled her eyes in silence. His presence sickened her.

His daughters attacked him with a series of questions about his lengthy absence, making him realize how big a fool he had been.

"Let's watch a movie, Daddy! Can we, Daddy? Can we?" Winter suggested.

"Yeah, Daddy, let's watch a movie," Summer echoed, pulling him toward the den, where the large flat-screen TV was located.

"Today is your day, girls. It's whatever you two wanna do." He desperately wanted Jasmine to join them. With his eyes, he pleaded with her, but he knew better than to ask.

Jasmine returned upstairs and wasted no time calling Deja.

"Can't you see he still loves you?" Deja said. "Surrounding himself by you and his daughters not only makes him realize how much he screwed up, but it also comforts him. He's aiming to win back your love and confidence, and these are his first steps. He's probably afraid to make any direct, aggressive moves toward you, fearing you'll reject him. But because you were his first, and he was your first, he'll always think he'll have a chance to win you back."

"Yeah, whatever!" Jasmine spat out. "The only way I'll take him back is if you take crackhead Garnell back!" She guffawed. "That nigga put his hands on me; therefore he don't deserve me."

"Just like Garnell's lying, cheating, married-with-children, drug-addicted ass didn't deserve me," Deja stated. "But seriously, though, you think it's something you won't ever get over? I mean, Garnell and I wasn't married, but you talking about your husband and kids. You've gotta learn to let go and let God in. Shamar probably is planning on askin' you to remarry him."

"Re-what? You must be out of your mind! As long as I'm black and breathing, I'll never give Shamar the time of the day, ever again, and I mean that! The only things we have in common are the girls! He demonstrated just how much he appreciated me and the things I did for him by laying me on the floor."

"Yeah, but something it took years to build doesn't just dissipate overnight or in a few months. And you can't act like that high rent ain't breaking your back."

"Whatever. Anyhow," she said, walking downstairs, wanting Shamar to hear, "I'm going to the club tonight and get my life on."

"Girl, you need to quit. You haven't been to a club in your life, but I know what you're doing. You're tryin' to make him jealous by saying that, aren't you? He must be nearby."

"You know it," she admitted. "Anyway, he's picking me up at eight on the nose, so I really need to start getting myself together."

Shamar shot her an angry glare.

Jasmine made her way upstairs, smiling, thrilled by the bamboozled look on Shamar's face.

I've gotta do sumthin'—sumthin' that will tear his yellow ass apart! I may not ever fully pay him back, but I've got to do sumthin'. Sumthin' effective enough to make his ass break down and cry. Sumthin' he'll never forget. It's payback time; and as they say, payback is a mutha!

She took the next hour and a half to primp and fit into the tightest, shortest dress she could find, along with a pair of boots that had a three-inch heel. When she came back downstairs, Shamar was lying with a girl under each arm; he was pretending to be asleep.

If I pretend I'm asleep, maybe she might let me spend the night. Then I'll put this dick on her and change her mind about goin' out. If I can just eat her pussy or put this thang on her, I've got her.

"Wake up, girls! Wake up so I can drop y'all off at the babysitter's. And, Shamar, you can go back to your momma's house."

"Can we just stay here with Daddy?" Summer asked, stretching as she stood.

"Why you dressed up like that? You didn't dress up like that when we were together."

"A special occasion."

He snapped at her. "A special occasion? What kinda sh . . . mess is that?" he asked, quickly changing his word choice in the presence of the girls.

"I'm single and I'm goin' out."

"Goin' where?"

"Are we not divorced?" she directed at her ex-husband. "Y'all go wash your faces, get your overnight bags, and put your shoes on," she said to the girls.

Once the girls were out of the room, Shamar continued his tirade. "Those papers don't mean a damn thing to me! As far as I'm concerned, you and my girls still belong to me!"

"Well, we'll see about that."

"That's fucked up, Jasmine. That's fucked up!"

"It's what you made it—that's what it is. You can come see the girls tomorrow, if you wish, but I've gotta get goin'."

"Who you goin' with?"

"Excuse me?"

"Who you goin' with? You heard me!"

"None of your business."

He stood for a few seconds, fuming, but Jasmine's firm stance told him he wouldn't win. Nearing rage, he grabbed his keys and headed to the door. "That's some bullshit!"

"And if you ain't off my block in the next minute, I'm calling the cops, so don't get no ideas," she warned.

Five minutes later, she peeled out of her sexy clothes, took the girls for ice cream, returned to the house, parked her car in the garage, and went to bed alone.

The following week, Shamar changed his driving schedule, to take only short-distance runs, which allowed him to be home more, particularly on the weekends, so that he'd be in a better position to ease his way back into Jasmine and his girls' lives.

Shamar made it his business to visit his daughters as frequently as he could; but, secretly, his aim was to spy on Jasmine. He wanted to find out if she talked excessively over the phone and exploited him in any form or fashion; did she have an admirer or several men she talked with over the phone; whether a man would show up on her doorstep; whether she would give Shamar a green light for at least a quickie; or whether she hinted around to put the past behind them, possibly remarry, and move forward together. He was dismayed to see that Jasmine treated him as if he didn't exist.

Shamar apologized to Jasmine each time he came over, but she would always respond silently. She would roll her eyes, turn up her nose, and walk away, obviously thinking, *Kiss my ass!*

"Teach that punk a lesson!" Tracey angrily said, empathizing with her friend. "You're a betta woman than me, 'cause I wouldn't even have him around me, regardless of the kids! If he hit me, then every time I saw him, I'd be attacking his punk ass! He ain't just comin' over to see the girls; the nigga ain't doin' nuttin' but tryin' to see what you're doin'. I know what'll really rock his world; start goin' out every weekend and give a couple men your cell and your home phone number. Watch what happens when they call you, and Shamar is around. Keep him wonderin', girl, keep his mind goin'. I had to do a nigga like that before, and it works. I'm tellin' you, it works. The thought of another man getting what he thinks belongs to him will drive that muthafucka crazy. Anyhow, the best way to get over a nigga is to replace him with another one."

"Sounds like a plan," Jasmine replied, admiring the suggestion. "Thanks, Tracey. Phase one is about to go into full effect."

"Don't say it if you're gonna get weak. You've gotta learn to mean what you say, and say what you mean."

"I got this."

They talked awhile longer, then broke the connection.

Afterward, Jasmine began thinking, *Tracey's right. I've got to make that bastard feel what I felt! I want him to feel a woman's wrath in a nonviolent but effective manner! Kiss my ass, Shamar!*

Wasting no time, she immediately initiated phase one. She unplugged the phone and went into her act in Shamar's presence. She pretended to be setting up a date with a man. During her fake phone call, she giggled and appeared happy; and she even went as far as to say, "I'm single and free, and it's been a while since I last had sex."

Shamar's stomach literally turned, and jealousy began brewing. This pleased Jasmine, confirming she was doing an effective job.

He suddenly kissed the kids good-bye and went to his mother's house, where he instantly called Jasmine.

"Jasmine, I just want you to know that I'm sorry for—"

She cut him off. "Don't bother coming by tomorrow. The girls are spending the night with their friends, and I'm going to the club."

"To a club!" he shot back.

"Do I detect an attitude? If I'm not mistaken, we're no longer married. So what's the problem? Anyhow, we won't be back until late Sunday evening."

Her calmness agitated him even more.

"You're tryin' to pay me back, aren't you?"

"You're the furthest thing from my mind, Shamar. Believe that."

"Men go to clubs to meet one-night stands, and women go to clubs to get laid by a new dick!"

"And what's your point?"

"You know what the hell my point is! You tryin'a get fucked. I know what's up!"

"Again, what's your point, Shamar? If I want to fuck two men a day, at the same damn time, you ain't got shit to do with it."

"So you're just gonna give up my pussy to a stranger and disrespect me, yourself, and the kids, right?"

She hung up in his face.

When he called back seconds later, Jasmine added to her bag of tricks.

"I'll be ready at eight, sweetheart. My ex is trippin', so I'm runnin' a little behind; but I wouldn't miss this date for anything in the world. I'm so excited! My panties are wet!" She giggled.

"This is me, Jasmine," Shamar snarled.

"Aw, damn! I'm sorry, Shamar," she replied, tickled by her deception. "Gotta go. I'm runnin' late." She hung up in his face again, triggering him to throw the receiver at the wall.

"Bitch! I'll kill you and that muthafucka!"

"You bet' not break nothing in this damn house! I don't care how much shit you done bought," Cyreese barked. "You're stupid, weak, naïve as hell! Why are you goin' crazy over a got-damn woman, especially an uppity bitch like that, when they come a dime a dozen?"

"Momma," he said, pacing the floor, "I ain't in the mood for hearin' your bullshit! I shouldn't have listened to you in the first place; then I wouldn't be in this mess!"

"Lower your damn voice, boy! Don't blame me; blame your got-damn self! Who the hell do you think you are? I may be Southern Baptist and sixty-six, but I'll put my foot deep up your pretty ass if you keep throwin' those disrespectful comments my way! I didn't put a gun to your head and make you do what you did; I was only tryin' to look out for your best interest!"

"Well, good lookin' out, Momma, good lookin' out, and thanks for screwin' up my life!"

"Listen, boy. You can't stop that woman from fuckin' another man! Ain't a got-damn thing you can do about it! That's her pussy and she's gonna do what she want with it, includin' goin' to a club and fuckin' a stranger, if that's what she wants to do!"

He frowned.

"You've been eavesdroppin', haven't you?"

"You don't pay no bills around here, so you can't tell me what to do or what not to do in my got-damn house! If you want some privacy, then there's the fuckin' door!"

"I shoulda known your nosy ass was listenin'. I shoulda known! You the one who put me against my wife! You did this, Momma! You did this! I hate you right now, so do yourself a favor and get the hell outta my face!" he yelled, doing the unthinkable and shoving his mother.

She stumbled backward. Her eyes were as wide as saucers as she fell, seated, onto her recliner. Right away, her eyes filled with hurtful and angry tears.

"You done forgot whose house you livin' in! I gave birth to and raised such an ignorant and pathetic child. I don't believe this shit! I fuckin' don't believe it. I got a trick for your high-yellow ass!"

With that, she went to her bedroom and slammed the door. She used her cell phone to call the police department.

Shamar stormed out of his room, grabbed the house phone, and constantly called Jasmine, leaving messages.

"Jasmine, I just wanted you to know that I'm sorry for what I did and for hurtin' you. Please don't cheat on me, baby. Please don't do it. I still love you, and I'm madly in love with you, baby. I want us to get remarried and start all over; all I need is another chance, baby. I just need one more chance. I want my family back. I miss you and my girls something terrible. We've got too many years invested in one another, baby, for it to end this way. I'm sorry. I was wrong for doin' what I did. I'm sorry, baby. I'm sorry." He began crying. "Every single day, I regret what I did, but I can't erase what I did, baby. The only thing I can do is try and make it up by makin' things right between us again. Please forgive me, Jasmine. This shit is killin' me, baby. It's fuckin' killin' me! Please don't allow another man to come between us, and please don't give my pussy up. Please don't, baby! Please don't!"

His words didn't mean a thing to Jasmine as she laughed, getting a kick out of listening to him beg and cry.

Shamar spent his weekend drinking and smoking weed, which he had started as a result of being stressed about the divorce. He was drowning himself with regrets and distress.

Chapter Thirty

"Eureen told me you done put that Chinese stick on her," Tracey said, taking a slow ride on Derrick's dick. She had cleansed herself with an alum douche that morning, making her pussy as tight as a virgin's, causing Derrick's face to contort into a number of expressions as she rolled her body on his. "Do her pussy feel this good?"

"Hell naw! You got the bomb-ass pussy right here, girl."

"Mmm-hmm. Can she work it like this, baby?" She circled her hips a little more, easing farther down on his dick, while pinching her own titties.

"Hell no, Tracey! Damn, girl! Work that shit!" he shouted out.

"She said you told her she fucked you up," Tracey said knowingly. "I thought only I did that."

"I had to tell her something, baby, to get some money. You know how that shit work." He grimaced in pleasure. "You act like you jealous or something."

"Suppose I am? How you gonna make it up to me?"

"How you gonna make up letting Jermaine fuck my pussy? You wearing his fucking ring on your finger, and shit. You think I like that?" Derrick whispered back, now holding Tracey by the hips and thrusting upward.

"Fuck me like you hate it then," she replied.

"You think I like sharing my shit with him? You think I like the idea of him sticking his dick where I eat," he asked, watching Tracey's eyes roll in the back of her head. "Spin it around and bring that pussy up here," Derrick ordered.

Tracey wasted no time moving into a sixty-nine and dropping her mouth on Derrick's dick.

"Yeah, baby, suck on this religious dick!" he mumbled before he lifted his head into Tracey's pussy. "Mmm-mmm!" he moaned. "Yeah, this my pussy right here."

He lapped greedily, while Tracey sucked and moaned wildly.

"Lick my asshole," he told her. "Oh shit! That's it, baby! Ahhhhhh."

The speed of her tongue flicking across his ass made him gobble up her pussy faster, until she came in his face.

"Do Jermaine do you like that, baby?"

"Yeah, he do that shit!" she answered, panting. "You gotta do it twice to outdo him," she said, wanting more. "You used to fucking around with them hard-pressed women, like Eureen, who will take any old thing. This is a grown-woman pussy right here. Don't come over here with that little-boy shit, thinking you gonna satisfy me."

"Oh, hell naw!" In an instant, Derrick flipped Tracey on her back and put his dick in her so deep that she screamed. "Say that shit again! Say it again!" he growled. "Whose pussy is this?"

"It's yours, DK! This your got-damn pussy!" Tracey spread her legs as far as she could and let him fuck her for all he could get.

"Who rule this shit?"

"You do, baby. This your kingdom! Get it, baby!" she yelled. "Hit the top!"

"Shit, you making me come, girl," he said, looking at the pleasingly pained expression on her face. "Shit!" he yelled, releasing his load, then easing into a satisfied smile for a few minutes. "Whew, that shit was good." He sighed.

"Yeah, it was, baby," Tracey agreed, lying against his chest in Jermaine's bed.

"You know I missed this pussy, don't you?" he said, sliding his fingers between Tracey's lips and tickling her clit.

"Yeah, I know, but you know I was tryin'a get myself together. You didn't want to marry me, and I thought I found somebody who cared about me a little bit."

"I did wanna marry you. I just wasn't ready yet. I kept tryin'a tell you that I had to get some things together first. And, obviously, you still think Jermaine care about you 'cause you still got on his ring," Derrick said, lifting Tracey's hand up.

"That's 'cause I haven't figured out a way to fuck him up real good yet," Tracey admitted.

"You don't think laying up in his bed with me is enough?" A chuckle escaped Derrick's lips.

"Nope. I'ma hurt his ass just like he hurt me. Did I ever show you the pictures?"

"No, you didn't."

"Be right back." Tracey got up and walked naked out of the room without a care. She returned a few minutes later with the envelope that had been sent weeks before while she did Eureen's hair. "Look at this."

"I can't look at that, for looking at all that ass you got." He grinned with lust.

"Whatever, DK!" She giggled, shoving the packaging into his hand.

Derrick pulled the papers out, which included a handwritten letter and photos of Jermaine, Heather, and Alexis lying in bed, naked and tangled together. It was hard to tell if there was a fourth person holding a camera, or if the camera had just been set up, but it wasn't so hard to tell that Jermaine was eating pussy, squeezing titties, and getting his dick sucked by the two gorgeous Latino women. Another picture showed both women naked and showcased large, pregnant bellies and huge smiles.

"He done got these bitches pregnant?"

"That's what this letter says."

Derrick fished through the photos and glanced at the letter, which was written in Spanish:

Jermaine,

Espero que no creo que jodido jugar con usted! Cuando estos bebés hasta aquí es mejor que tengas tu mierda juntos, o nos vienen a por ti. Este poco de dinero que se nos da parar por aquí no es suficiente para cuidar a dos bebés. Puede actuar como estos bebés no es tu es todo lo que quiere - pero vamos a tener algo por el culo!

"What the hell does this say?" he asked, crinkling his brows.

"I typed all of it into Google Translate the day I pulled it out of the mail, and it says, 'I hope you don't think we fuckin' playing with you! When these babies get here, you better have your shit together, or we coming for you. This little bit of money you be giving us stopping through here ain't enough to take care of two babies. You can act like these babies ain't yours all you want—but we gonna have something for your ass.'" Tracey read from the back of the paper where she'd written the translation.

"Damn. Cheating and leaving a trail." Derrick shook his head. "So this nigga had to fuck up like this to bring you back to me, huh?"

"We ain't back together, DK. You was cheatin' too."

"I had the sense to get a damn vasectomy, though, so I ain't making babies all over the place. And second, you was fuckin' everyone who was buying you dinner too, before you tried to get superholy."

"And I'm still tryin'a be superholy. Your big dick just happens to be my weakness. I just can't believe I tried to do the right thing and still got burned. I knew something was wrong when he said he ain't want nothing to do with God, and I had been praying for a sign, and if this ain't one, I don't know what is," Tracey revealed. "And it didn't make sense to me then, but this is what Jasmine must have been talking about when she was telling people I was pregnant. Jermaine must have told Shamar he got somebody pregnant, and Shamar must have told Jasmine, and Jasmine thought it was me. "

"You shoulda just stayed with me in the first place. I had a plan."

"What's the plan now, especially since you got Eureen sprung?"

"You know what that's about, baby. I'm in it for the benefits."

"Well, you know I don't like to share. So whatever benefit package you after, you better hurry up and get it," she demanded.

"What about you? What you tryin'a get out of this deal? Look to me like you fuckin' this nigga for free." Derrick shrugged.

"Naw, I'ma make this house mine. I just gotta set some stuff up right."

While Tracey spoke, the home phone rang. She reached across Derrick's chest to grab it; then she rolled over on her back as she answered.

"Hey, baby," Jermaine cooed in her ear.

"Hey, Jermaine." She rolled her eyes, still looking at the photos that his twin lovers had sent.

"What you doing?" he asked.

"Laying in bed, wishing you was here to eat this pussy the way you do."

"Mmm! Girl, you gonna make my dick hard. Why don't you touch it for me then?"

"Okay," she answered as Derrick slid down her body, landing his face in her hot spot. "Mmm, baby, just like that," she said to both Jermaine and Derrick. "Do it nice and slow."

"You miss this tongue, baby," Jermaine asked as Derrick did the work.

"Yeah, I miss that tongue. Stick it in me. Lick my insides."

Derrick followed her commands, making her gasp.

"You working that dick for me?" Tracey managed to ask.

"Hold on, baby, let me get some baby oil. Hold on! I ain't know you was gonna be ready like this tonight." Jermaine returned a few seconds later. "Yeah, I got it now, baby. I'm pumping this dick for you. Pinch them titties for me."

"Sssssss!" Tracey responded to both men. "Mmm, that feels so good. I'ma have to put you on speakerphone, baby, so I can work my hands."

"Do what you gotta do. Get it right."

Tracey leaned to the side a bit and pressed a button on the cordless base; then she planted her hands on Derrick's head. "Yeah, now I can do something," she said.

"Tickle it for me, baby. Let me hear you moan."

"Ahhhhhh," Tracey cried out, pumping her pussy in Derrick's face.

"Yeah, I like that! Feed it to me, baby. Feed me my brown sugar."

"Oh, baby! You makin' me come already," she said, opening wider to Derrick.

"I'ma come right with you, baby. I'm right behind you; I'm right behind you," Jermaine grunted. "Uhh, uhh, uhhhhhh. Shiiiiiiit!" he huffed as Tracey let out a satisfying moan of her own.

"That felt good, baby." She winked at Derrick. "I'ma need a little bit more of that in about an hour.

Derrick bit his lower lip and smiled.

"Well, call me back when you ready and I'll give you a little more. Have that big vibratin' dick out next time, so I can hit them walls," Jermaine told her.

"Mmm, I'ma love a piece of that big dick," she cooed as Derrick climbed on top of her and slid inside. "Yesss! I'ma love that! I'll call you back in a little while."

"All right, baby. Keep my pussy warm for me."

"I will, babe," Tracey said, ending the call with the press of a button.

"No, I will!" Derrick corrected as he motioned his hips, sending Tracey on her way to ecstasy.

The next morning, Tracey rolled out of bed, still groggy, but satisfied from the night before. She showered and got ready for church.

Derrick had already slipped away, needing to head out early to pick Eureen up for church, but he promised Tracey he'd make it up to her with some of Eureen's cash.

While she showered, she prayed, asking God to forgive her for once again sleeping with Derrick.

He is my weakness, Lord. And I did try to break it off—but why couldn't you have sent me somebody for real? I mean, do you want me to be with Derrick? At least he love you a little bit. I'm tired of always being on the losing end. I'm wrong if I have sex, and I still get screwed over if I don't. She sighed. *I don't know what to do. Please just have mercy on me 'til I get myself together.*

An hour and a half later, she slid into the pew beside Jasmine and Deja just as praise and worship ended, and Pastor Gardner stood to give a special announcement.

"I just wanted to let everyone here know that I had a chance to visit with Brother Garnell Sutton yesterday, and God is showing him mercy every day. I was recently informed that a few months back he was jumped by a gang as he did some work for his job out in L.A. He has been in the hospital ever since. He's suffered massive injuries, including several stab wounds, fractured ribs, broken bones, damage to his spine, and a fractured skull."

Deja gasped internally as Pastor Gardner recited Garnell's injuries. Although she had begged her father to tell her what he'd done to him, he refused to tell her—again reminding her that the less she knew, the better off she would be.

"Daddy, please tell me you didn't kill him," she'd begged.

"If he dead, I didn't leave him dead" was all he would say. "Anybody could have come along later and shot him. He mighta been hit by a car, overdosed, or whatever. Last I saw him, he was living and breathing. Now don't ask me about it again, hear?" His tone left no room for a rebuttal.

Sitting in the congregation, Deja felt extremely guilty and responsible for his injuries.

"He has a long way to go, but he is making improvement," Pastor Gardner continued to share. "And we need to keep him and his family in prayer, saints. His wife is here today, having come all the way from South Carolina. I'm going to ask her to stand and come forth.

We just want to have prayer with her and these precious babies that God will continue to heal her husband."

Deja, Tracey, and Jasmine couldn't whip their heads around fast enough to see the woman who would identify herself by standing as Garnell's wife. The woman stood five foot eight, weighed 135 pounds, and looked like a supermodel, despite having children, whom she held by the hands as she walked forward. She wore a sophisticated black wrap dress, black-and-gray snakeskin stilettos, with matching accessories, and tasteful jewelry. Her hair was pulled back neatly in a bun, which gave her a classic and elegant look.

Deja felt like a troll in comparision, having gained a few pound and missed a few touch-ups over the past two months.

"Wife! He was married?" Tracey whispered.

"Yeah, I'll tell you about it later," Deja said, ducking her head to blot away a tear, still feeling very hurt and violated by Garnell's deception. She mostly kept her head down for the remainder of the service.

"Why didn't you tell us?" Jasmine started to ask as soon as the three of them piled into Jasmine's car, where they could talk freely. Shamar had the girls that morning, so they weren't around to listen to grown-folks conversation.

"I was too embarrassed," Deja admitted, shrugging. "I just felt so stupid for falling for him the way I did, believing he was single and all this other crap, giving him a chance after he told me he had a record. Y'all know how we laugh at people."

"But we're your friends," Tracey offered. "And we need to be there when we need each other. I mean, here I am thinking my man is being faithful to me, and he done got two women preganant on the road!" Tracey angrily spilled the news.

"Shut your mouth!" Jasmine slammed her hand against the steering wheel. "So Jermaine *is* having a baby!"

"Yep. Not just one, but two, and not with me."

"Oh my God! What did you say to him?" Deja asked.

"I haven't said anything yet. I've been too busy trying to plan some revenge."

"'Vengeance is mine,' saith the Lord,'" Deja quickly responded.

"Yeah, his and your daddy's, huh?" Jasmine threw in. "We all know that Garnell didn't get done in by no gang. Your daddy put a hurtin' on that boy that he might not ever fully recover from."

Deja gulped and swallowed. "It's not like I told my daddy to beat him up."

"Then what did you tell him for? You knew that as soon as you told him what was up, he was gonna beat Garnell's ass—I mean, tail. I'm tryin' not to cuss so bad on Sundays," Tracey said, giggling. "But you told him, anyway."

"Yeah, and I regret doing that, because I feel so guilty about it. There isn't a day that goes by that I don't ask God to forgive me for moving ahead of Him and taking things into my own hands. I probably would have lost my mind if Garnell would have died. And those kids would have been left without a daddy."

"Pssh! Girl, please, they was already left without a daddy, 'cause their daddy left them!" Jasmine shot back. "Let Shamar mess around and get killed out here in these streets. He the one left me and the girls. We didn't leave him. Then he gonna put his hands on me too? Shooooo! Girl, I wish I had a daddy like yours. Shamar mighta been pushing up daisies right now. He 'bout to go crazy right now, thinking I'm seeing some-body."

"Jasmine, you're playing a dangerous game," Deja warned. "You need to stop before somebody get hurt."

"He wasn't thinking that when he knocked her on the floor and left her when their rent went up," Tracey interjected.

"He come calling me the other night, talking 'bout 'You made it back, huh? Was it good? Did you have a good time ridin' and suckin' his dick?'" Jasmine laughed, mocking her ex-husband. "I told him it was so good that I wanted to slap his momma!"

All three ladies laughed.

"Well, you know what they say. Don't ask a question if you can't handle the answer."

"I know that's right, Tracey," Jasmine replied.

"Girl, you gonna have that man out in the streets chasing a ghost." Deja chuckled.

Little did they know, but that was exactly what Shamar was doing.

Leaving the girls with his mom, Shamar jumped into his car in a rage, hitting the streets and driving like a NASCAR racer, talking to himself out loud.

"That's my pussy, and I ain't gonna just lay down and accept anotha nigga takin' mine! I don't give a damn about a funky-ass piece of paper with divorce on it. That's still my pussy!"

He drove to "Fruit Town" in Compton and met with his cousin, a reputable Blood gang member/high roller named P.C., in order to get a gun.

"Be careful with this, Blood," P.C. advised him. "You know I just did eleven straight, so you didn't get this from me. Know what I'm sayin'?"

"I'll ride my own, homie, I got this. Need you to front me a hundred pack 'til payday too."

"The last three niggas who told me they'll ride their own are the same muthafuckas who testified against me to get me those eleven years."

"I don't get down like that, P.C., I'm family. Blood is thicker than water."

"Family is the muthafuckas you gotta worry about, but like I said, Blood, family or not, you didn't get this heat or this dope from me."

"I got this, P.C., don't trip."

Shamar took the complimentaries and peeled out, distracted for a few seconds as he dialed Jasmine's cell phone number. When her voice mail picked up, he didn't hesitate to leave a message.

"I love you, Jasmine, that's real talk, baby, real talk. I'll kill a muthafucka over you, and don't think I'm just frontin'! Don't make me do sumthin' stupid, 'cause I will. You know I ain't neva been to jail or neva had a gun, but I got one now and don't make me do nothin' stupid! When it comes to you and my girls, I'll do what I gotta do, and don't give a fuck about circumstances! I apologized to you thousands of times and all I want is my family back—that's all I want. I know my actions caused you to fuck another nigga, but I'll forgive you for that. Just please forgive me, baby, please! I'm still in love with you, Jasmine. That's all I know. And I'll do whatever to get you back. Keep my side of the bed warm, baby. Do that for me, okay?"

He ended the call. Shamar purchased a forty ounce of Old English 800; then he rolled a joint in the store parking lot.

"Somebody 'bout to die. Yeah, somebody 'bout to die around this muthafucka," he said out loud.

"Might have to lay both of 'em down. Gotta do what I gotta do! She fucked anotha nigga; but I know deep down inside, she still loves me. I know she does! But she done let another nigga stretch my pussy all out of shape. Damn!"

As anger brewed, he sped out of the lot. Approaching a traffic light, he accidentally dropped the joint on his leg, causing him to take his eyes off the road momentarily and run a red light. A police car spotted him and instantly threw on its lights and siren, and pursued the violator. Shamar panicked and sped up, instead of pulling over. He impeded traffic and turned corners at excessive speed, triggering the policeman to radio for backup.

"Ain't no way in hell I'm gonna get busted with a gun, some dope, a got-damn open container, and all these damn GPSs in the trunk! Catch me if you can, cracker!" Shamar said out loud.

Minutes later, eight police cars, joined by a police helicopter, were in pursuit of Shamar. Approaching an intersection, he noticed a roadblock and numerous officers with drawn weapons aimed in his direction. With no other options, but to dive from the car and attempt to run, he brought his vehicle to a halt and stuck his hands out the window, surrendering.

The gun found in Shamar's possession was traced to three murders, which the district attorney pressed forward on and charged him with all three. Shamar was also charged with evading arrest, reckless driving, driving under the influence, possession of a firearm, possession with intent to commit a crime, and possession of stolen goods. Due to the severity of the charges, Shamar was held without bail and was facing life sentences for each murder at his arraignment.

When the news reached Jasmine, she was instantly remorseful, despite all the junk she'd talked to her friends. Had she not had him thinking she was seeing someone, divorced or not, she knew in her heart that Shamar wouldn't have been in the predicament he was in. She blamed herself.

Suddenly she wanted to forgive him for everything he'd ever done, including hitting her. She cried each day, begging the Lord for forgiveness; and more so, she begged Him to step in and see to it that Shamar be freed of all charges.

Whenever he phoned, she sympathetically accepted Shamar's numerous collect calls and had begun visiting him dutifully. Jasmine made it her business to be present at each of his court appearances, which inevitably caused her to face his snobbish mother, who'd cursed her out over the phone and also in the courthouse hallways.

Cyreese had even gone to the extent of disrupting court, yelling, "It was all her fault! She's the one who needs to be locked up! Not my son! She tricked him into believin' she was foolin' around with another man! If she hadn't lied, then we wouldn't be here right now! Lock the bitch up and throw away the got-damn key!"

After reviewing the police report, and assessing the case, a defense lawyer named Attorney Bridgewater promised Jasmine that since Shamar had no criminal record, he would receive probation, a few hours of community service, and have to pay a small fine as his penalty. This outcome would be a cinch to achieve. He also stated that the sentencing would result in Shamar's instant release. The attorney was so convincing that Jasmine took out a $25,000 loan and paid him a retainer.

Behind the L.A. County Jail walls, each and every day, Shamar would meet an inmate who had masterminded a crime or one who had been a willing participant. He met a man named San Diego Mike, who'd been shot in the eye by the police during a high-speed pursuit after having snatched an ATM machine from a bank wall. He was introduced to a reputable, notorious drug dealer named Bookie Ru from 30 Piru, who was incarcerated for six murders, extortion, and also for beheading a rival gang member. He met another reputable drug dealer, Moe Town who'd been set up by his cousin to deliver four kilos to an undercover federal agent. He met bank robbers, carjackers, kidnappers, home invaders, countless criminals, and addicts from all over the United States.

Shamar found it strange that instead of being remorseful for their acts of crime, and utilizing their time inside to change their way of thinking, the vast majority of them plotted more crimes upon release, whether they had one more year to serve or twenty more. He felt like a puppy alone in a jungle filled with ferocious animals, trapped in a breeding ground for evil and the criminally insane.

Never before had he missed his home, his wife, his kids, and his freedom as much as he did right then.

Chapter Thirty-one

Deja couldn't help but break into tears every time she thought about Garnell. Sometimes her tears were inspired by how much money he'd taken; other times it was because her heart had been broken. Sometimes it was because she'd let herself down by not sticking to her moral standards; but mostly it was because of the guilt she felt regarding the injuries Garnell had suffered. At least one hundred times over, she thought about what she could have done differently, and what would have happened if she'd not told her dad.

"I should have left it in your hands, Lord," she prayed aloud. "I was stupid to think I could handle this by myself. Forgive me, Lord, for not seeking and listening to you first. I let my flesh get the best of me, and look what has happened. I have just about caused death to come to this man's front door," she said, shaking her head.

She had been heading to the grocery store, but she suddenly made a U-turn, pulling out her phone to call Tracey.

"What are you doing?" she asked, once Tracey answered.

"Nothing really," she said, silencing Derrick, who had just rolled off her. "Why?"

"Come go with me to the hospital."

"For what? Who's in the hospital?"

"I wanna go see Garnell."

"Deja!" she chastised.

"I just want to see how he's doing. I feel bad, and the least I can do is pay him a visit."

"And what do you plan on telling his wife, or did you forget that part?"

"She might not be there."

"And she might just be there," Tracey countered.

"I'll just say we the church missionaries or something."

"You must think that woman is stupid. Her husband been here for months and months. You don't think she think he was out here, screwing around with somebody? Then here you go, shaking your fast tail over there." Tracey painted quite a vivid picture. "She might stand up and knock you out, laying you up in the bed right beside his."

"Well, if I see her in there, I won't stop. I will just act like I got the wrong room or something," Deja reasoned. "Or I can call the room and see if she answers the phone. I just need somebody to come with me. Will you?"

Tracey rolled her eyes as she rolled out of bed. "I guess so. You gonna come get me?"

"Yeah."

"All right, I'll be ready in an hour or so." She ended the call and looked at Derrick. "DK, give me some money so I can shop while I'm out that way."

"What you need?"

"Two thousand." She shrugged.

"Damn! I told you, I told Eureen I was gonna put this money in the women's shelter. You tryin'a eat it all up?"

"Oh, please, like that ain't what you doing. How much did she give you?"

"Ten grand." He grinned. "And you want damn twenty percent."

"I gave you one hundred percent of my pussy, didn't I? And this new mess of licking your ass ain't free."

"And I don't mind paying for that, baby! Whew!" Derrick commented. "Let me get a little bit more before you leave," he said, leaping from the bed and following her to the bathroom and into the shower. Tracey was just able to pull herself together when she heard Deja tapping her horn out front.

"You gon' be here when I get back?" she asked.

"I don't know. I might gotta go back to the Bank of Eureen and make a little more money; you done broke a brother down."

"Well, lock the door and set the alarm when you leave," she said, leaving Derrick laid out in Jermaine's bed. She hopped in the car with Deja. "Hey, girl."

"Why is DK's car over here?" Deja started.

"You gotta ask?"

Deja gasped. "Why are you doing that, girl? You know he ain't no good. And then why you gotta do it in Jermaine's house?"

"Look, don't start judging. Especially since you got me out here rolling with you to go see your married boyfriend."

"Touché," Deja said, shutting her mouth for only a few minutes. "But DK?"

"DK got an extra large dick and a magic tongue." Tracey didn't even bother to look Deja's way. "What other questions do you have?"

"How you gonna stop Jermaine from killing you, once he finds out you bringing another man in his house?"

"This is my song!" Tracey said, ignoring the question and turning up the radio. She popped her fingers and sang along with Alicia Keys; but in actuality, she was working on a plan of stealing Jermaine's property from right under his nose.

The two ladies walked into the hospital together, found out Garnell's room number, and headed for the elevator. Deja's stomach dropped with every other step, unsure of what she would find, and what she planned to say when she saw Garnell.

After easing to a stop on the seventh floor, the elevator doors slid open, ushering the women to a pretty quiet hallway. Almost tiptoeing, Deja found room 743, peeked inside, and saw no one other than the patient. He had both legs in casts, which were suspended in slings, and it made her eyes widen.

Deja and Tracey both stepped in softly, taking note that Garnell was asleep. His head was wrapped in a thick bandage that covered emergency-surgery wounds; his face was disfigured. His lips seemed to be twisted to one side, like a person afflicted with cerebral palsy, and his nose looked wide and flat. She could tell by the droop in his upper lip that his teeth had been knocked out, and he was connected to a breathing machine. Tears burned in Deja's eyes and rolled down her face as she covered her mouth with her hand.

"Damn," Tracey whispered.

Deja shook her head in remorse and guilt; then she slightly touched Garnell's arm. He stirred a bit; then he opened his eyes, as much as he could, which wasn't very much at all. One eyeball was misaligned and refused to turn toward Deja. His lips parted; and in a barely audible voice, he spoke.

"What the hell you doin' here?"

Deja was taken aback, never expecting in a million years that those would be his first words to her.

"I . . . I just found out what happened, and that you were here, and I wanted to come see you."

"For what? To see if your got-damn daddy did a good enough job?"

"I came because I care about you, Garnell."

"You care?" he said in a chuckle, which turned into a cough. "You better be got-damn glad I don't have the strength to move outta this bed; 'cause if I did, I'd strangle your scrawny black ass."

"Garnell, I never meant—"

"Bitch, get the fuck out of my room. And when I start walking again, you best watch your back. You and your black-ass daddy," he threatened.

Deja stood in disbelief for a few seconds, feeling sadder than she had when she arrived. Without saying another word, she left his bedside and exited with Tracey, who followed in silence.

Deja didn't speak again until she and Tracey were in the parking lot.

"Do you mind driving back?" she asked, wiping her nose on the sleeve of her sweater.

"I got you, girl."

Shamar quickly learned that inmates were not polite or humorous by any means. The majority were repeat offenders fighting unthinkable sentences: eighty years, double life, triple life, life without the possibility of parole. This kept them angry and always ready to fight or kill.

Shamar was caught up in a racial riot between black inmates and Mexicans the day before his next court appearance after being handed a weapon and instructed to fight and kill.

"If you don't get down wit' us," a black felon warned, "then we'll kill you!"

Afraid for his life, Shamar stabbed and severely wounded five Mexicans while under attack. He was also stabbed numerous times himself, ending up in the jail infirmary.

***

Having seen the disturbing news coverage of the racial riot at the jailhouse, Jasmine found herself crying a river of tears during praise and worship that Sunday. The choir sang an old favorite, "Jesus Can Work It Out," which normally had Jasmine standing, clapping, and rocking. But today, even though she stood, her eyes were tightly closed and her hands were lifted, beseeching the Lord for a miracle where Shamar was concerned.

Keep him safe, Lord, she prayed inwardly. *Hold him in the palm of your hand and move the heart of the judges and decision makers that he will be able to get out soon.* Jasmine even took the time to pray for reconciliation.

In retrospect, she was beginning to regret being so quick to divorce her husband.

"We were arguing over a damn rent increase," she said, stirring a packet of sugar into her tea.

Tracey and Deja sat with her at a table in the corner of their favorite Sunday afternoon restaurant, Outback Steakhouse. She had just dropped her daughters off at Chuck E. Cheese's for a birthday party.

Tracey was the first to throw in her two cents. "That is what you were arguing about that particular day, but you know it was more than that, Jasmine. He put his hands on you, remember?"

"I know, but I provoked him," she said, excusing his behavior.

"And? So that makes it right?"

"No, I'm not saying that. I'm just saying, I miss Shamar, and we could have probably worked things out if I had tried," Jasmine answered.

"You thinking about getting back together?" Deja

asked, working her knife through a segment of her chicken quesadilla.

Jasmine nodded somewhat shamefully. "And before y'all start judging and criticizing, I've thought about it and prayed about it. Shamar and I have a lot of years invested into each other and the girls. And he ain't never put a hand on me before; that was just a onetime thing, which I'm sure will never happen again," she explained.

Slightly rocking back and forth while rolling her eyes, landing them across the room, Tracey said nothing. Deja only nodded her head.

"I mean, all marriages have their ups and downs, right? Well, y'all have never been married, so maybe you don't understand my position or feelings."

"Sho don't," Tracey commented.

Only because Jasmine hadn't expected them to be fully bought into the idea, she was not offended. "Seriously, y'all. Please don't do this to me. I love Shamar, and it's a big decision that I would appreciate having your support on." Silence hovered for a few seconds; then she spoke again. "All of us have been in not so great situations. Deja, look at your involvement with Garnell. And, Tracey, for some reason, you are hanging on to Jermaine, even though you know he cheated on you and got somebody—I mean, two other women— pregnant. Even with you going back and messing with DK, I've not said a word. Not one time have I tried to talk y'all out of your relationships. I've always been there for y'all, and I'm asking you to do the same for me."

Later on, when Jasmine got home, she was finally able to connect with her husband.

"Hi, baby, are you okay?" she asked, pleased to hear his voice.

"Yeah, I'm all right. What's up?" His tone implied sadness.

"I saw what happened in there on the news, and I've been worried out of my mind about you. I'm so sorry, baby. I swear, I didn't mean to put you through all this chaos."

"Can't bring back the past, but I'm straight for right now."

"You need anything?"

"Hell yeah, I need something; I need you back in my life, baby. I need my wife," he said, pulling on Jasmine's heartstrings. "I swear, when I get out of here, I'ma make up for everything I've ever done to you, and everything I never did for you, baby."

"I love you too, Shamar," she said, shocking him but bringing a smile to his face. "I'm ready for you to come home."

"I need you to get me the hell outta here, Jasmine. What's that lawyer talkin' about?"

"He's been tryin' to visit you, but they told him you lost visiting privileges 'cause you were in the hole."

"But what's he talkin' 'bout? Is he gonna get me out or what?"

"I haven't heard from him in—"

"Call his punk ass right now on the three-way, so I can holla at him! All that fuckin' money you paid him, and he ain't done a got-damn thing yet!"

"Calm down, baby, and I'll three-way him."

The answering machine picked up.

"Ain't that a bitch!" he angrily yelled.

"Calm down, baby, and leave him a message."

"This is Shamar, man! I need you to come holla at me and get me outta this human zoo, ASAP!"

Then suddenly the line went dead, indicating his five-minute phone time had expired.

Checking his messages minutes later, Attorney Bridgewater immediately made his way to the county jail.

The attorney's dreadlocks turned Shamar off, but he was in no position to be selective.

This Bob Marley–lookin', dreadlock-wearin' muthafucka probably just smoked ten joints and now wanna holla at me! If this nigga represents me in front of a white judge, I'm really fucked! Why couldn't she hire a white lawyer to deal with white judges? I'm so fucked.

"You want the good news or the bad news first?" Attorney Bridgewater asked, thumbing through several papers.

"Give me the bad news, man," Shamar replied with an angry demeanor.

"I spoke with the two previous public defenders and also with the DA prosecuting the case. From my perspective, you'll do a year or so in prison, but that's better than a life sentence. The good news, my friend, is that because you were out of state driving trucks during the time the murders took place with the gun that was found in your possession, the DA agreed to drop life sentences. However, that still doesn't give you a pass on your additional charges. The DA is offering a sixteen-month prison sentence, but he is willing to suspend them, since you don't have a record. As soon as I get your signature on these documents, we can proceed."

Shamar let out a sigh of relief. "Thanks. I love you, man, thanks."

The attorney handed Shamar a few documents to sign; then he shook his hand and left.

Yes! I'm outta here!

Shamar's release from jail sparked new emotions in Jasmine. She was glad to see him free, and was comforted by his arms wrapped around her. Nuzzling against his chest after a long session of lovemaking, she whispered words that were worth gold to Shamar.

"Let's get married," she suggested, looking up at him with a smile.

Shamar planted what seemed to Jasmine to be a million kisses all over her body while uttering the words "my wife" over and over again.

Wanting to keep the arrangements simple, the couple decided on a backyard wedding on Memorial Day weekend, which was only a couple of weeks away. They would just have their two daughters as part of the bridal party and then would host a huge cookout for a reception.

Jasmine's friends could only pretend to be happy for her, even though they spilled out congratulatory words when Jasmine announced the wedding.

Tracey was lost in a sea of emotion about being faithful to Jermaine, only to be cheated on, and wondered how Jasmine could be getting married twice when she couldn't even find a man to marry one time.

Deja felt the same way, still reeling from her failed relationship with Garnell.

Eureen, on the other hand, really couldn't have cared less. She was living out with Derrick every sexual fantasy she'd ever dreamed, saw on tape, or read about. She was getting done so much that she'd stopped wearing panties around him, ready to give him pussy at the drop of a hat. She felt that a marriage would not sit well with her daughters just yet, and it would take away from her focus on trying to manage business, with which she struggled greatly.

And because Derrick was the keen and conniving

man he was, he had made his way slowly into her business affairs, offering to manage several entities of which she was clearly ignorant. He was careful to make her feel that she was being kept in the loop on everything; while behind the scenes, he set himself up for a takeover.

"You going with a color theme?" Deja asked, unenthused. She was sitting at Jasmine's kitchen table with the other ladies, snacking on chicken salad sandwiches and fresh strawberries.

"I'm going with ivory, and the girls will have on lavender," Jasmine gushed. "Look at this picture of the cake we want." She flipped through magazine pages, stopping at an elaborately constructed wedding cake, which stood more than four feet tall.

"How many people are you expecting? That's a big cake," Eureen commented.

"Well, I said we wanted it, not that we were gonna get it. We had an increase in our rent, so the budget is a little tighter, especially with Shamar not working. We're crossing our fingers that he can get back on with somebody's fleet. That's why we're going with the backyard wedding. Shamar told me not to worry about it, but I can't help but be a little budget conscious."

"I know that's right," Deja quipped. "Girl, my finances are torn out the frame ever since that bozo Garnell got ahold of my stuff."

"He ain't have no business with your debit card and bank account information in the first place," Tracey uttered, covering her filled mouth with a napkin. "We always trust men with stuff that they shouldn't be trusted with."

"Monroe wouldn't let me have access to nothing," Eureen added. "Every dime I had, I worked for it for myself or had to ask him for money, like I was sixteen years old."

"Well, you knew what you were doing by sticking by his side, girl, 'cause it sho paid off in the end." Tracey held up her hand for a high five. "God had a blessing in store for you, girl."

"Money doesn't replace love, though." It seemed like the right thing for Eureen to say; although she was so sprung on Derrick's dick and Monroe's estate, there were some days that she didn't think about Monroe in a romantic sense at all.

"So y'all are coming with your dates, right? No offense, Deja," Jasmine asked, guiding the conversation back to her wedding. No one gave an immediate response as they cut their eyes at each other. Eureen would have loved to be escorted by Derrick, but she wasn't ready to expose their relationship to the world. Tracey would have also loved to be escorted by Derrick. However, she also didn't want to expose their involvement, especially to Eureen.

"I ain't got no man," Deja said, rolling her eyes.

"Me either," Eureen added, focusing on the magazine and looking at no one.

"Neither do I," Tracey painfully admitted, although her eyes dropped to the ring still displayed on her finger. "His cheating ass."

"Whatever! If you still living in his house, he still your man," Jasmine teased, but she stopped giggling when she noticed Tracey wasn't smiling. "So why you still living there?"

"I just need some time to get my own place back. I can't live on the streets." Tracey shrugged.

"So he don't know that you know?" Deja asked.

"Nope. And I ain't telling him, until I got somewhere to go. But he's definitely not my man anymore. This ring don't mean nothing but some extra cash in my pocket after I take it to the pawnshop."

Silence filled the room for a few seconds while Tracey poked her lips out at the ring.

"Well, as long as my girls come, I'll be happy," Jasmine commented.

"We'll be there" was the promise Deja made.

Chapter Thirty-two

At Tracey's recommendation, Jermaine sat across the table from Derrick with a stack of papers in front of him in consideration of refinancing his home.

"Yeah, man, they want you to believe that you need to drop two percentage points before you refinance. But just half a point might save you a lot of money if you gon' stay in your house at least five more years." Derrick followed that statement with a bunch of number scenarios that Jermaine didn't really understand, but he nodded his head as if he did. "And you got enough equity in your property to pay for a nice wedding for you and your fiancée."

"Yeah, I think she is planning something pretty fancy," Jermaine answered, shaking his head. "Just the invitations she wants alone are outrageous!"

"You know what they say the key to a happy marriage is, right?" Derrick paused just a second. "Give the woman what she wants. Happy wife, happy life."

The two men chuckled; then Derrick rattled off more convincing reasons why Jermaine needed to refinance, focusing greatly on how much money he could pull out of the property.

"So how soon could I get a check, man?"

"Well, we would go to closing at the end of the month. Then usually about a week after that, you'd have a check."

"Punch up those numbers for me one more time," Jermaine requested.

Derrick fingered some numbers into his calculator while he talked about Jermaine's current percentage rate, points, the current market value, a comparative market analysis, and other real estate lingo, which again confused Jermaine.

"This is what you'd be looking at, bro," Derrick said, spinning the calculator to face Jermaine, who couldn't help but smile at the figure.

"So how would that change my mortgage payment?"

"Well, from what you told me your credit score is currently, you would definitely get a lower interest rate; and even with pulling out the equity, you're looking at keeping the payment almost the same as what you paying right now," Derrick assured him. "It will stretch your loan out back to thirty years, but, man, who know where we will be thirty years from now? Most homeowners in America sell their home before they pay it off; and then they take that equity and put it in another home. You know what I'm saying? I mean, Momma and 'em, they living in the same house they been in for thirty years, but everybody else move and buy a new house every five or ten years, you know?"

"Yeah, you right about that," Jermaine agreed, chuckling and nodding.

"Our dreams get bigger, and our families grow, or we get a new job out of town; and all of a sudden, the house you thought you was gon' keep forever don't fit no more."

"All right, man! Let's do this." Jermaine lifted a pen from the table after glancing at the calculator once more. "Where do I need to sign to get this ball rolling?"

Hiding his anxiousness, Derrick pointed to places that required Jermaine's initials or complete signature, providing a lie-filled explanation of each document as they went along. Trusting Derrick rather than reading the tiny print that covered the legal-sized documents, Jermaine initialed and signed in every place Derrick indicated; then he shook his hand.

"I'ma get these to the underwriter right away and let you know exactly what day we gonna go to closing," Derrick promised, squeezing his hand a bit more firmly.

"Thanks, Derrick. We will be sure to send you a wedding invite." Jermaine saw Derrick to the door; then he turned to Tracey. "I guess you can have the wedding of your dreams," he said, pulling her into his arms and kissing her lips.

"Thank you, baby," she gushed. "I won't spend it all in one place." She kissed him and spoke again. "I got something for you, since you so generous."

"What's that?" Jermaine answered, biting his bottom lip.

"Whatever you want, however you want it." She tugged his arm and led him upstairs for the night.

Having flirted with a few girls in the office and enticing them with money to overlook a few important recruiting processes, Shamar was able to secure employment again with another freight company. It wasn't long however before he was back to his old hustle. Hauling enough stolen goods across state lines to earn a twenty-year federal sentence, Shamar headed for California to prepare for his wedding day weekend. He and Jasmine were expecting more than 200 guests between that Friday evening and Monday, since Jasmine thought it would be fun to have a four-day event. Shamar phoned a thief contact to fulfill what would have been an incredibly high grocery order. Due to his connections, he'd get the food for close to nothing.

"What's up, Magic? This is Shamar."

"What it do, nigga? What's the business?"

"I got an order for you."

"Talk to me."

"You got a pencil?"

"Never answer the phone without it."

"I need seven slabs of beef ribs and five slabs of pork. Four big bags of quarter legs, three cases of hot links, ten large bags of wings. Gimme 'bout twenty pounds of ground beef and six buckets of that ready-made potato salad, eight cases of water, fifteen cases of soda, eight big cans of baked beans, and ten cases of Bud Light."

"Don't you need some bread with all that meat?"

"Yeah, hook me up with some bread, rolls, and hamburger buns."

"When you want it?"

"By the time you get it, I'll be at the crib or nearin'."

"It's a done deal, my nig."

"I'll holla," Shamar ended.

"Call me if anything changes. I don't want to be stuck with all that shit."

"It's all good, Magic. Ain't nuttin' gonna change."

Shamar spent the next few hours dropping off merchandise to other contacts and filling his pockets with the cash, prior to heading home. On his way, he called Magic back.

"You got me?" Shamar asked.

"I deliver, that's what I do," Magic replied.

"I'm about to drop my rig off at the crib, and I'll be right there."

"Hurry up, man."

"I'll make it up to you. Just wait right there."

Shamar parked his rig on a lot next to his home; then he climbed into his wife's Navigator and headed to the store. Pulling into the lot, he spotted Magic sitting on his bicycle next to the cart that contained the goods. He parked at the far end of a row and waited.

Seeing Shamar coming, Magic climbed off his bike and pushed the cart toward the Navigator; in no time, they were loading the goods into the cargo area.

Suddenly a store employee, who'd spotted Magic stealing, crept out of Food-4-Less toward Shamar's vehicle and jotted down the license plate number; then he sprinted back inside and gave the information to the waiting manager.

"That muthafucka wrote down my license plate number."

"He ain't nobody. Don't worry 'bout him."

"What the fuck you mean, 'He ain't nobody'? He wrote down my got-damn plate number, nigga!"

"That stupid Mexican probably got shit all twisted up. Quit trippin' and pay me so I can get outta here."

Shamar quickly handed Magic a wad of cash; then he climbed into his vehicle and peeled out. Magic stupidly returned inside the store to purchase a forty-ounce can of Old English 800. Before he could make it to the beer cooler, an officer approached him.

"Sir, I need you to put your hands behind your back, lock your fingers, and come with me."

Turning onto his block, Shamar noticed four police cars at his driveway. One of the officers caught sight of him, jumped in his cruiser, and burned rubber toward him, needing to get a closer look at the license plate. Shamar's cell phone rang, which he immediately answered.

"Babe," Jamsine started to say.

"What's up?"

"The cops just left, lookin' for you. What's going on?"

"I don't know. I'm down the street from the house, but they got me blocked in and got guns drawn on me."

Jasmine dropped the phone and ran outside.

"Turn off your vehicle," an officer yelled, walking toward the Navigator. "And throw out your keys!"

The additional officers held aim at him while neighbors began emerging from their homes. Jasmine approached, with her hair half done and half sticking up on her head, trying to prepare for her wedding scheduled for the next day. She was wondering what the hell was going on. Shamar cooperated with the officers and was quickly cuffed; then he was placed in the backseat of a police car. A sergeant searched the Navigator and instantly discovered the stolen groceries.

"What's goin' on, Officer?" Jasmine asked, staring at Shamar, who held his head down in shame.

"Your husband here has been involved in several thefts."

"Unh-unh, you've got the wrong man. He ain't that kinda person," Jasmine argued.

"Unless he can produce a receipt for these items, I have to proceed with an arrest."

"I'm sure he has a receipt, 'cause he don't get down like that. We got money to buy food."

"As I said, ma'am, if he can't produce a valid receipt, I'll have to take him downtown."

The sergeant phoned the officers at Food-4-Less, who were taking statements from the employee, and instructed them to bring both the employee and Magic to the scene in separate cars in order to identify Shamar as an accomplice. Several minutes later, Shamar was instructed to exit the police car and face the police cars containing the witnesses.

"That's him," the Mexican said. "He was the driver."

"Yeah, that's who sent me in there to get stuff for him," Magic snitched.

As the sergeant proceeded with paperwork, and an officer gathered the stolen goods, Jasmine approached the police car and stared at Shamar.

"Why?" she asked, shedding tears. "Why did you do it? It's the day before our wedding, and in front of all these damn people!"

Feeling humiliated, not only because of the presence of nosy neighbors, but more so by being caught, Shamar hung his head.

"How can you embarrass me like this, like we ain't got no money? What the hell you doin' stealing some damn food? All our family is here at the house for the wedding tomorrow, and you pull some shit like this!" she screamed. "What the hell! Stay your ass in jail this time!"

She turned her back and stormed away, cussing all the way up the street. Angry, frustrated, and utterly embarrassed, she walked back into her home, facing a sea of inquisitive faces; some of whom had stepped out on the porch, including Cyreese, to try to see what had been going on, while others peeked out the windows.

"The wedding is off!" she announced. "His ass out there stealing some got-damn chicken and ribs and shit!" she hollered, stomping up the stairs.

"Sir," Cyreese called after the officer, "how much is it gonna take to get him outta jail?"

"That's up to the judge, ma'am," one officer said, getting into his car.

"I don't believe he did it! He make too much money to be stealing hot dogs and hamburgers. He done brought me stuff from all around the world that half y'all cockamamy cops could never afford!" she spilled out, banging her fists on the hood of his car and catching the attention of another officer. "I got stuff from Eygpt, Timbuk-tu, Italy, and Sweden that he done bought me, so I know he ain't stealing no cookout food."

Unbeknownst to Cyreese, she had rattled off vital information to a cop who had been assigned to track Shamar's activity, as the police had already been tipped off on his criminal behavior of trafficking and selling stolen goods.

"You said he didn't do it, huh?" Officer Pate asked. "So what do you think happened?" Officer Pate's mind-set was to gather as much information as he could.

"I don't know what happened, but I can tell you what *didn't* happen! That boy ain't steal no damn food," Cyreese barked.

"He was getting married tomorrow?"

"Yeah. Him and his wife s'posed to be getting mar-ried, again, tomorrow afternoon, right in their back-yard. He ain't got time for this shit."

Pate looked at his partner. "That explains all the cookout food."

At that point, Cyreese panicked, realizing that she may have said too much.

The officer looked back over at her. "Do you mind if I come by your home and ask you a few questions about his job and income? You might be able to give us some valuable information that will prove his innocence, or at least speak for his character."

"What you got to ask me? Naw, you can't come over," she growled, remembering that her garage was full of hot property. "I told you he ain't did nothing. All you can tell me is what time I need to pick him up tonight." At that, Cyreese walked off, nervous about what she'd ignorantly shared with the police. As she walked back to Deja's home, she thought about how she could twist everything around to make it seem that it was Jasmine who had done all the talking.

As soon as she crossed the threshold, she screamed, "Jasmine! Are you some kinda damn idiot? Where the hell she at?"

"She went upstairs," a few guests said in unison.

"She need to bring her ass down here and explain to me why she runnin' her mouth to the got-damn cops! Jasmine!"

With red eyes, Jasmine appeared at the top of the stairs. "Why are you screaming my name?" she asked calmly.

"What the hell you done told them cops?"

Jasmine pressed her lips together in complete silence.

"Ain't no need in you standing there like the cat got your tongue now! You was saying all kinds of shit while you was outside with the police. Tellin' them how much shit he done bought you from all over the world," Cyreese stated, more so to the people in the room than to Jasmine. She wanted and needed them to repeat that it was Jasmine who'd tipped the cops off. "Now they tryin'a come to my got-damn house and ask me a buncha questions. You don't give a damn about Shamar! I keep telling him to leave your ass alone!" she finished, not caring that her granddaughters stood nearby listening. "How the hell you expect him to take care of these girls when you always getting him into some stupid shit? He just got outta jail because of you!"

"Get out of my house, Cyreese," Jasmine ordered.

"Who the hell you think you talking to?"

"I'ma tell you one more time to get the hell outta my house," Jasmine warned a second time.

"You want me out? You be woman enough to bring your ass down here and put me out!" Cyreese's defiant stance was a clear indication to everyone that she didn't intend on going anywhere. "What the hell you gon' do? Huh?" she bullied.

In an instant, Jasmine reached behind her and picked up a large vase filled with decorative branches, which sat on a table on the stair's landing. She hurled it at Cyreese's head, fully intending to hit her. Only because her aim was off, it smashed against the wall, causing a startled Cyreese to jerk her arms toward her head for cover while she ducked.

"You done lost your got-damn mind!" she spat out after taking a quick look at fragments of ceramic and scattered twigs, one of which had whipped across her arm and left a welt.

In a snarl as vicious as a bulldog's, Jasmine replied, "Am I gonna have to tell you again? I swear, if I come down these steps, mother-in-law or not, I'ma beat your ass."

Cyreese immediately cowered, calling for her purse and keys, and quickly made her way out the door.

Chapter Thirty-three

Sitting in the hallway of Antelope Valley Superior Court, discussing options with his public defender, Jordan Roussaw, Shamar was distraught by the unfavorable offer. Due to his mother's ranting, they'd shown up at her door, shortly after taking Shamar in custody, with a search warrant. It hadn't taken them long to find property that belonged to neither Shamar or Cyreese. It was enough to charge Shamar with grand larceny three times over, while Cyreese was given a charge of harboring stolen goods.

"Like I said, you're looking at a sixteen month minimum and that's a hell of a deal," Jordan repeated. "I strongly recommend you take it."

"You've gotta be kiddin' me," Shamar said to his attorney, frowning; but realistically, he knew he couldn't expect much.

"No, I'm not. That's what the DA offered, and I can assure you that if you refuse it, the offer will be taken off the table and the sentence will significantly increase."

"Man, no way in hell can I afford to be gone all that time over some fuckin' groceries! Get me probation and a fine or community service; or get me another court date and I'll hire my own lawyer."

"First of all, don't do the crime if you can't do the time. Secondly, your request will deliberately be denied; so I'll shoot for another court date, but make damn certain you've got an attorney when you return.

If not, Judge Hanky will lock you up immediately. And furthermore, the groceries are the least of your worries. We haven't even got to all that shit you had stashed in your mother's garage. She could end up being your cell mate, by the way."

"I'm not a bad person. I just made a dumb mistake."

"Looks like you made quite a few of them. I will make your request for community service known to the DA, but I can just about guarantee you that it will be denied." His attorney closed his portfolio and stood to his feet. As the public defender predicted, Shamar's request was denied, and the sixteen-month offer was off the table. He was instructed to return in two weeks with a private attorney.

He rushed to Cyreese's house after court, locked himself in the bedroom to keep her from endlessly cussing him out, and thumbed through the Yellow Pages, seeking a nearby, affordable attorney. An hour later, he was sitting in the law offices of Bret & Sikes, twenty minutes from his home.

Attorney Bret was highly impressive and said all the right things, as did most attorneys. "I can guarantee you probation or a slight fine. Just sign on the dotted line and I'll have a talk with my DA buddies to change their minds." He smiled and pointed at a wall picture. "Is that the DA handling your case, and is that the presiding judge?"

There was a picture of the private attorney playing golf with the prosecuting DA and the presiding judge. In another picture, the attorney was at a country club dinner with the same exact judge and DA.

An overly impressed Shamar smiled at the photographs. "Yep, that's them."

"I've got both of them in my pocket. Today is your lucky day, pal."

Suddenly relieved of all stress, Shamar handed the attorney $5,000 in cash as a down payment on the $20,000 total; then he signed the necessary contracts and left the office, well pleased.

Two weeks later, he confidently returned to court, but he was stunned when his attorney informed him that the DA had increased the sentence from sixteen months to thirty-seven years in a state prison for all of his charges combined.

"What happened, Mr. Bret? I thought you had this shit all worked out?" He was on fire.

"I thought I did too, pal, but apparently you pissed a few people off when you turned down their initial offer."

"What does that have to do with what you promised me?"

"I never made you any promises, pal. Promises are one thing I never make," lied the attorney. "What I said was that I'd provide you with the best representation possible."

"Bullshit! You knew I turned down the offer before you took my money, and I know what you told me!"

"Listen, pal, I'll put this to you in layman terms. They won't overlook your prior record and they're pissed off at you, okay? You and I can sit here and engage in a tug-of-war verbal riot with one another, or you can accept the five-year deal. Time is money, and I've got more clients than just you to tend to."

"Y'all lawyers ain't nothin' but a bunch of smooth-talkin', lyin' muthafuckas!"

"I don't have to listen to this, and you can bet your ass your balance will still remain."

"I gave you five thousand fuckin' dollars to get me five years? Kiss my black ass, Bret!" he yelled as he was dragged from the courtroom in cuffs. "What the fuck did I need you for? This is bullshit, man! I should sue your ass for perjury or some shit."

"Make yourself comfortable, sir. Because you're not going anywhere for a while," Bret laughed as he shook hands with the DA.

Jermaine pulled his rig into his yard and wondered what Derrick Kelly's car was doing there. "Maybe he's hand delivering my check," he said out loud, jumping down from the driver's seat. He thought it strange that he had just talked to Tracey a few minutes before and she'd not mentioned that Derrick was there. "What the hell . . ." he uttered, sliding his key into the lock, but the knob was not turning.

Jermaine jiggled the key, trying again, but he was unsuccessful in getting the door to open. Like a visitor, he first rang the bell; but a few seconds later, he pounded heavily with his fist, growing angry.

Tracey had already set up for the police to arrive, once she'd gotten Jermaine's call. Right on time, they coasted into the driveway, which was when Tracey opened the door.

"What's going on, baby?" Jermaine asked, confused not just by the changed locks and the arrival of the police, but also by Tracey's practically naked body, only dressed in a short gown and robe. "Where is Derrick? Why are the locks changed?"

"You need to get the hell off my property," she said, staring at Jermaine coldly.

"What're you talking 'bout?"

"Thank you for coming, Officers. Please escort this man off my property," she instructed.

"Sir, is this your home?"

"Yes, it is," Jermaine answered, becoming frustrated. "This is my fiancée."

"No, sir, this is *my* home," Tracey announced. "He used to live here and then he gave the property to me. We have since broken up."

"What? What the hell you talkin' about, Tracey? This is my house, Officers. I let her move in some months ago. I don't know what the hell she talking about, saying I don't live here."

"Do you have a key, sir?"

"I did, but she done changed the damn lock! I just got off the road, 'cause I'm a long-distance truck driver," Jermaine began explaining. "And I ain't been home in weeks, and I get here tonight and my key don't work."

"Because this is no longer his house," Tracey added.

"You got in, baby," Derrick called from the doorway, standing bare-chested and in a pair of pajama pants.

"What the fuck!" Jermaine bellowed. "You got some nigga in my house!" He moved to grab Tracey, but the officers had anticipated his movement once they saw Derrick appear in the door. They quickly reached for their weapons.

"Sir, don't move."

Immediately Jermaine rethought his movements. "What the fuck that nigga doing up in my house!" he raged.

"I have all the documents inside, including the deed to show this as my property," Tracey offered. "If y'all wanna step inside, I'll be glad to show it to you."

"I'm going to ask you to wait out here while I take a look at these documents," one of the officers said to Jermaine.

Now seething, Jermaine could do nothing else but wait. *I'ma beat her ass when the cops leave,* he promised himself, but he was smart enough not to make his thoughts audible.

Two minutes went by before the officer emerged and spoke to Jermaine. "I'm going to have to ask you to leave, sir. The documents clearly show that this is her property."

"What! What the fuck! Fuck that!" he yelled, dashing to the front door. The officers drew their guns, warning Jermaine to stop, and quickly fired a warning shot, but Jermaine paid it no mind. In an instant, he had both hands gripped around Tracey's neck and began to squeeze as he slammed her multiple times into the wall. "You bitch!"

Tracey's eyes bulged as she gasped for air, flailing her arms about wildly, looking for Derrick to come to her rescue. Derrick, however, stood calmly out of the way, with a smirk on his face, finding the fiasco quite entertaining.

"Sir! Sir!" an officer yelled before firing a shot that forced Jermaine to weaken his grasp slightly, but not before Tracey completely passed out. Seeing that he still had Tracey firmly around the neck, although her body was now limp, the officer fired a second time, which released her from Jermaine's hands as he collapsed on her. The 9.5 seconds of compression against her jugular veins cut off the oxygen supply long enough to cause cerebral ischemia.

And when the paramedics arrived, Tracey and Jermaine were both pronounced dead.

Jasmine, Eureen, and Deja stood under the awning at Joshua Park Cemetery behind Tracey's family. Their faces were hidden by pairs of dark shades in an attempt to mask their tears. Pastor Gardner read the appropriate words from his church manual, while Tracey's parents and siblings held on to each other for comfort. Minutes later, Tracey's family and friends were released to their vehicles, and the trio slowly walked away in silence. Each woman was adrift in her own sea of thoughts of what she had experienced, lost, and gained, if anything.

Jasmine had lost her marriage and couldn't think of a single thing she'd gained. Shamar was away in prison (while his mother served a brief, partially suspended sentence), leaving Jasmine alone with her two girls. She regretted the fact that she had taken matters into her own hands, instead of seeking counseling. While she found domestic violence unacceptable, she wished she'd handled things differently, but she was thankful that she still had her life.

Deja seemed to have lost her thirst for forbidden love after being terribly harassed by Garnell once he was released from the hospital, but he finally moved back to the East Coast. Deja thanked God for His mercy that her outcome with her involvement with Garnell hadn't turned out more disastrous. She vowed never again to fall for the simplistic, easy-to-mimic church theatrics as her measuring stick for a good, godly man. She turned her head and looked back at Tracey's casket, and she wiped away a tear.

And Eureen ended her explicit relationship with Derrick after the news reported that he was there when Tracey and Jermaine met their untimely demises. Soon after, she found out that Derrick had been robbing her blind and had swindled her out of more than half her fortune. Disappointed that love still hadn't come her way, she was grateful that it wasn't her or one of her daughters lying in a casket. Her focus would now be solely on her girls and strengthening her family, allowing God to lead the way.

Pastor Gardner watched at a distance, shaking his head at the ladies, feeling sorry for each of them.

"It's sad, isn't it, babe?" Felicia Gardner asked, taking hold of his arm.

He gave a silent nod, thinking of what he knew of all of them. "It's a good thing that Jesus paid it all," Pastor Gardner commented, "because the price of sin is too big a debt to pay on our own."

ORDER FORM
URBAN BOOKS, LLC
78 E. Industry Ct
Deer Park, NY 11729

Name: (please print): _____

Address: _____

City/State: _____

Zip: _____

QTY	TITLES	PRICE

Shipping and handling-add $3.50 for 1st book, then $1.75 for each additional book.

Please send a check payable to:

Urban Books, LLC

Please allow 4-6 weeks for delivery

ORDER FORM
URBAN BOOKS, LLC
78 E. Industry Ct
Deer Park, NY 11729

Name: (please print): _____

Address: _____

City/State: _____

Zip: _____

QTY	TITLES	PRICE
	16 On The Block	$14.95
	A Girl From Flint	$14.95
	A Pimp's Life	$14.95
	Baltimore Chronicles	$14.95
	Baltimore Chronicles 2	$14.95
	Betrayal	$14.95
	Black Diamond	$14.95
	Black Diamond 2	$14.95
	Black Friday	$14.95
	Both Sides Of The Fence	$14.95
	Both Sides Of The Fence 2	$14.95
	California Connection	$14.95

Shipping and handling-add $3.50 for 1st book, then $1.75 for each additional book.
Please send a check payable to:
    Urban Books, LLC
Please allow 4-6 weeks for delivery

ORDER FORM
URBAN BOOKS, LLC
78 E. Industry Ct
Deer Park, NY 11729

Name:(please print):_____

Address: _____

City/State: _____

Zip: _____

QTY	TITLES	PRICE
	California Connection 2	$14.95
	Cheesecake And Teardrops	$14.95
	Congratulations	$14.95
	Crazy In Love	$14.95
	Cyber Case	$14.95
	Denim Diaries	$14.95
	Diary Of A Mad First Lady	$14.95
	Diary Of A Stalker	$14.95
	Diary Of A Street Diva	$14.95
	Diary Of A Young Girl	$14.95
	Dirty Money	$14.95
	Dirty To The Grave	$14.95

Shipping and handling-add $3.50 for 1st book, then $1.75 for each additional book.
Please send a check payable to:
Urban Books, LLC
Please allow 4-6 weeks for delivery

ORDER FORM
URBAN BOOKS, LLC
78 E. Industry Ct
Deer Park, NY 11729

Name:(please print):_____

Address: _____

City/State: _____

Zip: _____

QTY	TITLES	PRICE
	Gunz And Roses	$14.95
	Happily Ever Now	$14.95
	Hell Has No Fury	$14.95
	Hush	$14.95
	If It Isn't love	$14.95
	Kiss Kiss Bang Bang	$14.95
	Last Breath	$14.95
	Little Black Girl Lost	$14.95
	Little Black Girl Lost 2	$14.95
	Little Black Girl Lost 3	$14.95
	Little Black Girl Lost 4	$14.95
	Little Black Girl Lost 5	$14.95

Shipping and handling-add $3.50 for 1st book, then $1.75 for each additional book.

Please send a check payable to:

Urban Books, LLC

Please allow 4-6 weeks for delivery

ORDER FORM
URBAN BOOKS, LLC
78 E. Industry Ct
Deer Park, NY 11729

Name: (please print): _____

Address: _____

City/State: _____

Zip: _____

QTY	TITLES	PRICE
	Loving Dasia	$14.95
	Material Girl	$14.95
	Moth To A Flame	$14.95
	Mr. High Maintenance	$14.95
	My Little Secret	$14.95
	Naughty	$14.95
	Naughty 2	$14.95
	Naughty 3	$14.95
	Queen Bee	$14.95
	Say It Ain't So	$14.95
	Snapped	$14.95
	Snow White	$14.95

Shipping and handling-add $3.50 for 1st book, then $1.75 for each additional book.

Please send a check payable to:

Urban Books, LLC

Please allow 4-6 weeks for delivery

ORDER FORM
URBAN BOOKS, LLC
78 E. Industry Ct
Deer Park, NY 11729

Name:(please print):_____

Address: _____

City/State: _____

Zip: _____

QTY	TITLES	PRICE
	Spoil Rotten	$14.95
	Supreme Clientele	$14.95
	The Cartel	$14.95
	The Cartel 2	$14.95
	The Cartel 3	$14.95
	The Dopefiend	$14.95
	The Dopeman Wife	$14.95
	The Prada Plan	$14.95
	The Prada Plan 2	$14.95
	Where There Is Smoke	$14.95
	Where There Is Smoke 2	$14.95

g and handling-add $3.50 for 1st book, then $1.75 for
ional book.
check payable to:
Books, LLC
eeks for delivery